PIG TALE

PiG TALE

VERLYN FLIEGER

Hyperion

New York

First Edition
1 3 5 7 9 10 8 6 4 2

Printed in the United States of America

Library of Congress Cataloging-in-Publication Data on file.
ISBN 0-7868-0792-X (trade ed.)
Visit www.hyperionteens.com

This book is for Neal and Kristin and Erik,
with love from Mom

ACKNOWLEDGMENTS

Many people helped with the making of *Pig Tale*. Thanks go first and foremost to Vaughn Howland, in-home editor extraordinaire, who patiently read every draft and told me whenever things weren't working, which was often.

I am grateful beyond words to my agent, Richard Abate, who believed in a story I thought no one would buy, and to Andrea Pinkney, who bought a story I thought no one would believe. Heartfelt thanks to my impeccable editor, Susan Chang, whose incisive comments did so much to shape the final product. Thanks to Anne Diebel for designing such a beautiful book.

Thanks go, too, to those who read drafts along the way, made sharp comments, and gave encouragement: Rose Solari, Doug Anderson, Paul Thomas, Joyce Kornblatt.

Contents

PART TWO—FOUND

PART THREE—MOKIE

PART ONE

LOST

ONE

DUST MOTES

It feels like we've been here forever.

Forever's not very long, Lally. You know that. We have to take things as they happen.

You mean if they happen, don't you, John? Are you so sure they'll happen?

Ask The Skimmer if you're not sure.

Well, Skimmer?

They'll happen. We're like motes of dust in a sunbeam. You can't hurry a sunbeam.

I don't want to hang about in a sunbeam. I want to get on with it. Don't you, John?

We'll get on with it.

Yes, but when? When will that be?

When time comes. Right, Skimmer?

Right. Time's coming. It's moving now. Moving fast . . .

TWO

STORMBORNE

THIS IS HOW IT BEGAN. In late afternoon, the sun disappeared behind a bank of slate-colored cloud. A wind started, spinning up dust devils out of the dry earth. Folk took shelter in their houses, barring shutters against the rain to come. Then the storm broke. Lightning cracked the sky. Fireballs of blue-white light played above the trees and fell like stars into the depth of the wood.

The wind increased. Thunder crashed, rolling above the fields and forest with a sound like a drumming of many hooves on the earth. Rain came driving over the village from upriver, battering the fields and flattening the long grass on the hillside. Trees thrashed, and branches sailed through the air on a wind that stripped them of their last, clinging leaves.

In the heart of the storm, a woman with deep-shadowed

eyes and a heavy belly lay down in the Farrow Field just outside the village of Little Wicken. No one saw her come. No one saw her pains begin as the night wore on and the storm raged. No one attended her labor except the wind her midwife and the rain her nurse. No one heard her cry in the night—the red, jagged cry of one whose body was being torn apart.

No one saw her leave.

Huddled in houses, snug in their beds, the villagers rode out the storm. With the rising sun the world was reborn. Wind and rain had passed, leaving earth clean and clear and ready to begin again. The woman, too, was gone, leaving as the only mark of her passage a squalling baby girl, as minute and insignificant a scrap of humanity as ever came unwelcome into the world.

A farmer—a hulking slouch of a man named Grime going early to his field in the rain-washed dawn—heard a tiny cry that scarcely carried on the air. It was both shrill and weak, the feeble mew of an abandoned kitten. Following the sound, he found the mite, blue and shivering in the wet grass. It was to his credit that although he didn't want her, he at least took her out of the field.

Grime's wife was not best pleased when he walked in unexpected and laid the infant on her wooden sink. She took her hands out of the greasy water and regarded the gift with distaste.

"What's that?"

"Don't be daft, woman. It's a baby. Use your eyes."

"I can see it's a baby; I'm not blind." She tucked up a

straggle of graying hair. "But what you going to do with it? Where'd you get it?"

"Found it. In the field."

She looked at him sideways. "Now, that's a likely story." She sniffed. "All alone? Nobody with it?"

"If there had been, I'd have left it."

"Should have left it anyway." She scrubbed her wet hands down her apron, and settled them on her hips.

"Wherever you got it, we've no use for it. Just another mouth at suppertime." She peered closer. "A girl, at that. A girl's no good to us. Ought to drown it. And how we going to feed her, anyway, a suckling babe?"

He shrugged and scraped a callused hand over his unshaven chin. It made a sound like a wood rasp on splinters. "I dunno. How would I know? Give her milk in a rag, I guess, same as when a sow goes dry."

She shrugged in turn, but fished a piece of torn sacking out of the ragbag and rolled the baby in it. "We'll keep her for now. Maybe someone will find a use for her."

But no one did. No one in the village knew what to do with her, and it took them all her life to find out.

❦

The village was called Little Wicken, mainly to distinguish it from the much larger town of Great Wicken, a day's travel down the river. It was a decent enough place, if you just looked at the village and not the people who lived there. The slope up from the river leveled off at a straggle of cottages fronting a dirt lane, then climbed to where the Wickenwood began at the crest of the hill. Just behind the village, an ancient apple orchard flowered in spring and supplied a modest crop of fruit in autumn.

Above the orchard, the Farrow Field rose to where the hill crested and the Wickenwood began. Only a few villagers with long memories could remember why it was called the Farrow Field, and lately folk had taken to calling it the Fallow Field as making more sense, since it was never plowed nor planted nor even mowed, but left wild season after season. Nevertheless, the name was as old as the field itself and the old ones of the village continued stubbornly to call it the Farrow Field.

Young or old, the villagers scraped a bare living from the thin soil. A few blade-hipped cows for milk and some equally bony goats for cheese supplemented their chief business, which was pig keeping; their survival dependent largely on the meat of pigs. Their field crops were meager, and the grazing for goats and cows hardly more, but the oaks of the Wickenwood supplied a feast of acorns, and the pigs thrived.

The wood was ancient, a dense forest left over from a past before the past. Stands of oak and ash, beech and thorn and wicken tree alternated with stretches of thick underbrush full of tangled paths and dark hollows. No roads led through the wood, only narrow ways that wound about and about but seemed to have no destination. Black, swift-flowing brooks threaded the trees, creating a labyrinth of interflowing channels that seemed also to have no destination. Their hidden voices could be heard, by those who listened for such things, in the clatter and mutter of water over rocks.

Like folk everywhere, the villagers wanted their little world to stay neat and orderly and within their control. They were afraid of what they didn't understand, and things went on in the Wickenwood that they didn't understand. The trees murmured to themselves in voices that sounded almost human; the shadows of the branches against the forest floor looked like ghost shapes moving just beyond sight; strange lights sometimes flickered deep in the heart of the wood where no people were.

Mothers cautioned their children. "Don't you go near that wood or I'll wallop you. Go in too deep and likely you'll lose yourself and stray through the Door that opens into the Crystal Country." Once through that Door, they warned, those who have passed are cut off from all they know and remember, suspended like dust motes in a sunbeam.

The village children obediently kept their feet away from the wood, but their eyes betrayed them, slanting in sideways fascination at the dark under the ancient trees. The villagers told them to keep their eyes to themselves, but unlike their parents, the children were drawn to the forbidden, even as they feared it.

The Wickenwood was also known to be the haunt of more ordinary folk, thieves and beggars, tramps and vagabonds. "And worse besides," some muttered. The villagers called them "outsiders," folk from the larger world outside their concerns. The business of the village was farming and pig keeping, but the entertainment was gossip, a stew pot bubbling with spicy tidbits that the village wives kept always on the boil. When the breakfast washing up was done and the household chores were seen to, the women gathered over their back fences to turn up the fire under the pot, to stir and taste and smack their lips.

—I heard—

—never does a lick of work—

—there they were—

—didn't come home all night—

—in the barn—

—told her to her face—

—broad daylight—

—behind the dairy—

Any new activity, any new person, any departure from what the wives of Little Wicken considered right and proper was meat for the stew. Busily they spiced and stirred and simmered it over the back fences in the mornings and dished it up hot to the menfolk along with the rest of the evening meal.

For a while, Grime's foundling made a tasty tidbit, a toothsome morsel to simmer in the gossip pot.

"Heard about that baby over to Grimes'?"

"A baby? Didn't know Grett Grime was teeming. Not but

what her apron's big enough to hide a full belly." A sniggering laugh.

"This one isn't hers."

"Well, now, I'd have thought she was done with birthing. They got that lump of a boy, Dommel, and she lost the next three. Where'd this one come from?"

"He *said* he found it, but you know Grime."

Eyebrows raised. Heads nodded. Tongues clucked.

"Where'd he say he found it?"

"Just lying in the field, he says, newborn and squalling and not another body in sight anywhere."

"A likely story."

"Unless it's a changeling."

"Get away! A changeling? You don't mean . . . ?"

"I do mean. Wouldn't be the first time the Crystal Folk have left their get for humans to raise."

Heads drew closer, voices lowered.

"Happened once in my grandma's time, or so my ma told me. My gram knew how to get rid of it, though."

"How's that?"

"It's an old spell. You save some eggshells from your cooking and fill them with water. Then you set them by the fire and let the water boil. When the changeling baby sees water boiling in eggshells it'll be so surprised it'll talk, and that's how you know it's a changeling. The one my gram had sat right up in the cradle."

"Did it speak?"

"Aye, it did, clear as anything."

"What did it say?"

"It said:

'By ash and thorn,
by rowan tree.
such little pots boiling
I never did see.'

Then it jumped out of the cradle and ran over the door sill quick as a mouse and was never seen again."

"Maybe Grime's baby'll do the same. What's it look like? Have you seen it?"

"Aye. Funny-looking little thing. Nose all squashed and its eyes two different colors. Wriggles too much for a newborn, if you ask me. It's as hard to hold as a yearling pig."

Time passed, however, and no preternatural speech or changeling strangeness marked the foundling; indeed, she seemed more than usually plain and ordinary. And so the gossip died down. No one ever came forward to claim the baby, and she was too small yet for any behavior odder than the manner of her arrival. Grime's wife kept her for a while, but finally tired of the trouble and handed her on to someone else. Passed from household to household as each in turn tired of her, she was never kept in any one home for very long, and it was many years before she was called anything more than "the lost 'un."

11

THREE

LiTTLE WiCKEN

WHEN MOKIE WAS VERY YOUNG, before she got her name, she did not know that she was unhappy. She rode the surface of her life like a leaf on the river, carried by a current of which she was unaware, only half conscious of the surges that sometimes swept her against rocks and sometimes spun her into eddies. Unknowing, she took the shifts and changes that came to her as the pattern of the water.

In much the same way, the village folk gave her little more attention than the river would give a leaf. They smacked her or cuffed her when she got in the way, and for the rest they paid her no mind. When they called her "lost 'un," this not with affection but indifference, she never asked why folk called her that, or wondered where she was lost from or how she had come to the village. She was just there, like a leaf, or a twig, or an acorn.

12

Mokie learned early not to play with the other children. As the lost 'un, she wasn't really part of the village, and children being children, primitive, cruel, and savage, they made her their scapegoat, drove her off when she approached, and kept her out of their games. It took her some time to absorb the lesson.

She was five or thereabouts when she came upon a group of girls playing jump-the-rope in the middle of the village's dusty lane. The chanting that accompanied the jumping seemed part of some mysterious ceremony, a ritual that everybody knew but her. The girls fitted the name of each jumper to the rhythm of their turning.

> *Here comes Zary!*
> *Right in the middle!*
> *Jump, Zary, jump,*
> *like fat on a griddle!*

Rocking back and forth to get the swing of the rope, Zary launched herself into the center and began to jump. Ammie and Meggit, turning the rope ends, let her jump for a bit, then speeded up until the rope was whipping dust from the ground. Zary kept up as long as she could, jumping faster and faster until her feet tangled in the rope and she was out. Meggit grinned, and her missing front tooth made it seem like a grimace.

There goes Zary!
Fat as a pig!
Had to stop jumping,
'cause she got too big!

Mokie drew closer. The rope turners saw her first and called to the others waiting their turn to jump. "Look what's coming," said Meggit. "It's the lost 'un. And she's still lost."

A shrill whoop of laughter hit Mokie in the face. She stopped, not sure what the joke was. The girls looked at one another and sniggered.

"Can I have a turn?" Mokie asked, as politely as she knew how.

"What?" called Ammie, pretending not to hear. She kept the rope turning. "What did you say?"

"I said—"

"What?" said Ammie loudly, drowning her out. "Can't hear you!"

Mokie tried shouting back, but not very loud. "I said can I have a turn."

"Did somebody say something?" Meggit asked Zary. "Did you hear anything?"

"Not me," said Zary happily. "I didn't hear anything."

Mokie came closer, so close she could feel the dust the rope kicked up as it slapped the ground with every turn.

"Can I play with you? I can jump the rope. Here. I'll

show you." She jumped heedlessly into the turning rope, missed her timing, got her feet hopelessly tangled, and fell heavily.

With herd instinct, the girls all at once tired of the game of pretending. When the rope stopped turning, Zary looked down at Mokie, then at the other girls.

"Look at that," she said. "Wants to play jump-the-rope and she can't even stand up."

She looked at Mokie lying in the dust. Delicately she prodded her with one pointed toe. "Go away," she said. "We don't want you."

"Why not?" asked Mokie.

"Because we don't," said Meggit with supreme illogic. She bent to scoop a small palm full of dirt, which she trickled artistically over Mokie's upturned face.

Mokie scrambled awkwardly to her feet, brushing the grit out of her nose and mouth. The girls were in a circle now, and she was in the middle.

"Lost 'un," taunted Ammie. "Lost 'un, lost 'un, lost 'un!"

The others joined in, chanting and pointing. Zary took a handful of dirt and flung it in Mokie's face. Suddenly they were all flinging dirt by the handful. Mokie stood her ground long enough to feel it sting her face and get in her eyes. As they closed on her, she burst out of the circle and began to run, stumbling, near-falling, catching herself and running on. The pack followed her for a little way, pelting her with dirt, but became as suddenly tired of the sport and went back to their game. They made up a new rhyme.

There goes the lost 'un,
crying in her shirt!
She can't jump,
'cause she's made of dirt!

She heard them as she ran, tears making muddy tracks down her face.

FOUR

THE CRYSTAL COUNTRY

MOKIE WAS HOPEFUL ENOUGH and unwise enough to make more attempts to join games, so the hard lesson was brought home to her again and again. She learned from the girls in pinafores who threw dirt at her. She learned from the boys who threw stones when she tried to join their games of skip-stone, who chased her away when they fought and wrestled and tumbled like puppies in the Farrow Field. It took her some while, but she learned to stay away.

But nothing could keep her away from stories of the Crystal Country, that enchanted, beautiful place that played such a vivid role in the imaginations of the folk of Little Wicken. Its shining brilliance offered a contrast to the drab, colorless life of the village, and made it seductive and frightening in equal measure.

After supper, when the children snatched at the last precious

17

moments of play before full dark, they congregated in the gathering dusk to tell stories. Whenever she could, Mokie crept within earshot and hovered, not near enough to be noticed and hurt, but near enough to hear the stories. She stayed silent, a shadow just within hearing, while the boys and girls told each other tales of the hard, glittering Crystal Folk who live in that magic world. Stories of adventure and romance where Crystal heroes triumphed over strange beasts that roared in glass forests, or fell in love with Crystal princesses and took them away to live in sparkling, many-towered palaces.

"They say the wind in the Crystal Country is green," the children whispered to one another, "and the grass and the leaves and the flowers are shiny like glass. The sun is a big, shiny marble and it rolls through the blue glass sky like a ball. The clouds are spun glass like sugar icing. Next to the Crystal Country, Little Wicken is a dull old place."

Others took up the tale. "The Crystal Folk are happy all the time. No one ever whacks them or makes them do chores. They do nothing all day but laugh and sing and play with balls of colored glass that never break. They live in beautiful silken tents that they can fold up and put in their pocket when they travel."

"Of course they laugh and sing," said Dommel. "So I would, too, if I had nothing else to do but play with balls. But they're jealous of us humans because we can cry. That's why they hate us. The Crystal Folk can't cry. That's how you can tell who they are."

"But," said one of the littler boys timidly, "don't they look different from us? Don't they look like Crystal Folk? All shiny and bright colored? Can't you tell who they are without they can't cry?"

"Sometimes," said Dommel. "But sometimes they look just like us, to fool people. And then you have to watch and see whether they cry."

What's so special about crying? wondered Mokie. I'd much rather not cry. It hurts too much.

The older ones took special pleasure in frightening the young ones with tales of Red Sorcha, the Queen of the Crystal Country. Red Sorcha was Mokie's favorite.

"Red Sorcha is a giant sow; her pig skin shines like snow." Ammie chanted the words like a jump rope rhyme. "Her ears are red, and in the dark they gleam like polished amber."

Meggit continued, "Her mouth is like an open door, her teeth are sharp as glass. She can bite through solid wood."

The children gasped in delighted horror.

Ammie picked it up. "Red Sorcha leads the Phantom Herd. They stampede in the moonlight. That's pigs just like our own pig herd, except they're all transparent."

The little ones shuddered deliciously and huddled together, begging to be told more. Mokie was not frightened. She hovered closer to listen.

"When they are hungry," another girl took up the tale, "and there are no people for them to eat, the Phantom Herd forages for silver acorns with golden caps that fall from oaks whose black trunks are twisted out of spun glass and whose leaves are clear green crystal."

Mokie's eyes grew round with wonder.

"Sometimes you can only hear them. On windy nights in autumn Red Sorcha and her herd run wild through the wood. Even if you're in bed with the covers pulled over your head, you can hear the pigs grunting and the sound of their hooves crashing through the underbrush. That's how you know the herd is running. If you're caught out-of-doors when the herd passes by, you'll be trampled by their hooves, run right over, and squashed flat and left for dead."

And the children would squeal and huddle closer and the little ones cry from fright.

"That's not what *I* heard," said Ammie. "My mum told me if you get caught by the Phantom Herd, they'll surround you and carry you off to the Crystal Country. They rush so fast you can't get away, and before you know it . . ." She stopped dramatically, letting her listeners imagine the rest.

"*My* mum told *me*," whispered Meggit, her eyes gleaming round like polished stones, "that Red Sorcha can take the shape of a beautiful woman with hair of changing colors. She dances to unheard music and captures you with her magic and you never get free. You belong to her and the Phantom Herd forever after and have to run with the ghost pigs. And you can never get home again."

Mokie thought about that, as much as she thought about anything. She imagined Red Sorcha, a magic figure shimmering between pig shape and woman shape, racing through the Wood with the wild herd running behind her. I wouldn't mind being captured by magic, she told herself. I wouldn't want to go home again. Not if home was Little Wicken. I'd stay in the Wood and eat silver acorns and run with the Phantom Herd. I bet they're nicer than the people here.

There being no one in whom she could confide these thoughts, she kept them to herself. She yearned for the bright and shining beauty she sensed in the tales of the Crystal Country, a world she half dreamed, almost half remembered. For one day, while she was still very young, too young to understand but only feel, she caught a glimpse.

It was springtime. In the sunny, dusty road, the usual clumps of children were quarreling and playing and shouting. Avoiding them, she took the path through the orchard up to the Farrow Field. The air moved gently, carrying the scent of greenness. In a place where deer had slept and left the imprint of their bodies she lay down, and the earth received her. She felt as if she were being pulled down, no longer on the earth but in it, yet at the same time she was falling upward into a sky that closed like water over her head.

The apple trees were coming into bloom, the pink blossoms deeper pink at the center, the colors light and airy against the new green of the leaves. As they nodded, swaying in the wind, she heard a chiming far away like the memory of bells. The echo of apples breathed in her nose. Then she saw that the blossoms were made of the most fragile tinted glass, crystalline and shimmering. The trees were black glass that glittered in the sunlight, the leaves were sharp green spear points of glass, the sky was a green glass bowl. The whole world was green glass, clear and bright as a river pool when the sunlight strikes into its depths. And she knew that she, too, was glass and filled with light. She felt herself chime in tune with the apple blossom bells. So sudden was the sensation that she cried out in pain, pierced by joy sharp as a killing knife.

It was well that it lasted only a moment; she could not have borne it any longer. Then it was over and everything changed back. The grass was simply grass, and bent under her hand. The trees were gnarled and twisted growths with aged, blackened trunks; the sky was thinned by far, high clouds; and the wind bore a breath of winter still.

The experience was so unlike anything else that had ever happened to her that she did not know what to do with it. All she could do was put it carefully away in a secret room in her mind. But she never forgot that it was there. Sometimes—not often, for fear of tarnishing—she took that moment out of the secret room and looked at it, turning it around and around in her mind's eye as if it were a green jewel that she treasured. She had no name for what had happened, and so she simply called it the Crystal Time.

FIVE

PLAYING

UNLIKE THEIR OFFSPRING, the grown-ups were not actively cruel to Mokie; they were mostly just uninterested. Occupied with their own children, they had nothing left over for one unwanted foundling. Oh, they fed her enough to keep her alive, and clothed, and sheltered from the weather. But she was not loved. For the most part she was either invisible or in the way, and when she got in the way, she was likely to be pushed aside, occasionally slapped or kicked, not from malice so much as impatience. She took the blows for granted. She survived because she must. And so she scrambled through the passing years any way she could, growing, but always on the edge of things.

If Mokie had been a pretty girl, pleasant to look at and soft to touch, she might have won a place for herself. But she was neither pretty nor soft. Instead she was tense and wriggly, from infancy hating to be held and fighting to get down as soon as picked up—which was seldom and then only to be moved aside like as not. As she grew she ran about in cast-off clothing always either too large or too small, but always torn and ragged. She was dirty because no one ever took the trouble to wash her. Her hair might have been ginger colored if it had been washed. It might have curled if it had been combed. But it never received any such attentions and was so matted with dirt, so tangled in snarls, that it looked more like thatch than hair.

Her eyes did not match, the left one being the somber brown of winter fruit and the right one the hopeful green of apples in springtime. Both kept a sharp lookout against the cuffs and blows that were part of her daily experience. Her nose wandered to the left, and her mouth followed it. Her chin was defiant. No one knew, least of all Mokie herself, that the defiance was an empty sham, a precarious defense against the hard knowledge that in a village so small that everyone knew everyone, no one wanted to know her.

There was nothing for her but pain in the laughter and the shouts of the village children, and so she found for herself a quiet place away from them all. Behind a ramshackle, abandoned shed on the edge of the village was a midden, a trash heap of useless, discarded items: broken pots and dishes, saucepans with holes burned through the bottom, straggly broom stubs with the straw worn away, scythes with split handles, gap-toothed rakes, pitchforks with broken tines.

Undisturbed among these rejects, Mokie made for herself a place of her own. When the taunts and mockery of the village children struck her like flung stones, she retreated to the shed of broken things. There she was free to follow her thoughts and feelings where they led, out into a world whose only horizon was the reach of her own imagination. Still, it was not enough. She wanted something . . . more? . . . something else? She wasn't sure.

One day in spring—it was her birthday, but she didn't know that, and she was ten years old; but she didn't know that either—she fled the laughing pinafores and the shouting boys and retreated to the shed. The ground there was dusty and easy to draw on, and it gave her an idea. She began to make a village. She smoothed out an area for the fields, marking off the boundaries with lines traced in the dust, and drew a wide curve for the river beyond. Then she began on the pebble houses.

Absorbed in outlining the houses, Mokie was unaware that someone was watching. A small, skinny boy with black hair falling untidily over his eyes as rainwater at night was standing at a corner of the shed. In one grubby hand he clutched the marble he had been playing with. It was made of green glass and he loved it, but he forgot it now in the fascination of the world he saw growing under the lost 'un's fingers. Step by step he crept closer, until he could almost touch her. Still Mokie did not look up. Hesitantly he reached out and placed his marble in the dirt beside the stones. Turning, she flung up a hand to ward off the expected blow, but stopped in midair when she saw him. For a moment she stared in puzzlement, for she knew him from somewhere. The fugitive half recognition teased at her memory, but fled even as she looked. She lowered her hand to scoop up the marble and place it in line with the pebbles, glancing up at the boy from beneath lowered lids.

"You're making it wrong way to," he told her. "It goes the other way. The houses on this side are closer to the road than the ones on the other side. Bigger, too."

She paid no attention, but went on lining up pebbles.

"Don't do that," he said. "You got it all wrong."

She went on.

"I said don't. Look what you done now! You spoiled the road."

"What do you know about it? It's not your road. I can make it how I want." But she stopped lining up the pebbles.

He explained carefully. "The road don't go like that. It turns at the last house, here, see?"

"Does not."

"Does too!"

"Does not!"

"Does so too. And it goes right the way down to the river. Like this, see?" He squatted beside her. "The river's a longer ways away than you made it. The road has to turn to get there."

"Well, anyway," she said, "it's not this road and it's not this river."

"What do you mean, it's not? The road's this road and the river's this river."

"No, it isn't. Not my road. Not my river."

"Your river? What's 'your river'?"

"It's the one—" She stopped to worry it for a minute, then began over. "I'm pretending a river. Not the real one. A play one, in . . . in my head. Sort of . . ."

She trailed off, stalled by the gap between her imagination and her limited store of words.

He sat back on his heels, head cocked to one side, thinking it over. Then he said, "Can I play too?"

She considered it, made her decision. She nodded—graciously. "All right. But I'm in charge."

"All right," he said. He smiled then a curiously sweet smile. "But let's make the road turn." He dragged a curve through the dust toward her imaginary river, disarranging the careful arrangement of stones.

"Now *you're* messing it up!" Angrily she pushed his hand away and began repositioning the pebbles.

With an equal burst of temper, he grabbed them away from her and began rearranging them to his liking.

She tried to grab them back, but he held on.

"Stupid!"

"Stupid yourself! Look now. The house goes here, and the

road turns here, and the river's down here." His hands moved with childish care, painstakingly rebuilding the house, realigning the road, directing it toward the river.

She saw that he was right.

"But it doesn't turn that much; it only bends a little." She brushed aside his track and began again.

"And the house sits sideways, not flat on the street like the others." He took pebbles and carefully arranged an off-angle outline, putting his marble where the door should be.

"Wait, leave room for the shed and the barn behind."

"I know," he said impatiently. "Give me those pebbles. I'll put how it should be." He grabbed for the pebbles.

"You give those back! I know how it should be, and I'll do it!" She grabbed them back again.

He pushed her. She fell. She got up and pushed him back. In a moment they were ruffing and scratching at each other like cats while the pebbles spilled careless into the dust. The two little figures closed with each other in miniature wrath, clinging and pummeling and rolling over and over while the pebble village went scattering in all directions. Like kittens they fought and like kittens they suddenly tired of fighting. They lay for a moment tangled and panting in the road and then, in perfect amity, began picking up the scattered pebbles and restoring them to order.

SIX

PAYiNG

ALL THE REST OF THE GOLDEN, DUSTY AFTERNOON they arranged and rearranged, as intent as craftsmen to make the finished product as perfect as could be. Two heads bent close over the task at hand, two shadows grew long and longer in the dust. So intent were they on their work that they failed to see the woman who suddenly loomed over them, skirts rustling angrily, forehead creased in perpetual frown. Her voice rasped like a rusty pitchfork against stone.

"Janno! So here's where you are, is it! I've been all over looking for you! What you doing here?" She grabbed a handful of Janno's hair and hauled him to his feet.

"We were playing." He gulped, tilting his head to ease the pull.

"I'll give you playing!" She gave his head a rough shake. "And who said you could? And how did you get so dirty? Look at you!

29

All over dust and your clean shirt too! And this—" She gestured contemptuously at his playmate. "You keep clear of her, the dirty little pig that she is and you'll be just like her if you're not careful! You stay away from that field brat! She's nothing but trouble!"

Why am I a pig? wondered Mokie. And she didn't know what Janno's mother meant by trouble, but she could see Janno's face screwed up with pain and she wanted to stop it.

"I'm not trouble," she said softly, timidly. "I wasn't—we weren't—"

That was as far as she got before Janno's mother, keeping firm hold of her son's hair with one hand, used the other to deal the little girl two ringing slaps, one on either cheek.

"I'll give you trouble, you little pig!"

At that, all Mokie's smothered rage erupted in a torrent she could not control.

"Pig yourself! I hate you! You mean old woman, you're worse than any pig that ever was! I hope the Phantom Herd tramples you and leaves you in the dirt! I hope Red Sorcha eats you up!" She stamped her foot and glared furiously.

With a hissing intake of breath, Janno's mother let go her son and took the child by the shoulders. She turned a look on her that chilled the little girl's bones.

"Don't! You! Ever! Say! That! Again!"

With every word she shook the child until her head rattled, then flung her down in the dust. Mokie lay where she had landed, terrified, bewildered, and uncomprehending. As Janno's mother dragged him away around the corner of the shed, he looked back at Mokie in frustrated pain until he lost sight of her, hustled by the hair back to where he belonged. When he was gone and Mokie was alone again, she picked herself up and looked around her at what they had made and marred and made again together.

Janno's marble lay in the dust of the road where it had rolled when the fight began. She picked it up and flung it violently against the shed wall. It made a loud *clunk*! But it didn't help the pain. With her two hands she smeared the patterns in the road back into uncreation. As hard as she could she kicked the pebble rows that had formed the houses until they were only scattered stones in the dirt. Then she stamped on the stones. Then she took them and threw them by handfuls after Janno and his mother. When all the stones were gone, she squeezed her eyes as tight shut as she could. If I don't cry, I won't cry, she thought, but the hurtful tears escaped despite her. They trickled down her cheeks and dripped off her chin one by one, making splash marks in the dust like summer raindrops.

She rubbed out the marks with one grimy foot. Then she walked over to the shed, scanning the ground with every step. She began casting about in ever widening circles. The search grew desperate, and anyone watching would have thought her life depended on finding the thing she sought. She stooped suddenly by a clump of grass at the base of the shed wall. Parting it carefully, she reached down and picked up the marble.

It was clear, bright green, the color of young leaves with the morning light shining through them. She balanced it on her palm, feeling its coolness, watching its slight roll as it responded to her heartbeat. As if its depths held a secret, she peered into it, sinking into its greenness as into a clear pool. She was enveloped, surrounded, held and buoyed up by green light. For a long moment she gazed. Then she blinked hard, closed her fist tightly around the marble, and marched away.

She saw Janno playing by his front door the next day. Their glances crossed briefly before he looked down, scratching his toe in the dust. He looked up for one moment, and their eyes met again. She would not close hers, would not cry, would not even look away. She held hard to the marble in her pocket. Mokie could not see the look on her own face then, defiant and beseeching. Janno saw and understood and shut his eyes. A hand reached from behind and yanked him indoors. Mokie stood her ground until he was inside and the door had closed behind him. Still clutching tight the marble, she turned and walked away, never seeing his face at the window, never knowing that he watched her until she turned the corner out of sight.

He was aware of her after that, every once in a while, as a flicker in the corner of his eye, as a hesitation in the distance when he played with the other children. Just a shadow under the trees, a movement in the grass, footprints in the dust of the road.

SEVEN

PiG GiRL

MOKIE KEPT THE MARBLE, took it out and looked at it often, but she never went back to the shed of broken tools. The raw wound Janno had left gradually scabbed over, but stayed sore and tender underneath. She schooled herself not to think of him or the shed, and most of all, not to cry ever again. As the years passed, it became her chief goal never to let anyone see her hurt. When the tears came, as they would despite her, she squeezed her eyelids and forced them back and said her prayer. If I don't cry, I won't cry. That made her feel strong, but the tears pushed inward made her stomach hurt, a dreadful, sick feeling that knotted her insides. She worked hard not to let anyone see, nor to let anyone come close to her ever, ever again.

Only the animals understood. They were as easy with her as if she were an animal like themselves, and she felt closer to them than to the people who treated her like one. The bony, emaciated cattle submitted to scratchings behind the ears and offerings of cow parsley, and the goats nibbled buttercups from her outstretched hand. What she liked best was that the pigs, especially the piglings, came at her beckoning and gathered around her like children when their mother calls them, grunting and squealing for the acorns and occasional windfall apples she bestowed on them.

The villagers, observing this, began to regard her as truly different from themselves—not as a real animal, of course, but as something a little less than a full member of the human community. The old changeling rumors and stories began to circulate again, and folk recalled to one another how she had simply appeared one day, born from no apparent mother, but from a storm. The older she got, the more they lumped her with the animals, and by the time she reached adolescence, her place in village life was fixed.

When in late autumn the farm beasts were driven wild-eyed through the bonfire smoke to make them fertile in the coming year, Mokie was set to wait for them on the other side. When they came through, bawling and snorting, it was Mokie who gentled them and calmed their terror.

Since she had a way with animals, she was set to watch the pigs. In this way she came full circle, for her welfare was given back into the charge of Grime and his flint-eyed wife. Grime was the pig keeper and had charge of the village herd. It was Grime who built up the herd, choosing which pigs to keep and which to sell off. It was Grime who decided which pigs would be slaughtered in pig-killing time. If crops were poor and there were too many bad years, so that an offering was needed, it was Grime who chose the pig sacrifice and saw to its carrying out. He was a man of substance, as substance was defined in Little Wicken. This meant chiefly that he had a cottage with two rooms instead of the usual one, and his wife had three dresses instead of the usual two—one to wear, one in the wash, and one for feast days.

"I suppose we have to find a place for you," said Grime's wife the first evening.

Her son, Dommel, standing behind her, smirked. "Put her in the pig yard," he suggested, glancing sideways at Mokie. "She'll be right at home."

Mokie looked at him.

"Not in the yard proper, she'd be underfoot of the pigs," Grime's wife continued. "But here'll do."

"Here" was the wattled lean-to at one side of the pig yard, a dirt-floored shelter with a straw roof. It was used as a birthing stall when the sows farrowed and was littered with sticks and straw. It smelled rank and sour, a combination of pig sweat and old blood.

Grime's wife tossed in a shapeless piece of rough sacking. "You can sleep on this."

Mokie picked it up and laid it against the wall.

"About the pigs," said Grime. "That big sow over there, the one with red ears, she leads the herd. Mornings, she'll take 'em up to the wood. You go along to keep 'em together, see they don't get into the corn. Bring 'em back at sundown. Make sure they're all in the yard and the gate's closed. You got to watch 'em close to see the little ones don't get trampled."

Mokie nodded. When the three Grimes had left, she looked about her. The sun was down, and gray twilight was shading into night. The sagging lean-to door opened into the pig yard where the pigs were gathered, staring curiously at her. She called to them, low and sweet, and the red-eared sow ambled over. Mokie took a stick and scratched the sow between her shoulders. The sow grunted gently and lay down on her side so Mokie could scratch her belly. Mokie squatted companionably beside her and continued scratching.

"Well," Mokie told her confidentially, "this is not so bad. I'd a heap rather be underfoot of the pigs than underfoot of the Grimes. If I had my choice of herds, I'd take the pig herd over the human herd any old time."

Then she dragged her sacking over to the open door and laid it in the soft dirt next to the sow. Snuggling up to the broad, warm back she was soon asleep. So was the sow.

Dommel brought her food the next morning, a loaf end and a rind of hard cheese.

"Sleep well, pig girl?" he asked. When Mokie made no reply, he grabbed her arm just above the elbow and pinched it hard, rolling the muscles painfully against the bone. She winced and tried to pull free, but he held her, grinning.

Grime's wife called from the kitchen. "Dommel! You come back here! Stop fooling with that pig girl and get in this house. Food's on the table."

He released her then, so suddenly that she staggered and fell in the muck of the pig yard. "That's where you belong," he told her. He left her sitting and swaggered off. She rubbed her arm, where a purple bruise was forming.

If the Grimes were no worse a family than any other in Little Wicken, still, they were no better, and it was not to her advantage that her job as pig herder made her a hanger-on in Grime's household. It gave her, however, the only name she ever had. For it was then that folk began to call her Mokie, though that was no more a real name than lost 'un.

"Why 'Mokie'?" inquired a stranger passing through the village on his way to somewhere. "That's just a word, isn't it?" His moist, mournful monkey eyes rested inquiringly on the outcast as she stood engulfed in the swirling, milling pig herd. "Not a real name at all. Not even a nickname. Doesn't it just mean 'pig'? Why would you call her that?"

It seemed an idle question, but he listened attentively to the reply.

"Oh, there's reasons," said Grime the pig keeper. He gestured roughly to Mokie to go on up the hill with the pigs, then turned back to the stranger.

"But you have the right of it. Not a name, 'mokie' isn't, nor even a real word. Nor it doesn't mean just 'pig' either. The word is just a kind of byword. It just means 'little girl pig,' or in her case, 'little pig girl.'"

And that was how Mokie got her name.

Grime continued. "She's not good for anything but running with the pigs. She's a pig, all right, you can see that well enough. As wild and dirty as they make them. Not but what she might turn out well enough when her bleeding starts and she's ready."

"Ready?" asked the stranger, a quizzical look on his round, wrinkled face. "Ready for what?"

"Why, for breeding, man." Grime gave the stranger a wincing poke in the ribs and followed it with a wink and a snigger.

"I'll see how she does. She's coming into her growth, you can see that, ripening into season. I'm keeping an eye on her." He stretched his mouth in a gap-toothed grimace that passed for a grin.

The grin was not a pleasant one, and the stranger did not respond in kind, or even acknowledge the nudge. Instead he watched the girl go her way up the hill with the pigs and disappear into the wood. Then he went on his way to wherever he was going, the tail of his green overcoat dragging after him in the dust.

EIGHT

ANOTHER COUNTRY

I N MOKIE'S MIND, she was not just the pig girl, but Red Sorcha of the Gleaming Teeth, Queen of the Pigs, and the village herd was her Phantom Herd. In the mornings, she led the village pigs in the Wild Hunt, driving them out of the pen, up through the orchard and the Fallow Field into the Wickenwood. All day they gobbled and foraged in the loose earth under the trees, busily feeding while Mokie watched the wood. She liked the deep, cool shade of many leaves, the rich, damp smell that filled her nostrils when the pigs snuffled the newlyturned earth for acorns.

The wood had its own life and sound. Mokie soon learned that even though all was quiet and watchful when she entered, if she kept still and waited, it never took long for things to happen. A slate-colored mockingbird with watchful eyes and an arrogant tail sang his signature song of three clear descending notes with variations. Once, twice, three times the call would ripple through the trees before the bird flirted his tail, spread his wings, and took off for fresh woods and a new audience.

A chipmunk came streaking across the glade, a bolt of brown-striped energy, and stopped abruptly on seeing her. Presently it sat up, front paws clasped to its chest, looking so comically sober and solemn that Mokie burst out laughing—at which it leapt away and dived under a tree root.

"Your mother wants you," she called after it. Then, in rude imitation of Grime's wife, "You get right in this—um—burrow!" She laughed, mostly at herself, but she missed the little darting thing when it was gone.

Lit by a shaft of sunlight on the forest floor, a cluster of minute blue-and-white butterflies pulsed and fluttered. Mokie thought they looked like flowers playing.

The wood was another country.

Pigs do not need a great deal of watching, so while the Little Wicken pig herd snuffled and rooted and dozed, Mokie beguiled the time by playing let's-pretend. When she tired of being Red Sorcha and found her Phantom Herd to be more interested in acorns than in her royal self, she created another world of tiny acorn and twig people whose lives she arranged in patterns vastly more interesting than her own.

"You," she told a small acorn in the palm of her hand, "are a found baby, a changeling, left in the human world by the folk from the Crystal Country. No one but me recognizes you or knows that you are special."

She laid the changeling tenderly in a hollow between two roots.

"There, now. While you sleep, I'll sprinkle you with magic dust. I am your Crystal mother, and when you wake I'll claim you, and we'll run away to the Crystal Country to live in my scarlet pavilion."

The pigs were un-enchanted, and continued to gruntle and root.

The stories centered on transformations and had always some grand conclusion that changed character from day to day with Mokie's chameleon imagination.

"This one is a poor orpheling." She held up for the pigs to see a twisty twig with two scrawny leaves for arms. "She was lost out of a red-and-yellow-painted caravan, but the raggle-taggle gypsies are coming to town with their jingling bells and juggling knives, and they'll know her as one of their own. They'll carry her off in triumph and dress her in swishing skirts and put shining rings in her ears. And then the mean old villagers will be sorry they treated her so bad. But it will be too late."

A sprig of fern wrapped round the twig became the swishing skirt, and the gypsy queen danced for her pig audience. The pigs looked up briefly, but soon returned their eyes to the earth.

"Shall I tell your fortune?" Mokie asked a large green acorn with a jaunty little cap set sideways. "I see with my extra sight that you are a royal princess, and you are disguised as a lady-in-waiting to save you from the Dark Magician. He is searching for you, but you are safe here in the wood, where he will not find you."

One or two pigs looked around to stare stolidly at the lady-in-waiting and then went back to their own, far more interesting occupation.

When these adventures waned with the setting sun, Mokie put aside the changeling child, the poor orpheling, and the lady-in-waiting until tomorrow. She came reluctantly back to her own world, calling to the pigs to round them up. They were sated with acorns and eager to get home, so that she scarcely needed to whack them with her staff to set them trotting homeward again. All running together, the herd made a sound like distant thunder on the dry earth, and Mokie, surrounded and nearly engulfed, had to take care that the pigs—her company and her kingdom—didn't accidentally trample her underfoot in their hurry. But she knew them all, and called to them by the names she had given them according to their habits and looks—Spotted, Lop Ears, Brownie, Snuffle, Long Tail, Squinny, Mud Snout.

So the years passed. Spring, summer, autumn came and went. Mokie dreaded wintertime, for it brought the Dark Month that was pig killing time. That was Grime's busiest time, and he was in his element. In late summer he marked out the pigs selected for slaughter and penned them separate from the rest. All through the autumn Grime's wife fattened them with extra scraps from the kitchen. Then, on a special day, their throats were cut and their bodies hung upside down for the blood to drain. The housewives caught the blood and thickened it for pudding. They cleaned out the carcasses, throwing the offal to the dogs, saving the guts to rinse and use for sausage casings. With bloody hands and blood up to the elbows, they cut out the heart as a special morsel and carved the loin to roast for the pig feast that followed the slaughter. Then they salted down the rest of the meat for winter. When the time for planting came in the spring, Grime directed the farmer to bury the bones in the field along with the planted seed so that the grain would grow.

Mokie hated the Dark Month. She hated the sight of the scaffolding and ropes they rigged to hang the carcasses. She hated the harsh, screaming rasp as the bright knives were sharpened on the spinning whetstones; she hated the coarse, easy laughter of the men as they went about the work and the shrill chatter of the women. Most of all she hated Grime, who was in charge of the killing. Worse than anything and almost more than she could bear were the high, almost-human death squeals of the pigs. Every winter Mokie lost friends, sometimes three or four, sometimes more. She always fled when the killing time came and stuffed her fingers in her ears, going as deep into the wood as she dared to shut out the dreadful sounds.

One year when she was quite young—before she was the pig girl—a worse thing befell. On the day before Killing Day, one particular pig, a little brown sow, was deliberately let loose from the pen. She scampered through the orchard up to the Farrow Field, her little snout lofted to sniff the air of freedom. She rolled in the tall grass, wriggling and scratching her back ecstatically. Then she got to her feet, ready for more running, only to see Grime standing over her.

She ran in the other direction, but Grime made no move to chase her. Another villager with a stone in his hand was waiting to head her off. She doubled back, only to meet another villager who ran at her, waving his hands and shouting. The little sow stopped short. All around her now were people, moving toward her and shouting. She panicked and began a stubby-legged gallop in a frantic circle, headed off by the villagers at every turn. She broke out of the circle at last and ran toward the wood, where Mokie stood watching.

The sow was almost there when the first stone hit her. She broke stride, veering wildly. Another stone, this time from the direction of the wood, hit her on the snout. Then they came fast and hard and from all directions. An especially big one made her stagger, and another struck before she got her balance. She went down. Then she was on her feet and running, but the stones had taken their toll and she had no speed left. When she fell again, she did not get up. The villagers closed in, battering her little body with more and more stones, stunning her into semiconsciousness.

One last time she tried to rise on her forelegs, but Grime

struck her hard on the forehead. At that she collapsed to the ground and rolled over on her side and lay dreadfully still. When it was clear that the little sow was dead and the drama was finished, the villagers made a circle around her. Grime scooped up a handful of earth and scattered it over her body. Then he and the villagers walked back to Little Wicken, leaving the poor, broken carcass lying in the field. When Mokie, drawn by a compulsion she did not try to understand, went to look the next day, the crows had already begun their feast.

Winter came early that year, with harsh winds and heavy snows that lay on the ground for months, thawed with reluctance, and froze again. With the spring melt, the ground was sodden, and the rains soaked it further and the river flooded, inundating the fields and delaying planting. When the water retreated and the sun finally shone, the late-planted crops seemed almost to leap up to touch it, so fast and high they grew. The harvest that autumn was bountiful.

In time the memory of the little sow receded and Mokie forgot her, except sometimes in dreams. When she dreamed, she was not only the watcher but also the little pig, feeling her terror and the thud of the stones as they hit her body. Mokie always woke up shivering and dry-mouthed, but she never remembered the dream.

NINE

A Likely-Looking Sow

NEXT TO THE DEATH CRIES OF THE PIGS, the sound Mokie hated most was the constant catcalling and derision of the village boys. They took to following after her as she drove the pigs, yelling and taunting. The leader in this was Dommel Grime, who took it as his right to persecute the pig girl since, as he saw it, she belonged to his father. He was just then beginning to get his growth, and went out of his way whenever he could to tease and torment her with furtive cuffs and pinches that left her spotted with bruises. She learned not to fight back, knowing that if she did, he would simply punish her more cruelly next time. And if he didn't, Grime would. Both Grime and his wife saw the teasing as part of normal young male behavior and made no move to stop it. She was, after all, only the pig girl.

The other boys followed Dommel's lead. "Yah! Yah! Mokie!"

they would yell. "Oink! Oink!" and, "Hey, piggy! Want an acorn?" A hail of acorns would come flying after her. In the summer the acorns were small and green and hard; in the autumn they were big and ripe and brown and even harder. Either way they hurt. At first she ducked and tried to run, but the boys kept after her. After that happened a few times, she turned on them in fury.

"Pigs yourselves!" she yelled. "You're not even worth herding! See how you like *these* acorns!"

She began hurling the acorns furiously back where they came from. One especially large acorn struck Dommel so hard his nose began to bleed. So then the boys began to laugh at him instead of Mokie. He never forgave her for that. The boys soon learned that she could throw as well as they and hit harder. When enough acorns had hit them enough times, they stopped. For a while.

So time went on, and no one, least of all Mokie, heeded that she was growing. But growing she was, as she had to, in the way that all female creatures must. And when her bleeding time did come, as Grime had foreseen, everything changed.

Between one day and the next she grew taller and softer, or so it seemed to those who began to watch her. Her legs got longer and her body stretched and softened into smooth curves. Tender, vulnerable breasts began to show through the holes in her ragged shift and to alter the balance of her body. Her eyes got larger and her mouth fuller. Even her nose looked less like a mistake and more like a piquant irregularity. The swing of her long legs caused a sway in her hips when she walked. The tilt of her chin seemed more a challenge than a warning.

There being no mirror in the wood, Mokie was unaware of this. She was only conscious that her body was becoming heavy and slow and would not obey her. An unaccustomed lassitude weighed down her legs, robbing them of swiftness. Her new breasts felt tender and sore. They hurt her, and she found that they got in the way whenever she tried to climb a tree. And not just her body changed, but so did her surroundings and the people in them, for it was then that her small world began to notice Mokie.

The first were the wives. Although some of them were little older than Mokie—Little Wicken girls were married off young and started bearing children early—they all rolled their eyes, shook their heads, clicked their tongues.

"Saw that pig girl again today, taking the pigs up the Wickenwood," said Ammie's mother, a round, rosy woman with a perpetually smiling face. "Somebody ought to get that one a new dress. Enough holes in the one she's got on to see everything she's got."

"Yes, and there's plenty that like what they see," answered Grime's wife, and her eyes narrowed.

"Bet she knows it, too. They're all alike, that kind. Can't blame the boys. She's looking for trouble."

"I told Grime when he brought her home no good would

come of it, and I'll say it again. You mark my words." She tightened her lips and nodded portentously.

And then the boys who had chased after her with acorns began to change their tactics. Instead of shouting insults, they looked at her under their lids when she went past with the pigs. They strutted and made comments and told each other smutty jokes, loudly, so that she would hear.

"There's a nice loin of pork. Make a hot roast, that would. How about a bite, eh? Go on, I dare you." They would grin and nudge one another in the ribs.

Of course the girls saw how the boys behaved. Of course they blamed it on Mokie. They gave one another meaningful looks whenever she went past. They rolled their eyes and looked slantways at one another. They never spoke to her, but they spoke at her, and they sounded just like their mothers.

—you can tell—

—looking for trouble

—looking for something—

—bet she'll find it—

—my mother said—

—way she walks—

The boys bothered her, but the girls hurt her. Still, both boys and girls were easier to deal with than Grime. He took to treating Mokie in a new and disturbing way. He would talk louder when she was about, making sure she could hear. "There's a likely-looking young sow. Ready for breeding she is. You can smell it, can't you?"

He would stand uncomfortably close when she took the pigs out. He found reasons to touch her. It made her nervous, and she devised as many ways as she could to avoid him.

Mokie was not stupid. She knew perfectly well what was going on. She had grown up around barnyards and she knew the behavior of animals in season. She understood the jokes and the snide comments. She knew too much and too little. It all made her want to run and hide more than ever. She thought she could run from her body, but as time went on, she would learn that she took it with her wherever she went.

Other things were changing as well, most of all the weather. The same years that saw Mokie grow and change from girlhood to budding womanhood saw the summers get progressively hotter and drier, the winters get colder and drier. Every winter there was less and less snow to soak into the iron-hard ground and soften it for planting. Springs came later and later, and the earth changed from frozen to dry with little or no snowmelt to moisten it. The spring rains, which should have made up for the lack of snow, fell sparser and sparser. The sun shone relentlessly out of a hard blue sky with never a cloud in it. Dust blew up in the faces of the men as they broadcast the seed. Heat hung over the fields, making the air quiver. In such times the pigs fared better than the villagers, foraging under the thick shade of the Wickenwood for the acorns that fell and were enough for them, but the grain as it ripened was meager in the head, the stalks brittle. If Mokie had been as slow to ripen, her life might have been different.

TEN

CRYSTAL CONSPIRACY

DEEP IN THE TREE DARKNESS OF THE WICKENWOOD, a faint glimmer shone from a ramshackle hut. Outside the hut an autumn wind tossed branches and whirled leaves skyward. Inside the hut a candle flame clear as glass, unwavering in the still air, threw against the walls the shadows of the three around the table.

Lally huddled into a patched and faded shawl pulled close around her shoulders. Her voice chimed clear as a glass bell.

Well. She's come, then, hasn't she? Then let's move. What bothers me is this hanging about like specks of dust in a sunbeam. We've been here forever. Let's get it over. We're running out of time.

Ah, no, Lally, that we're not. When you're out of time the way we are there's no running at all.

Hunched into a green overcoat many sizes too big, The Skimmer blinked his round, sad eyes against the candlelight. His voice was dry and husky, like last year's leaves.

It's her time I'm talking about, Skimmer. You know very well what I mean.

Of course I do, Lally. And you know what I mean, too, right enough. But time's coming. I know you're anxious to get on with it. Well so am I. So's John. We neither of us like hanging about any more than you do, any more than we like what has to happen. Right now we're just observers, you might say. We can watch, but we can't move yet. We're waiting on her — or rather, on both of them. And they'll take their time.

John said nothing. The candlelight struck gleams off his eyes, opaque as black glass. He tossed and caught a green glass marble, tossed and caught it over and over. As it rose and fell, the marble trapped the candle's flame in its depths, tracing the same green arc repeatedly through the air.

Whatever their time is. Can't we hurry it?

Lally, you can't hurry a pattern, any more than the seasons or the way the stars turn. Might as well try to hurry moonrise. We have to take things as they happen.

When they happen. If they happen.

They'll happen, all right, and well you know it. They'll come when they come and not a minute sooner. Nice fools we'd be to try to force things. Sure as we did, somebody'd notice, tip the balance, and then where'd we be?

53

Right where we are now. No place at all.

She shivered, snuggling her shawl closer about her thin shoulders.

Not that it's any better out there. It's dark out there. And it's cold. And look at the trees, how they're tossing like they're angry about something. You can see the wind is blowing a gale.

Well, of course it's dark out there, ninny.

The green overcoat's sleeve-ends waved toward the wood.

Of course it's cold out there. Of course it's blowing a gale. What you expect? Out there is—out there. It's their world, not ours. It's where things are moving, and not just trees. Have you forgotten so soon?

I was thinking of the people more than the weather. Have I forgotten? Do I remember? Not if I can help it. Some times . . . some times I can't help remembering, but it's different every time, and all the times run together so that they're all the same time. I do remember some things. Little snippets. Like—I think I remember scissors. Silver scissors with etched handles. But what scissors could have to do with anything I don't know.

She shook herself like a cat that has stepped in water.

And a tree. A big, old oak tree. It told stories. No, that's silly. But somebody told stories. And I think I remember a bird calling. Now why would I remember that? And I think I remember—no!

She huddled deeper into the shawl.

Not that. Whatever it was, it's something I don't want to remember. But I don't want to hang about here in the Doorway, either. This

54

*time is bound to be just like the last time, like any time. Whatever time,
I just want to get on with it.*

We'll get on with it, I promise you that.

Skimmer, if you say that once more I'll bite you.

When time comes.

The room hummed with the dark sound of John's voice, as if
a finger had been run around the edge of a glass bowl. The marble rose and fell, rose and fell, ceaselessly tracing the same airy
path.

*Things have to happen in their right order. They're just beginning,
just starting to happen now.*

*And quit it now can't you, John! Forever playing with that ever-
lasting marble! Why you brought it with you I can't imagine.*

She reached over and snatched the marble out of his grasp,
slammed it on the table where it wobbled for a moment, then
rolled immediately back to John.

Can't you imagine, Lally? Can't you?

Lally frowned and began to speak, then thought better of it,
and looked away.

John picked up the marble and began tossing it again.

ELEVEN

Storm Born

ONE THUNDERY SUMMER EVENING when Mokie was fifteen, or thereabouts, she was driving the pigs home from the wood as usual. It was the third year of the drought, and for once a storm looked to be making up, though the rain, if it came at all, would be too late to help the fields. The herd moved slowly, gruntingly down the Farrow Field toward the orchard. They were eager to get home, for it was late in the day.

The air grew close and heavy, and a livid, green-yellow light hung over everything. The sinking sun disappeared behind a bank of slate-colored cloud. Then the wind came up, spinning dust devils out of the dry earth. The storm broke. Lightning cracked open the sky. Thunder crashed and reverberated. The trees in the wood thrashed, their branches sailed through the air.

In the middle of the storm the big white sow with red ears who led the herd, the cranky one whose uncertain temper and tendency to bite had led Mokie to name her Red Sorcha, slowed, then stopped. She lay down in the field at the edge of the orchard. Pregnant out of season, she was full and heavy, urgent with the need to give birth. She let out a deep, unearthly groan, and Mokie could see well enough that her time was on her.

"Oh, Sorcha, not now!" Mokie prodded her with the stick. "Get up, you old thing! Come on. Only a little way more and you'll be in the pen and safe and warm."

Red Sorcha groaned, and her belly clenched, but she did not stir. Mokie looked down to the village. No one else was around, folk having fled indoors when they saw the storm coming.

"Well, then, no help for it. Stay there," she told the sow, who showed no sign of going anywhere. "I'll be right back." As quickly as she could, she drove the other pigs down to the village and into the pen, where she shut them securely. Then she came back to Red Sorcha and settled down next to her to attend the birth.

While she watched and the sow labored, the storm raged, drenching the orchard and soaking Mokie and Red Sorcha equally. Neither paid attention, for there was more important work at hand. Mokie held the sow's head firmly between her hands, and before very long out they came one after another after another, almost too fast to count—twelve piglings in the birth. Just to be sure, Mokie examined Red Sorcha's belly. Sure enough, there were twelve teats—just enough to suckle the piglings. They were small, curled, wriggling things of a uniform dun color, with miniature trotters and tight-wound tails like little springs, and their restless snouts quivered with the first breaths of new air.

Then, when all seemed over and a sodden, shivering Mokie was collecting the piglings to put them to suck, lightning opened a jagged crack in the sky over the heart of the Wickenwood. A final great heart-stopping concussion of thunder beat directly over her head. The sound jolted the air from her lungs and body like a blow from some huge hand. Mokie choked and gasped for breath. As she did so, out came a thirteenth pig baby that landed in the orchard grass like a flung stone. At the same moment, fireballs, three whirling globes of brilliant blue-white light, played above them and disappeared into the depth of the wood. The clouds broke, parted, and a setting sun drove its light through the rift in the sky.

Spent from her labor, Red Sorcha lay on her side, exhausted and empty. She was only just able to give suck, and all the work was done by the voracious piglings. They fought and scrabbled and squirmed their way to the teats, where they subsided into the bliss of their first meal. All but the thirteenth pigling.

Having all she could manage with the first twelve, the sow was completely unprepared to welcome this new and hungry little mouth. Unlike the other piglings, who were plain brown all over, this baby was parti-colored—white, with rust-red ears, like her mother. The likeness clearly did not impress Sorcha, who sniffed with weak suspicion at the unlucky thirteenth and would have eaten her if Mokie had not snatched the baby out of harm's way.

Mokie, usually so guarded against giving herself to anyone or anything, took an unexpected liking to the hungry, crying runtling. She picked her up and held her close, and the little thing, so warm and new and wriggly, snuggled close against her and tried to suck her finger. That gave Mokie an idea. First making sure that all twelve piglings were at suck, she took the squirming runt in her arms and went down through the orchard.

Grime was loafing about near the pigpen, watching, as he often did now, for her to come in with the pigs. "Eh, there! You! Young Mokie! Where's my pig, then? Sorcha's not in the pen. And what's that you've got?"

"Sorcha's up in the Farrow Field," Mokie told him. "She had her litter."

"And couldn't you get her to the pen in time? Should have driven her, carried her." This although Sorcha weighed easily three times as much as Mokie and would have been a heavy burden for any two grown men.

"Not much good, then, are you, pig girl? How'll I get them piglets safe penned? Likely to drown up there in the field."

Harsh as the words were, Mokie preferred his anger to the looks he had begun to give her lately, as if she were a sow whose worth he was calculating. So she bore his tirade in silence, and when she was sure he had finished, she told him

59

the size of the litter. Then he was pleased, and grinned his wolf's grin. It was well enough that Mokie had done his work for him, and Red Sorcha was the biggest of his sows—strong and well able to feed such a litter. So large a farrow, unusual in a lean year, was a good sign and promised well for next year's pig killing.

He was turning away to his own concerns when Mokie showed him the little extra one. The pigling was small and ill-favored, and didn't look likely to grow. It would only take milk from the rest of the litter.

"Drown it," he said without hesitation.

"Can I keep it?" she asked.

It was the first time in her life she had ever asked for anything, and she dared only because the baby was a throwaway, like the rubbish in the shed of broken tools. Grime looked at her closely. The little pig was quiet now, cradled in her arms, nestled up against her breast, and there was an unlikely softness in her voice and manner that caught his interest.

She bore his look and looked back without the defiance that usually marked her, and that caught his interest even more.

"Can I?" she persisted. "Keep it?"

He stood very close to her.

"What you want with a runt pig anyway? If you're wanting to cuddle, there's better ways to do it, and better things to do it with than a pig, eh?"

She froze like a rabbit in an open field, refusing to understand him. She dropped her eyes and looked as uncomprehending and stupid as she knew how, but stubbornly stood her ground.

"Keep it if you want, but you'll get more trouble than it's worth. How you going to feed it? You're no mother sow."

He reached a dirty, broken-nailed finger and prodded her breast, watching her from under his eyebrows. "Not yet, anyway. But we'll see about that."

She bore it as she bore all abuse, by pretending it wasn't happening. Only she went rigid, holding herself in suspension, not looking at him, not looking at anything, until it was over.

Getting no response, Grime tired of the game. "We'll see about that," he said again. Laughing at his own joke, he hurried off to count over his pig crop.

Mokie watched him go up through the orchard. I may not be a mother sow, she thought, but I'm better for this pig than you'll ever be, you mean old skinflint. We'll show you. The two of us. You wait and see. Then she stole off quietly to the dairy. The stoneware crocks, brimful from the evening milking, stood cooling in a row on the shelf, waiting to separate and for the cream to rise. She filled a little jar from one of these and returned for the first time to her own private place behind the shed of broken tools. There she settled down with her nursling in her arms. Mokie was ill prepared for motherhood, and her first attempts at feeding combined spilled milk and frustration in equal parts.

First she tried dipping her finger in the milk and letting the

61

baby suck from her finger end, and that went well enough but for the fact that a finger end holds very little milk for a hungry piglet. So then, tucking her infant under one arm for safety, she went back to the dairy and filched a clean cheesecloth from the ripening room. Back at the shed, she twisted the cloth into a makeshift teat, dipped it in the jar, and coaxed the baby to suck from that. It was slow going, for the little one had an alarming tendency to swallow the cloth along with the milk. The first few times it very nearly disappeared down the little pig's gullet and Mokie had to haul it out, an operation to which her child did not take kindly. But after a few false starts and a certain amount of temper on both sides, both she and the pigling got the hang of it, and the baby began to suck enthusiastically.

Mokie settled down comfortably, her back against the shed wall and her nursing infant in her arms. Cradling her close, Mokie felt a warmth she had never known before. In the rejected little pigling, so helpless and trusting, so eager to love and so ready to be loved, she found her hidden self.

"Pig child," she said, "little pig girl just like me, nobody wants us. Never mind, we can want each other. I'll be your mother now, and you can be my lost 'un, my orchard baby with red ears, my little red windfall apple."

And that was how Apple got her name.

TWELVE

LADY~IN~WAITING

IT WAS CLEAR FROM THE START that Apple was not an ordinary pig. She responded to her name after the first day, and right from the first she appeared to understand everything that was said to her. Unlike the other pigs, who slept in the dust or mud of the pig yard, Apple slept snuggled close to Mokie in the little wattled lean-to. Perhaps because of this closeness, she was uncannily sensitive to Mokie's moods and emotions—frisky when Mokie was happy, consoling when Mokie was sad, curiously protective when the village children teased.

She came perilously near to biting a girl one evening as the pig herd returned to the village. Meggit, who had trickled dirt on Mokie when she tried to play jump-the-rope so long ago, had hated her ever since. When Mokie and Apple passed with the pigs, Meggit voiced her opinion loud enough for Apple to hear.

In no time at all Apple had jumped out of Mokie's arms and before Mokie could grab her was nipping at Meggit's heels. The girl ran squealing to her mother.

"Calm down, Apple," Mokie said, "or you'll get me in trouble. And anyway, I'm supposed to be taking care of you, not the other way around. Who's the mother here, after all?"

To this last question Apple made no reply, but it was clear from the way she looked at Mokie that she had her own ideas.

While the village pig herd ranged far through the wood, rooting in the oak mast, Apple stayed close to Mokie. She trotted busily after her when she wandered, sat content by her when she rested, and nursed on stolen milk as often as Mokie could get it—which was regularly, for Mokie was a dedicated mother and became, in the nurture of her child, a stealthy and practiced thief. Her clandestine forays into the dairy were carried out with skill and intelligence. She never skimmed from one crock only, but divided her takings equally among them all so that none looked any less full than the others. And so Apple thrived.

So well did Apple prosper as a result of Mokie's mothering that she rapidly grew sleek and round. Though she had started out the smallest, she caught and surpassed the growth of her littermates in a surprisingly short time. Never having to fight for her place, nourished on stolen cow's milk and then on the tasty mash of milk and acorns that Mokie stirred up for her, Apple was rapidly becoming what any farmer would call a prize pig.

And that is just what Grime decided when he noticed her

trotting off one day to the wood with the other pigs at Mokie's herding. Forgetting his order to drown the runt, he came to think of Apple as his. He was content to let Mokie look after her for the moment, but he developed plans of his own in which Apple played a significant part, and Mokie, a rather different one. Mokie was completely unaware of all this, and that was just as well.

For the first time in her life, Mokie had a companion and friend. And something more, for she came to think of Apple as almost a part of her, another self reflecting back to Mokie all that she thought and felt and imagined. She and Apple took possession of a certain tree—a massive holly oak, ancient as days, that ruled the edge of the Wickenwood. The oak was so old, its branches spread so wide, that all the ground underneath it was bare of other growth, leaving the earth soft and welcoming. Great roots ran outward from the tree's base like knobbed fingers. Fallen acorns came to rest in the hollows between the roots. In Mokie's inner geography it was marked as the story tree, for it was there that she shared with Apple the part of herself that she hid from others.

See Mokie and Apple any summer afternoon in comfortable company under the shade of the story tree, Mokie cross-legged in the hollow between two of the largest roots, her back propped against the massive trunk. Apple sits facing her, all attention. They are alone and content, the girl with her imagination free to roam, the pig in sympathy, her little old wise face cocked to one side, her narrow eyes closed to mere slits, her sharp little ears pricked to alertness. Mokie looks up, seeking inspiration in the canopy of branches that spreads above her, searching for the words the leaves are whispering. Her head is tilted sideways, listening. Her face is open, receptive, her eyes are wide, her lips are half parted to repeat the words she can almost hear. So nearly beautiful she looks at this moment that Grime would scarcely recognize her. She plucks a story out of the air.

"Someday, Apple, when you're rooting for acorns, you'll find one made all of silver and its cap made all of gold. I'll plant it and a tree will grow with leaves of green glass and in the autumn it will bear more silver acorns with golden caps. They'll fall, and we'll gather them in heaps. Some I'll wear for a necklace, and one I'll tie to your tail. We'll dwell beneath the green glass leaves like kings and queens and live on silver acorns and gold."

Apple looks gravely up, waiting for more. When Mokie tires of telling stories, she puts her head back against the old tree's gnarly trunk and dozes or daydreams. Apple settles down next to her, folds her trotters, drops her snout, and closes her eyes. It looks as if she, too, is dozing. But from time to time her eyes open, and she looks long and hard at the girl beside her. Then Apple's eyes close again.

One unseasonably hot, dusty afternoon they settled themselves comfortably under the story tree, grateful for the shade and the coolness it gave. At some distance away in the wood, the other pigs snuffled and rooted, giving from time to time little grunts of pleasure. Mokie sat cross-legged with her back propped against the trunk, and Apple sat directly in front of her, with her little pig snout twitching in anticipation. Mokie began a new story.

"You are not an ordinary pig, you know, Apple," said Mokie, pulling her ears affectionately.

Apple looked inquiringly at Mokie and blinked.

"You were special from birth. You are the one over the dozen. You are the lucky thirteenth, born on the wings of the storm. Suppose you are—" she rummaged in her mind for something new and wonderful to build a story on.

"I know! Let's pretend you are not a pig at all, but a fairy queen, shape-changed by a dark magician. You are a royal lady who has been robbed of her kingdom and made to toil and trouble in the world."

The scatter of twigs and leaves on the fairy queen's nose from rooting in the dirt was no bar to the storyteller's eager imagination. The fact that the royal lady neither toiled nor troubled but was the happy gobbler of everything edible that came within her compass, this bothered Mokie not a whit. She continued to embroider her fancy.

"Shall I be a fairy queen too? No," she decided, "that's one queen too many. I'd better be your fairy lady-in-waiting. I wonder what a lady-in-waiting is supposed to be waiting for."

Instead of listening attentively, as she usually did, Apple nudged at Mokie with her hard little nose and whimpered.

Mokie looked up from her story to see a ring of village boys standing looking at her, six or seven of them.

The biggest boy stood a little in front of the others. He was a thick-bodied, bull-necked youth with greasy hair growing low on his brow, overhanging his flat, close-set eyes. She knew him all too well. It was Dommel, who was fast getting a reputation in Little Wicken as a troublemaker. Dommel had all the qualities of a successful bully, in which respect he took after his father. His usual method was to taunt the other boys into some act of random mischief—snatching bundles from a housewife, chasing a gathering of little girls happy with hopscotch or jump-the-rope. Once he and his gang had crept behind a bush to spy on an old man squatting to void himself, with his pants down and his bum bare. Dommel made them push him down in his own dirt and run away laughing.

Too often of late Mokie had seen him watching her when she led the pigs to the wood, and felt his eyes following her when she brought them home again. Mokie looked up at Dommel. His face had a look she had seen before. Her voice died away; she stood up and reached for her stick.

"Grab her," said Dommel, and two boys grabbed her by the arms while a third kicked her legs out from under her. She fell heavily and they let her fall, though they held on tight, closing in around her.

Dommel undid the rope that held up his pants. Mokie knew what he was going to do. She had watched the pigs often enough. What she didn't know, nor did the other boys, was that he had never done it before. That was his secret. This was his chance. "Hold her down," he said.

The two holding her arms tightened their grip. Another pushed her head back, one hand against her forehead, the other against her throat. Two others jerked her legs apart and held them. Mokie risked one desperate look at each of her assailants in turn. None of them would meet her eyes except the youngest boy, who stood a little apart. She recognized him. It was Janno, the boy with gray eyes, the boy she had played and fought with so long ago, the boy whose mother had called her a little pig. The boy whose green marble she still kept. Once only did Janno look at Mokie directly, his face expressionless. Then, as he had done that other time, he shut his eyes. After that Mokie lay still, too proud to struggle, too stubborn to beg.

Dommel pulled up her shift, ripping it in the process, for the cloth was thin and worn. She did not move. He looked around, daring his gang to dare him, but they were as silent as Mokie. None of them had ever done it either, though each of them kept that fact as his own secret. Now they would watch and learn. Dommel swallowed and dropped his pants, hoping desperately that he would not be shamed and inadequate. He was not shamed. His body was readier than he was. Well, then the thing was to be done. Before he could lose his nerve he dropped to his knees and straddled her, feeling all the while the eyes of the other boys watching every move.

Every muscle in her body tensed. The gnarled knob of a tree root dug into her back between her shoulder blades. Far off, in another country, a mockingbird called—three plaintive descending notes, over and over. Mokie closed her eyes as she felt Dommel push inside her, clumsy and rough and hard. Her body clenched itself against the intolerable insult. Something tore. She felt herself slipping, lost in the pain, until finally there was no Mokie, there was only the pain.

It did not take very long, only forever. The pain kept on. The bird sang. Suddenly he gasped and slumped heavily against her. She opened her eyes to the sight of his face hanging dark above her, blotting out the tree and the sky. She did not move.

The boys looked at one another, embarrassed and wondering if they would be expected to go next. After a long moment, Dommel withdrew and stood up. He pulled up his pants and tied his belt and looked around at the boys standing wordless, staring them down, daring them to fault his performance. He waited, but no one spoke.

"Let her loose," he said.

She did not stir when they released her and stood up. They waited for her to move, to say something, to beg or plead or admit that they had prevailed and it was done and she was what they made her. She could not speak. They thought it was that she would not speak, and they judged her accordingly. The silence grew. "Come on," Dommel said at last, and strode off. One by one, the others turned and went away, a silent line.

70

At the edge of the little clearing the youngest boy, Janno, hesitated, turned toward her, turned away, then came slowly back. Not looking at her face, not looking at his hands, he took her torn skirt and pulled it down to cover the blood on her thighs. Then he followed the other boys away out of the wood and back to the village.

THIRTEEN

THE WITNESS

AFTERWARD, MOKIE WAS VERY STILL. She did not move. She did not cry. She was very cold, but she made no effort to cover herself, no attempt to clean herself, or even to find out the damage. She did not want to look. All the while Apple had been circling, whimpering, trying to find a way in to her, blocked by the boys. Now she came and rooted against Mokie, sniffing her all over, uttering plaintive, nurturing little grunts. Without looking, Mokie reached an arm and pulled her close, cuddling the little pig warm against her side. "Apple," she whispered, "Apple. Apple."

All afternoon Mokie lay there lost to herself, never stirring, never shutting her eyes. Meanwhile the boys, excited and anxious, prideful and ashamed, were busily constructing their own memory of what happened, talking it up to make it true. As they talked, their fear receded and bravado took its place, covering over their shame. What they had done, what their leader had accomplished, became an exploit to be boasted of, and what they told each other they came themselves to believe. The pig girl was nobody after all, so who cared? She'd never been anything but the lost 'un anyway. Hanging around in the woods all by herself, what did she expect? Just waiting for someone to come along. She was a tease parading herself for their eyes; she had as much as invited them; she had been asking for it. They said it over among themselves to make sure it was true. Hearing them talk, the housewives smiled at one another with angry satisfaction. Just what they had predicted. Just what they had expected.

Just what they had wanted.

When the westering sun drove its level rays through the open spaces in the wood, Mokie stood up. The suddenness of her own movement and the pain in her body unbalanced her. The trees turned cartwheels around her and she nearly fell. Dizzy and sick, she reached out to the holly oak to steady herself. A pit of darkness opened at her feet and she stared into deep, empty, black nothing. She felt herself falling and knew that if she let go, she would fall forever.

She held on. She looked at her hand resting on the story tree, the witness. "Remember," she told it. Her skin felt the rough, scarred bark of the massive trunk, and with her hand she gave what had happened to her into the keeping of the tree, to hold it for her until she could bear to look at it.

Then slowly, methodically, as if her body did not belong to her, Mokie put herself to rights, carefully smoothing her shift down over her legs, pulling closed as best she could the rips and tears in the flimsy fabric, brushing the leaves and twigs out of her hair. Then she picked up her staff. Moving deliberately, she rounded up the pigs and drove them home, herding them out of the wood, down the field, and into the pig run.

The village wives were waiting for her, watching tight-lipped and narrow-eyed. They took note of the new tears in the shift. They observed the way she walked, stiff and awkward, as if she hurt inside.

"Slut," said Grime's wife conversationally to her neighbor, as one might say, "Nice day."

The neighbor, Ammie's mother, nodded. "Tramp," she agreed pleasantly.

"I always knew it," added Grime's wife. "I've seen her with the boys."

Ammie's little sister Del, half hiding behind her mother's skirts, flung a pebble. There was only a child's uncomprehending malice to aim it, only a child's feeble strength to launch it, and the missile fell short.

It hit its target, nonetheless.

Then the mutterings began.

—told you—

—scandal—

—half dressed—

        —no shame—

    —I heard—

           —mark my words—

—bad fortune—

The gossip pot was on the boil, and for the third time in her life Mokie was a choice morsel. She heard the wives, she saw their eyes, she understood the words, but she gave no sign, only tilted her chin and wrapped her defiance tight around her. When the pigs were safely penned and the pen gate latched shut, she took her stick and called to Apple. Together the two of them walked back into the Wickenwood, turning their backs on Little Wicken.

FOURTEEN

DARK TIME

WITH NO CLEAR NOTION of where she was going, Mokie headed instinctively for the heart of the wood. Apple pattered after her. If Mokie had been attending, she might have been aware that someone was behind her and tracking her passage. But she was not attending, and so she heard nothing of the careful, quiet tread along the forest floor, the barely perceptible rustling sound of someone slipping cautiously in and out of the shadows.

Mokie had no idea of her direction, but she did not care. She walked blindly among the trees, her feet following a slender thread of a track that wound around and around, in and out of the trees and underbrush, looping and doubling on itself like an animal in flight. It took her into the place where the dark was deepest, away from all sight and sound of folk. Outside the wood the sun was throwing its last light across the fields, but deeper within the wood the shadows were already somber.

Darkness fell. After a time the crescent moon rose, the silver Night Mother who births herself and devours herself afterward, only to give herself birth again—a ceaseless round with a promise of birth and death and renewal. Though she was only a spectral glimpse beyond the branches overhead, she shone dusty silver through the trees and lighted their way. A ripple of sound and an occasional glint or sparkle told of water over shallow stones, a brook that ran beside their path. Leading them deeper and deeper into the wood, the path suddenly disappeared. Mokie, putting one foot after the other as in a dream, was abruptly brought up short, her way blocked by the huge tree that loomed in front of her.

It was an ancient ash, its trunk as big around as a small shed, its substance riven and hollowed by lightning. Half of it was dead, its branches broken and singed into skeletal dryness, but the other half was vigorously alive, and there were fresh green sprouts springing around its gnarled and reaching roots. Apple, with her ancient pig wisdom, knew a good resting place when she saw one. She burrowed immediately into a drift of fallen leaves at the old tree's base, hunkered down, twitched her ears, and folded her trotters under her.

Mokie came aware and looked about her. It seemed as good a place as any and better than some. She was tired, chilled with moonlight, and stiff with fighting against pain she would not acknowledge. Her body ached. She was tired from the marrow outward, and she wanted desperately to sink into dark sleep, to have it cover her over and shroud her from the world. After a minute's hesitation, she too hunkered down, folded into herself, and closed her eyes.

But her body would not let go. It stayed locked against itself, guarded from unwanted knowledge. Her thighs ached, her neck was stiff and painful, and her stomach was in knots. All this she felt, but she refused to notice or acknowledge the other pain, the sharp, jagged pain somewhere inside. Presently she began to shake. Her teeth knocked against one another, her jaw muscles locked, her arms and legs jerked convulsively. She could not control the shaking. It took some time for the fit to pass, and it left her tired to the bone.

Distressed, Apple whimpered softly and crept into the hollow of her side, and the warmth of the little pig's body gradually penetrated Mokie's chill. She let go then, giving in to exhaustion, and curled herself around Apple, her arms cradling the only comfort she knew. At last Mokie slept, tucked against Apple in a nest of leaves in the hollow of the ash tree.

From the far side of the tree the watcher stood silent, looking at Mokie asleep. Then he turned and went back the way he had come. He was very late getting home, too late for supper, and with no appetite for the food his mother had kept hot for him, so she put him to bed, covered him well, and dosed him for fever. She made him stay in bed all the next day, and he did not protest. The day after, however, he insisted he was fine and played and shouted as boisterously as the rest of the boys. If there was a shade too much energy in all his actions for so quiet a boy, no one noticed.

FIFTEEN

WILL-O'-THE-WISPS

WHILE MOKIE, worn out with trouble and weak from fighting unwelcome knowledge, slept, Apple stayed wide awake, looking into the night, waiting for something. Finally, though she did not sleep, she nestled into the hollow of Mokie's body and closed her eyes. Later on, much later on, three will-o'-the-wisps came bobbing through the wood, flickering wisps of light that stopped at the ash tree and hovered just above the two sleeping bodies.

The lights dropped lower, almost touching the pig, who opened her eyes and looked at them straight. For a long moment the lights held still in the steady gaze of the pig. Then they dipped and bowed, circled once around her head, and went flickering away down the dark aisles of the forest. Apple closed her eyes. Mokie stirred restlessly in the leaves, half woke up, and clutched at Apple, who snuggled her little pig snout into the curve of the girl's arm. Sleep took them.

That's her for sure

Lost, poor thing

She'll find her way

In time

PART TWO

FOUND

SIXTEEN

WICKENWOOD

MOKIE OPENED HER EYES. She didn't know where she was, or why. All around her was new and strange—the dappled shadows in all the wrong places, the silver morning light that slanted through trees instead of the cracked boards of Grime's shed. Nothing made any sense. Something warm and wriggly nudged her, and she looked down to see Apple. Then she remembered the two of them walking into the wood, walking away from something.

Her mind veered. Never mind. Apple was here and begging for food. She heard her own stomach growl, and the sound was real and strangely comforting. It was morning, it was breakfast time, and she was hungry. While Apple went rooting in and around the tree roots, Mokie scavenged for what breakfast she could find. In a little clearing she came across a thicket of blackberries. They were past ripe, for it was midautumn, but fallen leaves had hidden them from birds and other foragers. Though they were less than abundant toward the end of the season, their sweetness was sustaining. They were all she could find, and she ate every one.

Following the sound of water, for the berries made her thirsty, she came to one of the winding brooks that threaded the wood. A little cascade tumbled over a fall of rock, and she cupped her hands and bent her head to drink. Out of the corner of her eye she almost saw a bright shape shining out of a dazzle of sunlight on the ripples, but when she turned to look it was gone. Behind the wind in the high tops of the trees a voice almost whispered, but it stopped when she tried to listen.

Mokie was not the only one. From time to time Apple would stop her digging, lift her snout, and search the wind. Sometimes she would look at the empty air as if she saw beyond it into something she almost knew was there. Whenever that happened, Mokie felt suddenly more aware. Colors got brighter; the edges of things cut more sharply against one another; her skin felt sensitive, as if water were being poured gently over it. Looking into the shadowy aisles, she could almost see the watchers—their faces hidden in a crossing of branches, their eyes peering out of the knots in a tree. On another day she would have been curious, but this day she was fully engaged in trying not to think.

The angle of the sun, though half obscured by the trees, told her the morning was getting on. In the village now she would be driving the pigs out to forage. With no pig herd to see to, the time dragged. Sitting under the holly oak, she tried a game of twig and leaf people, but they turned into the wives of Little Wicken and jeered at her until she could not bear it any longer and broke them into pieces. She tried a story, but the words withered in her mouth. A fallen acorn claimed Apple's attention. She chomped it, gazing at Mokie with pig sympathy and blinking. Mokie fished another acorn out of the soft earth, tossed it, and Apple snapped it deftly out of midair. It disappeared into Apple like magic.

Out of the depths of her memory came a vivid picture of a ragged troupe of tumblers passing through Little Wicken on their way to somewhere else. She saw again their one performance in the Farrow Field, lit with torches and looking splendid in the firelight. A tall man conjured some flowers out of three-year-old Elenny's pinafore and presented them to her with a bow. Another, older man pulled a basket of cakes out of Granny Gorlan's apron and passed them around, and then brought out a pair of high stilts, mounted them, and began to dance. A heavily veiled woman swathed in scarves and jingling with jewelry brought out a deck of cards and told a few fortunes—all good, of course.

Then the two men began juggling, tossing balls and sticks in the air and keeping them moving in an airy circle. They began tossing the objects back and forth to one another in a shifting, flickering dance almost too swift for eyes to take in. The woman joined them, and the duo became a trio. Then they let everything fall to earth, and went to tumbling, somersaulting, rolling over and over each other, the woman standing on the men's shoulders, the men tossing the woman back and forth between them.

The troupe did not stay long, for none of the villagers had any thought, much less any money, to spare for their antics. But Mokie was enchanted. These magical beings seemed exempt from the laws that governed ordinary mortals. They defied gravity, they made something out of nothing, they could see into the future. Although they were gone in a day, the tumbling folk had invaded her dreams for several nights. Now they invaded her waking.

"Apple!" she said so suddenly that Apple jumped and her ears stood up from her head like flags.

"Apple, how would you like to be a performing pig, hmmm?"

Apple made no reply, but her eyes invited explanation.

"A clever, trained, performing pig? You'd be so famous—no one would kill you for sausage."

Apple cocked her head on one side.

"We could be tumblers, you and me. We'd travel around like those tumblers who came to the village."

Apple looked quizzical.

"I forgot. That was before you were born. Well, let me tell you."

Apple looked interested.

"They did—um—tricks, sort of. Juggling and balancing and things like that. Well, it's hard to explain. Here, I'll show you."

She tossed another acorn. Like the first, it disappeared out of the air and into Apple.

"No, don't eat it. Bring it back to me."

Another acorn. The same thing happened. A snap, and it was gone. Apple waited expectantly for more.

"No, no, no!" Mokie thought a moment. "Maybe acorns aren't the right things." She fished around in the dirt and tossed a small twig. Apple caught it, but finding it inedible, immediately dropped it.

"Bring it here," ordered Mokie.

The pig looked at her.

"Here!" She held out her hand. Nothing happened. She picked up the twig, held it out, and said again, "Here!" Then she tossed it to Apple and again held out her hand.

After several more tries Apple began to cooperate. When Mokie said, "Here!" and held out her hand, Apple brought her the twig. Mokie gave her an acorn.

"You're wondering what this is all about, aren't you, Apple? Never mind. It may seem silly to you, but if it works we'll not have to starve or beg our food, or go back to Little Wicken ever, ever, ever."

With every word, the idea became more entertaining, more possible. She tilted her head to one side and looked thoughtfully at Apple.

"You'd like to be famous, wouldn't you, Apple? I'd be your trainer and you'd do tricks and they'd throw us pennies."

Apple seemed agreeable. By the time the morning was over, they were well along with Apple's training. Mokie tossed a twig. Apple caught and held it. Mokie ordered, "Bring it here!" Apple trotted up and laid it at her feet and got her acorn of payment.

Encouraged by success, Mokie attempted more advanced training, coaxing Apple when she had fetched the twig to sit up and beg for the acorn. That took longer—the bulky torso and solid center of gravity natural to pigs does not lend itself easily to sitting upright. Apple's hind legs were smaller than her hunger for acorns, and she kept falling over. Nevertheless, they persisted—Apple from a desire to please, Mokie with a circular concentration that kept going over the same ground, keeping at bay the memories hovering at the far edge of her mind.

The day passed. The sharpening of shadows and liquid golden light sifting through the trees told them evening was near. Apple was unusually full of acorns and more than usually ready for sleep. Mokie, who had forgotten her stomach as well as her troubles, suddenly felt drained and hollow. There was nothing for her to eat, so she filled herself with water from the brook and, as dusk gathered, rolled into the leaves next to Apple, hoping that sleep would make her forget the growling of her stomach.

Next morning she was sick and dizzy. She didn't want to wake up at all, but there was nothing else to do. She lay drowsy and listless for a while, then roused to look for food, but there were no more berries near the tree. She made her way to the brook and drank deep, but her head swam when she stood up, and she nearly fell over. She got herself back to the tree somehow and leaned against it, but her legs gave way and she half fell, half sat against the trunk.

"No tricks for a while now," she told Apple, and wondered at the feeble sound of her own voice. The colors in the wood suddenly seemed painfully bright and the air shimmered in front of her, dazzling her eyes.

"We'll take a rest till my head settles down," she heard someone say faintly, and did not know the sound of her own voice. Her eyes closed of their own accord.

Apple trotted off in search of acorns. Mokie could not have opened her eyes even if she had wanted to, and she did not want to. Presently she drifted into a half sleep. She did not see Apple heading in the direction of the village and the orchard. She had no idea how much time passed before she was roused by a hard little head pushing against her leg. Drowsily, she opened her eyes. Apple was standing beside her, a broken branch hung with three small, knobby apples protruding from her jaws. When she had Mokie's attention, she dropped the branch in her lap and settled down at her feet.

The first bite of apple was so piercingly delicious Mokie could hardly bear it. The firm, crisp flesh crunched under her teeth; the tart, tangy juice rushed down her throat. She held a morsel on her tongue for a little, just to savor it, then swallowed. Another bite, and another. She ate it all, core, seeds, even the stem. Nothing had ever tasted so good. The second apple went down a little slower, but came just as welcome to her stomach. When she had finished it, she put the third apple aside for supper and lay back, feeling the apple juice coursing through her veins like new blood. In a little while she was ready for work.

They began by going over yesterday's tricks—catch, fetch, sit up. Encouraged by success, Mokie tried her talented companion with somersaults. That proved surprisingly easy, for the little pig's legs were so short and her neck and shoulders so strong that she could put her head down and roll over herself almost before she began. Mokie was triumphant and so, it seemed, was Apple, for she continued joyously rolling over and over like a hoop. Then Mokie tried to get her to do it backward, but that didn't work at all, and after one or two tries she gave it up.

Feeling that she should at least keep pace with her pig, Mokie tried a few tricks herself, but her body was no longer a stocky, compact child's body. Taller and leggier, its balance altered by her physical maturation, it would not obey her. Not only that, when she tried somersaults, putting her head down made her sick and dizzy. The green marble fell out of her pocket and fetched up underneath her when, having managed to roll over, she landed flat and with a thump and with the marble right where it would hurt her backbone the most. The trees turned cartwheels around her head and she had to close her eyes for a long minute to make them stay still. Without changing position she fished the marble out from under her and put it back in her pocket. Then she abandoned that project.

She tried juggling with acorns, but that was no better. Conscious of her limitations, she began with two, passing one from hand to hand and keeping one in the air. This proved manageable, and after a while, she promoted herself to three. That was when the trouble began. She made the beginner's mistake of watching her hands instead of the acorns, with the result that while the acorns moved reasonably well from hand to hand, the one tossed into the air flew wild and fell to the ground before she could free a hand to catch it. She kept on trying until her eyes began to cross from confusion, and that brought back the dizziness and she had to drop all three acorns and sit with her eyes shut and her head on her knees until the ground stopped rocking. It was humiliating to think that she could not perform as well as a pig, yet she was proud of her pupil.

"I'm just a dud, Apple," she told the pig with a mixture of pride and chagrin. "You seem to have all the talent in the family. I'm too clumsy to do anything. So I guess you'll have to be the star and I'll be your trainer."

Modestly pleased with herself, Apple looked sympathetic.

The enterprise had succeeded in filling the empty hours. It gave Mokie something to do and occupied both her body and her time. Most of all, it kept her from thinking—or remembering. She saw with surprise that it was almost nighttime. In the depth of the wood, the sun's passage was hard to see, and even at mid-day the shadows stretched long. As the afternoon declined toward evening, the sky began to be covered with high, thin clouds that scattered the sunlight and diffused the shadows. Outside the wood time was moving. In a few weeks it would be pig-killing time back in Little Wicken.

Mokie hugged her pig close against her and ate her third apple. No longer so hungry, she was satisfied with her success as a trainer and reconciled to her own lack of talent. She settled down for her third night in the wood, burrowing into the drifted leaves and curling tightly against Apple to keep away the penetrating chill of the autumn air.

SEVENTEEN

TiME QUT

FOR THE REST OF HER LIFE, Mokie remembered her time in the wood as almost a dream. She was neither happy nor unhappy, neither well nor ill. She just was. The days came and went, darkness followed light with hypnotic regularity. It was a time out of time. She and Apple slept and woke, played and explored in a rhythm altogether separate from the world outside the wood.

Mokie was not a practiced forager, but she did her best, looking for berries, gathering mushrooms. Once she spotted a few wild carrots by their feathery tops and dug them up. They were past their prime and not much good to eat, being tough and fibrous, but they gave her mouth something to do, and they were at least ballast for her stomach. Quite by accident, on their fourth day in the Wickenwood, she came across a packet of food that some tramp must have forgotten. Hidden under a pile of last year's fallen leaves, not far from her shelter tree, were a stale end of bread and a rind of cheese wrapped in a ragged cloth. No telling how long they had been there, she thought, but by good luck no animal had found them. She and Apple shared the feast and had berries for dessert.

Mokie began to feel that there must have been more tramps and vagrants in the wood than she was aware, for such discoveries occurred from time to time. Never in the same place, and not nearly as often as she could wish, but often enough that she did not starve. One packet had some scraps of meat in it, another had a rib bone of beef with some bites still adhering. One wonderful day she and Apple came across half a pie stowed in a sack and thrust deep in a hole under the root of a tree. So occasional and fortuitous were these finds that Mokie grew to enjoy their discovery and made a game of trying to guess where the next one would turn up. Aside from wondering vaguely at the number of vagrants who forgot their lunch, she never questioned the presence of the food packets, and her tired mind, as bruised in its way as her body, and weary of all life that might be outside the wood, simply took the random benefices as part of the wood's magic and was content to let it be so.

Mokie could never have guessed that Janno's mother—a widow who took in sewing to make ends meet and had only the income from her needle to keep her and her son in food and clothing—began to find her scanty larder even barer than she expected. Not every day, but two or three times a week she would reach for something only to find it gone. She was positive she had put a cheese rind on the shelf in the larder, but when she went to get it, it was not there. Bones she had saved for making soup unaccountably went missing one day. A loaf end she had wrapped in a torn old petticoat to keep it from getting too stale for even her and her son to gnaw disappeared, petticoat and all. One disastrous day, the remains of a pie that a neighbor had given in return for some sewing—enough to feed a frugal mother and her son for several days—was stolen from plain sight on her windowsill.

She began to look suspiciously at the children as they played in the dusty lane outside her door, and for a while she even forbade Janno to play with them. He did not seem to mind, and took to going off by himself up around the Farrow Field. His mother was a busy woman, and since he was always home again in time for supper, she seldom watched him when he left the cottage. If she had, she might have seen that his solitary games brought him so close to the Wickenwood that he was sometimes swallowed up in its shadowy distances.

EIGHTEEN

Light in a Dark Place

WITH ANIMAL EASE, Apple nearly always nodded off as soon as she lay down at night. Sleep came more slowly to Mokie. When she lay still, all the old aches and pains revived, coming back like birds alighting. She could not stop them, though she tried desperately to fend off their meaning. She often dropped at last into a restless half drowse and dreamed she was falling into darkness. From this she would abruptly awake to phantom pain that lingered even when she opened her eyes. The real darkness of the wood around her was filled with night sounds—small insects calling, an owl hunting, a cricket chirping, far off the snap of a twig where the night prowlers roamed. When this happened, she usually stayed awake for a while and then sank into a quieter, deeper sleep that lasted until morning.

One night she came awake from the dream to find that she

was lying in a kind of quaking, living darkness. The sound of wind roared like a waterfall over her head, and she heard the trees crack like ship masts in a storm at sea. There was a rushing noise, as of a great many animals trampling though the wood, a snuffling and grunting together with the crackling of underbrush and thudding of many hooves. She sat up then and looked about, but the wood was suddenly quiet. There was no wind, no cracking of tree trunks, no noise of animals. But there was a light shimmering bright but distant between the tree trunks in the deep part of the wood. At first she thought it was the late moon rising, a clear white, almost silver luminescence gleaming through the trees. But it was coming from the wrong direction, and besides, the moon had eaten herself, Mokie knew, her lighted curve almost swallowed up. She was nearly consumed, ready to begin again.

It was like no light Mokie had ever seen. As she continued to look, she saw that it did not change position, as the moon does when your eyes follow her path. And not only that, this light flickered, sometimes going almost dark and then shining into brilliance again. But it never came any nearer or got any farther away. It stayed in one place. Mokie felt a sudden great desire to discover what that one place might be. Shaking off her covering of leaves, she discovered that Apple was awake and already trotting purposefully through the wood. Mokie took off after her. The rushing sound of the storm began again, and with it the grunting and squealing of many animals.

As she followed her pig, she had a dreaming sense that they were surrounded by many other bodies, that they were in the midst of a heaving, jostling herd of pigs, although no pigs were visible anywhere around them. It was then that Mokie remembered the stories. She recalled all she had heard about Red Sorcha, about the Crystal Country and the Crystal Folk. Maybe I'm being carried away to the Crystal Country, she thought with a little thrill half of excitement and half of fear. Then the old feeling of delighted power came back to her as she became Red Sorcha once again, leading her Phantom Herd on a rampage through the wood. Following the invisible herd as best she could, Mokie stumbled after her own pig, the little white Apple shape that bobbed in and out of the darkness like a will-o'-the-wisp, like a phantom light leading her toward an unknown destination.

Mokie knew, as everyone in Little Wicken knew, that outlaw folk, tramps and vagabonds and suchlike used the wood for refuge. And she had heard the other, darker stories about the entry to the Crystal Country and what happened to those who passed the portal. No one wanted to risk that, she was certain-sure. Yet that light drew her, and she could not and did not want to resist its lure. As she got nearer she saw a darker outline against the dark trees, a ramshackle hut of leaning walls and a sagging roof. The light came from its one window and floating on the light came a murmur of voices. Mokie was powerfully curious to see what was going on inside.

Making sure that Apple was still by her side, she snaked her way through the weeds and underbrush, creeping as close to the hut as she dared. A sharp noise startled her, and she froze, cowering in the weeds. The unlatched door was banging insistently in the tugging wind, knocking against the frame with every random gust. No one, however, seemed to be near the door or in the doorway, and after a long moment she went on. Keeping close to Apple for comfort, expecting she knew not what, Mokie cautiously approached. She pushed through the tall weeds that rose almost to window height and raised her head to the level of the window opening, which was sagging and latticed with cobwebs. A strange light, the light she had seen and followed, shone out through the window.

Elevating their eyes just above the windowsill, Mokie and Apple peered inside. Although she had had no expectations, Mokie's first look into the hut struck her with inexplicable familiarity. A thought came slipping into her mind. I have seen this before; I have been here before. I know this place.

She was looking into a room like a narrow cave that reached back into darkness. The light Mokie had seen came from a candle stub sitting in a puddle of its own wax, the transparent flame motionless in the still air. Beyond its little circle of colorless light, shadowy recesses ran back into darkness where wind swirled the drifted leaves. She saw the clear light from the candle flame shine weirdly across the faces of the three who sat around the table—a woman and two men. The flame had the luminescence of moonlight, and its shimmer turned the hut into another world. It hollowed the eyes and cheekbones of the three and threw their night-black, lightless shadows huge against the walls. The whole scene was grayed over, the colors faded, like a painting dimmed and dirtied with the grime of countless years. The door had stopped banging, but Mokie did not notice.

Apple nearly gave the game away by letting out little grunts, almost as if she recognized the three faces in the candle's light. Mokie had to keep a firm grip on her to prevent her from trying to clamber through the window. But Mokie, too, felt a kinship with the three in the little hut. It was clear from their ragged clothes and shabby, unkempt appearance that they were homeless vagabonds. Mokie, too, was a homeless vagabond, just as shabby and ragged as they were. They were tramps. She was a tramp. The village wives had said so. She listened to their conversation, scarcely breathing.

The woman was speaking.

NINETEEN

Through a Glass Darkly

"**I** WANT TO GET ON WITH IT."

The little man, the one in the green overcoat, answered. "We'll get on with it, Lally, I promise you that."

"Yes, but when will that be?" said Lally.

"When time comes," said the other man, the dark man. His black, gleaming eyes followed the path of a green glass marble that he tossed and caught, tossed and caught. Mokie's eyes widened when she saw the marble and instinctively she reached in her pocket. Her hand closed around nothing. No marble. Her pocket was empty.

The man smiled, caught his marble, and held it up like an eyeglass, looking at each of his companions in turn. Then he shifted and turned his green glass gaze to the window where Mokie and Apple listened. The color caught at Mokie's eye, filling it, so that all the air was turned to green glass, and she was looking through green air at the dark man who was looking at her. Within the marble their eyes met and held for the time of a single heartbeat. Something happened. All in a moment a connection was made, reinforced, tied into place. Mokie felt her heart lurch.

"Stop looking out the window, John," said the man in the overcoat. "Anyone would think there was something out there, the way you go on."

Lally shook herself, like a cat that has stepped in water.

"And I don't want to hang about in the Doorway, either, Skimmer. I want to get on with it."

"We'll get on with it, I promise you," said the one called Skimmer.

"When?"

"When time's here," said the dark man. He turned his green glass gaze toward the window again, looked directly at Mokie through the marble, and slowly, deliberately closed one eye.

Mokie's eyes widened, and she let out a little gasp. Echoing her, Apple grunted.

They were the smallest of night sounds, immediately swallowed, but the one called John lowered the marble. He did not move, but his eyes, glittering now in the candle flame like black glass, slanted toward the window. The woman called Lally followed his look, and a little smile started at the corner of her mouth. With the barest of motions, John shook his head.

"Here's my idea," The Skimmer said. "There's the Harvest Fair over beyond the wood at Great Wicken. Folk come from all around for it. Let's head for there, set up our pitch. We'll be tumblers, mountebanks. That always fetches a crowd." He slid a glance at the window.

"That's a start," said Lally. "I got a feeling. I think the luck's breaking."

"Well, then," said The Skimmer, "if it's time for starting, it's also time for eating."

"What a pig you are!" said Lally, and she waggled her tongue at him.

"Look who's talking! Pig yourself!" said The Skimmer. "I'm that hungry, I feel like I haven't eaten since—since—"

"Since before starting time," said John.

"See if it's safe, then," said Lally.

With elaborate unconcern, The Skimmer sauntered over to the window, peered vaguely into the dark.

Mokie clutched Apple tight and flattened herself against the wall, holding her breath. Did he see them?

"Not a soul in sight," said The Skimmer loudly.

"It wouldn't matter," said Lally, her silvery voice lilting out the window. "All anybody'd see is a bunch of tramps."

"That's right," said John, looking anywhere but toward the window.

Their eyes locked in agreement. Their heads nodded ever so slightly.

Before Mokie's gaze the dim light changed, as if a hand had wiped across a dusty windowpane, leaving it bright and clear. Then the shabby wooden walls thinned and vanished altogether. In their place Mokie saw a scarlet silk pavilion festooned with ropes of glass beads—beads like iridescent soap bubbles that changed from violet to blue to rose-red and back again. The air chimed softly, as if the beads were clashing delicately against one another. Light shone through the three figures. The scent of apples filled the air, rich with the taste of autumn.

Lally lifted the flame off the candle. Balancing it on her palm, she began to sing, and as she sang, the flame circled on itself and became a ring of fire. Her other hand swirled the wide, trailing shawl off her shoulders. It settled on the table like a cloth. Its fringe swept the shining floorboards while its embroidered butterflies—tiger-tawny and iridescent green and cobalt blue—flew up and lighted on the walls, glowing like fireflies. She blew gently on the ring of fire and set it on the table. Next she traced a round, flat-bottomed shape over it. A saucepan took form, and from it the rich smell of onion soup drifted out into the room. Finally she took a copper penny out of her pocket and rolled it between her hands until it rounded, lengthened, expanded into crusty brown crispness. The fragrance of new-baked bread joined the smell of soup.

Mokie's nostrils flared and her stomach growled as the good

smells reached her. Her mouth watered. Apple watched Mokie, not the scene in the hut.

The Skimmer surveyed the table. "I've a thirst that would swallow an ocean," he remarked.

Carefully folding back the lace ruffles at his wrist, Dogger John tossed the marble, which grew and hollowed and curved around itself, becoming a crystal jug brimming with wine. He set it on the table.

"There, now," said Lally. "Now we can have a feast. But we need a proper setting."

The Skimmer stood up inside his overcoat. From one pocket he pulled a handful of stars and flung them upward, where they arranged themselves into a chandelier. From another pocket he took four cut-glass goblets and set them on the table. Four cut-glass bowls went beside the goblets, and four crystal spoons went with the bowls. He reached in his inside breast pocket and, with a flourish, set down a large square of yellow butter and a comb dripping with golden honey.

Mokie's stomach rumbled alarmingly, and the pig let out a little grunt of sympathetic hunger.

Lally began to comb out her hair, a shining ripple of changeful silk that she tossed back and forth, first over one shoulder, then over the other. She tossed out flowers—violets, snow daisies, wood primroses—shaking them onto the table and floor until their scent filled the room.

The Skimmer snapped his fingers, and out of the flowers

arose a faint music. Then the three, like princelings at a festival, sat down to the banquet. John poured wine, broke thick chunks off the loaf, handed around the bowls that Lally filled with the brown, fragrant soup. The Skimmer passed the butter and the honeycomb, managing to drip some on the gold-braided cuffs of his velvet jacket.

Mokie was mesmerized, in two worlds at once. She breathed in the bitter damp of the forest and it tasted on her tongue like honey-buttered bread, warm from baking. The odor of rotting leaves mingled with the onion-smelling soup and the cool perfume of the wine. Her green eye took gold glimmers from the chandelier. Her brown eye brightened to amber in the glow of the candle flame. Cradled in her arms, Apple watched Mokie as Mokie watched the others, her little stubby pig body immobile, her eyes intent.

In the other world, the three laughed and ate and drank, savoring the food, chuckling at their own jokes, toasting one another with the fragrant wine. Sometimes their speech moved into song with the inaudible music that drifted like a scarf on the glittering air. The Skimmer found a glass flute in his hands and began to play a strange, haunting melody with odd stops and runs and sudden shifts of rhythm. Lally Dai stood up to dance, weaving a circle of magic around the little room, swirling and dipping in an intricate pattern. The butterflies left the walls to light on her hair, where they formed a wreath like live flowers. John clapped, picking up the rhythm, driving it faster and faster. Lally Dai turned and swayed, her silver-gilt hair toss-ing, her skirts swinging, her smile wide and generous as she came to each in turn.

Mokie was enchanted. She piped with The Skimmer. Her heart beat to the rhythm of John's clapping. Though she never moved from the spot, the muscles of her body echoed Lally's dance. She was a part of all she saw. She became the music and the dance, became Lally and The Skimmer and John. She was unaware of time passing, and she could have stayed suspended in the moment forever.

Suddenly it all changed, as if a play had come to an end. With a final trill the music stopped. With a last swing of her skirts, Lally's dance ceased. Skimmer beckoned the stars down from the ceiling, put them in his pocket, rolled the dishes into his overcoat, punched it once or twice to fluff it out, and lay down in a corner with his head pillowed on the bundle. In a minute he was snoring gently. Lally Dai blew out the flame on the stubby candle, wrapped her skimpy shawl as close around her as she could, tucked her bare feet up under her skirt, and lay down on the floor. Only Dogger John stayed awake, sitting with one leg over the chair arm, tossing and tossing the green glass marble.

His hand moved independent of his gaze, which, like that of a juggler, followed the arc of the marble. Only gradually did Mokie realize that the arc traced the shape of the very window opening through which she was peering, that it made a kind of second window through which she and John stared at each other. His look was unmistakable—their eyes locked with an almost audible click. She blinked. Dogger John's face did not change, but as before, he slowly, deliberately closed one eye and opened it again.

It was too much for Mokie. She ducked her head, and clutching Apple close to her, careful to make no sound, she backed carefully away from the window, treading softly until she was well clear of the hut, then hurrying as fast as she dared through the dark tangle of the wood. The way back seemed infinitely long and dark, a journey back to a world that felt strange, unreal, and unfamiliar compared to the one she had seen. Only when she was safe home, and tucked in her nest inside the ash tree, did she let out a long breath, a sigh in which relief, confusion, and exaltation were mingled. Worn out from too much excitement, she burrowed into the leaves and fell at once into sleep.

TWENTY

RAGGLE~TAGGLE GYPSIES

THE GREAT WICKEN HARVEST FAIR was the last big festival before the dark time that rounded off the half year's turn away from the sun. From every direction in the surrounding country-side, people would bring what goods they had, hoping to sell, looking to buy, ready to trade and bargain. It was the last chance before the iron cold of winter locked the countryside under a glaze of ice or a deeper covering of snow. Folk would not gather again until the deepest part of the winter, this time to mark the longest night with the need-fire that celebrated the sun's return and drove back the dark.

Even in a bad year like this one, the fair was a market for live-stock, produce, poultry, for home-baked pies and cakes, the last good-bye to summer. The sky was clear, for this year's long dry summer had kept bright days well into autumn. The air was dry and diamond hard, cold in early morning, warming as the sun mounted, hot enough at noontime. Evenings the air cooled again, and nights were biting with the promise of the greater cold to come.

On the first day of the fair, Great Wicken woke early, and the smoke of breakfast cooking hung in the still air. The sun was barely up, the night chill not yet burned off the air when over in the Fair Meadow the first arrivals were setting up stalls, roping off the enclosures for animal judging, putting up the pavilion for the prize giving on the last day. Back in town, a few early housewives sweeping their doorsteps halted their brooms in midsweep and stared, their jaws hanging open. Prancing down the main street as if they owned it was a sight indeed—a raggle-taggle, tatterdemalion crew making a real show of themselves, one of the wives told her neighbor. Two men and a woman. Or rather, a man and a woman and a green overcoat.

"Someone was inside it," confided the wife, "though you had to look hard to see. I thought it was a child at first, but no child has such knowing eyes. It's an old man. A very old man. The other man, the one you could see, was in a fancy red jacket all ruffles at the wrist. Buttons missing," she noted, "and holes in the sleeves. More patches than cloth on his britches and a yellow scarf around his head."

"I saw them too," said her daughter, peering over her shoulder.

"The gypsy and the overcoat were pushing a two-wheeled cart. And bold as daylight, right on top the cart, a brazen piece of work with long red hair—"

"Too red to be real."

Her daughter ignored the interruption and went on, "—a scarlet mouth and bold as brass; you'd have thought she was a princess instead of a no-good gypsy tramp."

"Beggars like as not," said the neighbor. "Or thieves."

"Both, if you ask me," replied the wife. "They had that look—you know? Steal your purse as easy as good morning. I stared right through them like they weren't there, and then I went in the house and slammed the door. Hard," she declared with tight-lipped satisfaction. "I don't want any of them sneaky folk coming around begging for handouts."

She went in the house with her daughter and slammed the door again, just for emphasis. Her neighbor did the same.

Fortunately no one saw the odd pair that came trailing after the procession a few moments later, a girl and a pig who came slipping warily in and out of the cold shadows cast by the early sun. Both were bone tired and leg weary from trekking through the wood after will-o'-the-wisps. All night they had followed the dancing lights that bobbed in and out of the trees, floating over brush piles, skimming along a few feet above the ground. All night they had stumbled after the lights through underbrush, tripped over fallen branches, gotten hooked and snagged again and again in brambles. Mokie's eyes ached from tracking the dancing lights, finding and losing and finding them again. In the gray dark before dawn she had watched as they flickered out of the woods, crossed a few stubble fields, and hovered over an open meadow just outside Great Wicken. Then they disappeared into the dark like sparks thrown out from a fire, and there stood Lally, The Skimmer swathed in his overcoat, and last of all, against the lightening sky, the dark shape of Dogger John.

When midmorning came, and the chores were done and the fair getting well under way, folk noticed a scarlet pavilion on the edge of the meadow next to the flower stalls. No one saw it go up, but there it was. In the doorway sat a woman swathed in bright scarves, jingling with cheap brass jewelry. She was shuffling a pack of cards, sliding them in falls from hand to hand, riffling them together. A dark man in a head scarf squatted on the ground, drawing patterns in colored sand. He was sifting lines of red and black and yellow between his thumb and forefinger, reading the picture the lines made, sweeping up the pattern and beginning again. Next to him, a tumbler who apparently had no bones was doing splits and back flips and handstands on a faded green overcoat spread to cushion his landing.

Color and commotion and sounds and smells were everywhere. Painted scarves and embroidered shawls hung gaudily from the display in the weaver's stall. The leather-goods man had hung up his wares on gaily colored ropes—tooled belts and worked-leather purses and sheathes for knives. A hot-drink seller poured out steaming tea or cocoa to warm early morning stomachs. At intervals the scissors grinder rang his bell, sending its little tolling across the meadow.

Half hidden behind a pile of brush at the edge of the meadow, a ragged girl and a pig crouched, watching the gypsies. The gypsies kept their eyes on the crowd, but a careful observer would have noticed glances flicking from time to time toward the pile of brush. A boy with his thumb in his mouth strayed from his mother's skirts and edged up to where the dark man was drawing his patterns. The man looked up and caught his eye. The boy edged closer and looked at the patterns. With a swift motion the man swept the sand up into his hand. He blew on it and a bouquet of salmon-pink roses flowered in his fingers.

"For your mother," said the man, holding it out. The boy was reaching to take it when his mother appeared, grabbed his outstretched hand, and dragged him briskly away.

Looking wistfully over his shoulder, the boy saw the man smile forgivingly. The roses fell back into sparkling pink sand, trickling down onto the ground and forming into letters:

BETTER LUCK NEXT TIME

Mokie's eyes met Apple's in a look of perfect understanding.

The tumbler folded away the overcoat and began to dance on clog stilts that clackered invitingly above the noises of the crowd. People drifted over. Someone threw a penny that landed between the tapping stilts. Without missing a step the tumbler bent in half, retrieved the coin, and tossed it in the air. It vanished. The fellow who had thrown it frowned—good money!—and gaped as the tumbler produced it from his left elbow. It was not a copper penny now, but a shiny gold piece. The tumbler tossed it again, caught it in his mouth, swallowed it, and spat two gold pieces out on the ground.

"One for me," he said gaily, "and one for you." The man hesitated. "Go on," the tumbler said with a laugh. "It won't bite you." The man picked it up warily. He bit it. It was gold. The tumbler gave him a wink. The man backed into the crowd to get away before the money changed again.

Now the woman came out, scarves fluttering, bracelets and earrings and necklaces jingling. She fanned the cards in her hand and held them out to a bystander. Looking around for approval, he took one. "Tell me what you hold," said the woman in a velvet voice. He looked and gasped. Pictured on the card was his own face grinning at him out of a ring of silver coins. "Good fortune!" she cooed. "You'll be rich before the year's out." Deftly she repossessed the card and slid it back into the center of the deck. Others came crowding, and soon she was sitting crosslegged with a ring of folk around her, all waiting to hear of fortune to come.

Nobody noticed Mokie and Apple, and that was good, that was what they wanted for now. There was too much to see. A flame swallower toasted cheese with his fiery breath. A vendor hawking roasted chestnuts made a winding progress through the crowd. The good smell of the chestnuts mingled with the fragrances from the food stalls, where spiced chicken legs and toasted cheese and hot sausages on sticks tempted the hungry with a late breakfast or an early lunch. A storyteller held a gathering crowd enthralled with tales of kings in exile and princesses saved from dragons.

The teeming, jostling crowd was more turbulence, more unshackled energy, more humanity than Mokie had ever seen in her life. Their noise frightened her; their presence threatened. She was safe while they didn't see her. When they did, they would surely jeer and laugh and throw stones. Only the magical three—the goals of her bold, timid, hopeful quest—offered anything else. As Mokie watched, the chaotic picture gradually took on shape and pattern; the crowd sorted itself into groups, chattering threesomes, hand-linked pairs, the odd loner. The people became individuals moving in a random pattern. One loner in particular caught her attention. He wore shirt and pants of a soft dun color. Although he looked interested in everything, he didn't buy anything, but moved unobtrusively from group to group. Mokie saw him mingle with the crowd around the storyteller, his face rapt with attention.

He stood quietly just behind a paunchy fellow whose hands were fat with rings. The girl behind the loner bent to tie her shoe, but lost her balance and stumbled against him, pushing him in turn so that he half fell against the man with the paunch. He put out a hand to steady himself while the other hand slid down to the purse at the fat man's belt. Mokie's eyes widened as she saw him deftly detach the purse and lose himself in the crowd before the fat man could regain his balance.

Mokie was fascinated. She tracked him as best she could, sidling around the edges of the fairground with Apple trotting at her heels. She saw the stumbling trick done twice more at widely separated intervals. She saw him linger by the shawl seller, admiring the pretty girl who stopped to finger the goods on the display rope. Glancing under her lashes for permission from the vendor, the girl lifted down a shawl and held it up to see the embroidery, swinging it coyly to test the fringe.

The shawl seller came from behind his counter to swirl it around her shoulders, patting and smoothing it a bit more than was necessary. The girl smiled, the shawl seller returned her smile, and the quiet man slid behind them, twitched three shawls off the rope while pushing the others to fill in the space, and was gone while the girl still flirted. Then, apologetic, she shook her head, handed back the shawl, and walked away, skirts swinging, allowing the shawl seller a last look.

Mokie observed the play with the seed of an idea growing in her mind. It sprouted as she and Apple followed the man's activities throughout the day. Things disappeared from counters and shelves, never very much, and never all in the same place. Often the pretty girl was nearby, tying her shoestring or fingering things on counters or flicking through a rack of goods, attracting attention with a laugh or a flutter of lashes. From time to time, near the edge of the fairground, their paths would cross. They never looked at each other, but hands met in passing and a great many things found their way into the pockets of the girl's voluminous skirt. As the day went on, Mokie's sprouted idea grew until she caught Apple's eye and realized that she and the pig were having the same thought.

"Mama, look there!" cried a little girl, one hand busy with a seed cake, the other tugging at her mother's skirt. But her mother was haggling with the knife seller and she simply batted away the child's hand.

"Not now."

"Mama, do look!"

"I said not now!"

"But it's a pig walking on its hind legs! Please look, Mama!"

Impatiently the mother looked down at her child, then in the direction the little hand was pointing. Then she looked again. No doubt about it. A small white pig with red ears was balancing upright on its hind legs and taking short choppy steps like a child learning to walk. The mother put down the silver embroidery scissors she was holding and let the little girl drag her over to where the pig was now sitting up on its haunches, forefeet held pleadingly in front of it, head cocked to one side.

"It's begging, Mama! It's begging for food. Can we give it something?"

A crowd was gathering. Someone threw a morsel of cheese, and the pig caught it out of the air, swallowed, and begged for more. The little girl threw the last of her seed cake and giggled when the pig gulped it. Soon there was a ring of people throwing bits of bread and cake and clapping noisily when the pig snapped them up. Applause turned to astonishment when the pig, having swallowed the last morsel, tilted forward onto its stubby head and rolled over in quite a creditable somersault, coming upright into the begging position again.

A boy tried to catch it, but it dodged, ducked nimbly under somebody else's feet, and scampered to the other side of the fairground, where the performance was repeated. Word got around, and soon the vendors were leaving their stalls—"just for a minute"—to see the show. Sometimes a pie or a pastry was missing when they returned to business, but no one thought to connect pies and pigs. No one knew who the pig belonged to and no one came forward to claim it. After a while the fun began to pall. The pig had only a few tricks, repeated over and over. People drifted on to the more elaborate entertainment of jugglers, sword swallowers, and acrobats, and the pig trotted away and out of sight.

TWENTY-ONE

Shape Changing

BY LATE AFTERNOON THE CROWD HAD THINNED. On its way to setting, the sun poured light like clear honey across the field. In front of the gypsy tent the tumbler climbed down from his stilts, the dark man swept up the sand, the woman folded her cards away into a capacious pocket. The last few hangers-on drifted away. The stalls were emptying, stall keepers packing up, looking ahead to dinner and tomorrow. The flower sellers gave their plants and cut flowers water to keep them fresh through the night. The leather worker stowed his purses and satchels, rolled up his belts, and put them in boxes. The shawl seller folded his wares and laid them carefully in the trunk to keep them unwrinkled until he hung them up again. A pie vendor counted up his profits against the pies he had left, but it didn't come out right. He shook his head and resolved to keep an eye on the customers next day. The knife seller lifted his wares off their display hooks and counted them. A pair of scissors was missing—silver sewing scissors with a pattern of intertwined flowers etched in the handles and along the blades. He looked suspiciously about him, but no one was near the stall.

In the yard of a house on the edge of town a housewife took in the washing left drying on the hedge while she went to the fair. A pair of breeches and a shirt were missing. Now who would want a pair of old, patched breeches and a worn work shirt? Strangers? Gypsies? She shook her head and resolved to keep an eye on the fairgrounds.

Evening came on. The gypsy tent flared bright with a cook fire, and the three sat companionably around it, dipping bowls into the stew kettle that swung from an iron stand.

"Well, Lally, things are moving," said The Skimmer. "Just like you wanted. We're waiting on her now. So where to? Stay in this world tonight? Go back to the hut?"

John looked at Lally Dai. She smiled at him, her lovely, spendthrift smile. "Let's stay," she said. "No one has to see us."

"Let it be her move," said John. "We have some time and we've still a few tricks we can pull out."

Alone in the colorless dusk, at a little rock pool just outside the town, Mokie and Apple shivered in the evening air. A creek flowed down a miniature waterfall into a rocky basin before brimming over and wandering down an arm of the Wickenwood, a tangle of trees flung out from the main forest. The girl and the pig were preparing to have a bath, something neither of them indulged in under the best of conditions, let alone in a chilly brook in cold weather. The pig was used to being without clothes. Mokie was not, and her unprotected skin found the frigid evening air only a little less cold than the water. She came out in goose bumps, and her skin shivered of its own accord. But she grabbed Apple firmly around the middle, held her up at face level, and looked her in the eye.

"That was a pretty good show you put on, Apple. I said you had all the talent in the family, and so you do. You kept them so busy looking at you, nobody saw me at all. I'm sure of it. And now we're going to scrub up and change our spots before we let them see us again. So be a good pig and hold still while I get you clean."

She dipped the protesting pig in the water, scooped up a handful of sand, and rubbed her firmly all over, ignoring the squeals and wriggles. Then she dunked her under again. Apple squeaked in protest. She was released finally, pink with cold, to scramble up the bank and roll in the grass.

"And keep yourself out of the mud," warned Mokie. "You don't want to make me wash you all over again."

Now it was her turn. Gasping at the cold, she waded into the pool. Then she inhaled deeply, held her nose, and ducked under the water, letting the breath-stopping iciness close over her head.

The cold was both numbing and invigorating. She opened her eyes and saw a new world—green and pale, with blurred and wavering underwater outlines. It's like the Crystal Country, she thought.

She stood up and, scooping handfuls of sand, scrubbed herself all over. She even washed her hair, though rinsing sand out of the tangles was an arduous task, and took longer than she expected. The sand was as harsh as the water, but she felt obscurely that this cleansing, the first she had ever given herself, was in some way a rite. The sandy water running off her body carried with it all the dirt of her old self. She treated herself to one last allover ducking, came up spluttering, and clambered out.

"There, now. That's enough. No sense overdoing it," she told Apple.

Mokie rubbed herself dry with her shift until her skin glowed red. Then she tore a wide strip off the hem and bound it tightly around her breasts, squashing them flat, or near enough. She could not escape her body, but suppressing it might avoid the trouble it caused. She gave her flattened chest an experimental poke. It still showed a slight but perceptible curve. However, a shirt would conceal that. Satisfied, she picked up the shirt and breeches that lay on the bank. The breeches were patched, and the rough cotton shirt was a grown man's. It hung almost to her knees, the sleeves falling so far over her hands that she had to roll them up several times.

The breeches were for a man twice her girth and well over her height. She pulled them up around her waist and they immediately fell down around her ankles. She pulled them up again and, holding them with one hand, used the other to stuff the shirttail well down inside and fold the pants twice around her middle. She cinched the whole affair tight with another strip torn off the bottom of her shift. The pants stayed up. But they still hung down over her feet, and she tripped with the first step she took. She rolled them to midcalf and hoped they would stay there.

"Have to cut my hair, too," she told the pig.

Apple looked wise, but did not offer to help. With a pair of silver embroidery scissors, Mokie hacked at her hair. Too thick to manage easily under the best of circumstances, it was soaking wet into the bargain. The scrub and a fairly thorough rinse had left it silkier than she was used to, but it was hopelessly snarled from years of neglect. The scissors, designed to snip silk thread, would have been inadequate under ideal circumstances, but Mokie persisted, sawing grimly until she got it above shoulder level. She could not see that it was ragged and uneven, longer on one side than the other, nor that a great hunk was missing from the back where she had to go by feel.

"I can tie the rest of it up in a rag," she told Apple, and stowed the scissors in a pocket of the pants. She ripped another length off her shift, rolled the remains into a damp bundle, and stowed it behind a tree. Flattening what remained of her hair close against her head, she wound the homemade scarf around it and tied it into a knot. It felt fine. She took a few steps, trying out the stiff, swaggering, male walk she had seen and hated in the village boys, keeping an eye on the pig to see how she took it. Apple blinked her approval.

"All right, then. Come on."

With Apple trotting at her heels, Mokie constrained her natural, loose-limbed gait to a stiff strut. The sky was full dark now, and the distant gold of windows against the evening showed where the houses in the town were lit with lamps. The fairground was deserted, the booths shuttered, the spaces in front of them emptied of the life that had teemed and jostled there so short a time ago. It had the loneliness of all places made for crowds when the crowds are gone—all the lonelier for the scraps and pieces their presence had left behind. A broken earring whose silvery half circle glimmered faintly in the dust, gnawed chicken bones, a wooden doll, scrunches of paper wrapping, a ribbon tangled in the grass, the overlapping prints of many feet. It took her eyes a minute to see beyond the discardings of trash, and what she saw was unbearable, a loss that echoed against the buried memory of another loss, another desertion, a place that once had been and was no more.

The scarlet tent was gone, the place where it had been was bare, unthinkably clear of any evidence that it had ever been occupied. No one was there. Cold stars shone down on the empty space where the man in the head scarf had drawn in the sand, where the juggler had danced and balanced. She could almost see the ghostly outlines of their bodies moving against the trampled grass, almost hear the jingle of brass jewelry ring faintly through the hollow air. Yet nothing was there. She stood blank, unable to face her lost hope, to accept so bitter a letdown. She willed the tent to be there, willed the three to be inside it, willed her fragile hope to be met.

Nothing.

All her carefully put on bravado ran out of her like bran out of a torn sack. Bereft, Mokie walked over to the place where the tent had been, where she had watched them, followed their every move as the day passed. Step by reluctant step she paced the vacant space. The air around her, the ground under her feet were as empty as her mind. Every other booth was there, firmly set in place. Only this tent was not, and clearly had never been. Miserably she roamed the fairground, searching, hoping and berating her foolish hope. Of course nothing was there. Of course nothing had ever been there. She should have known better. She did know better.

Hope was a dangerous indulgence and this feeling, the wave of disappointment and despair that almost drowned her, was the inevitable punishment for hope. It was what she deserved. She did not know what to do or where to go, so she didn't go anywhere. Her knees gave way, and miserably, with an ache in her middle as heavy as a stone, she folded up and sat on the ground. Desolation took her. Apple crept close, and automatically the girl cuddled her. Overhead the stars wheeled, shimmering their bright and distant light on the forsaken meadow, on the bright-eyed pig and the lonely girl. After a while the two slept. The stars wheeled on.

TWENTY-TWO

COMPANY

THEY FOUND THEM THERE IN THE EARLY LIGHT before the sun came up, curved into each other on the cold ground, the girl's arms and legs wrapped around the pig, the pig nestled close inside the curve of the girl. The girl was sleeping deeply. Aware of their presence, the pig woke immediately and looked at them.

She's ready? Lally's look inquired of Apple.

Apple blinked. *She's ready. As close to letting herself be loved as she can be right now. Now's the time to move.*

As if at a signal, then, Mokie came awake. At the first sight of dark shapes against the brightening sky, she ducked her head and flung up an arm to ward off the expected blow. The instant defensiveness of her response was not lost on her observers, who exchanged glances. Then she saw who they were, and her arm dropped. It was too much, too perfect an answer to her wish.

She would not let herself believe it. She shut her eyes. But she could not bear the darkness, and so she opened them again. The three figures were still there, solid shapes against the light.

"You're back," she said, and scrambled to her feet.

"We were never away," said Lally.

"You were so too. You went away. You were gone. I came last night and I looked all over. You were all gone, no tent, no nothing."

"Look behind you," said John.

She looked at the scarlet tent pegged solidly into the ground, its flap looped back to show the pillows, the sleeping rolls, the stilts leaned against the tent wall, the cooking pots hanging from their iron stand. She blinked.

"What you want us for, anyway?" asked The Skimmer.

Get ready for acorns, thought Mokie. She swallowed and tilted her chin. "I . . . I wanted to . . . I thought maybe I could . . . maybe if you . . ." Her courage drained away like river water. "Nothing," she said, and shrugged. "I didn't want anything. Just to look." She scooped up Apple and walked away, head high, chin lifted.

"Lost her," muttered John.

"Never mind, we can get her back," murmured The Skimmer quietly. His eyes surveyed the retreating figure, taking in the defiantly squared shoulders, the pathetic disguise of the too-large shirt and baggy, belted-in breeches that deceived no one. The picture was clear. As she reached the edge of the meadow, he called after her.

"Hey—ah—boyo! Hey, there! Stop a minute, can't you!"

Mokie stopped. The call sounded almost like the village boys, though he hadn't called her "piggy." "Boyo" wasn't bad. It sounded promising.

"Come back. Come here a minute."

She half turned and glared at them in an agony of hope and defensiveness, clutching Apple against her chest for protection.

"Come on back," The Skimmer insisted. "I can't shout across half the world."

For a long minute there was no response. A struggle was going on, and they could only wait for the outcome. They did not know about the acorns. At last Mokie turned, came a few steps, then stopped. In her face John read a confusion of defiance and longing that hurt him where he breathed.

Now for it, thought The Skimmer. "You look hungry, boyo. Well, so are we, and we're just going to eat. Will you have some breakfast with us?"

She took a few more steps, hesitated, came on. No acorns so far. Whoever they thought she was, they did not hate her and they seemed not to want to hurt her. Not right away, at any rate.

"I guess so," she said with ferocious shyness, and then in her best boy's voice—deeper, gruffer—"I mean, all right."

"Good," said Lally briskly. She disappeared inside the tent and reemerged with an iron kettle.

"Take this and fill it at the brook over there across the meadow. Make sure you pick a place where the stream is running fast, and make sure it's well above where the sheep come down to the water. We don't want to be drinking sheep piss." She smiled her wide gay smile.

Breakfast was well on its way when Mokie got back from the brook. They had lighted a fire. Butter was bubbling in a long-handled tin fry pan, and fresh mushrooms danced in the bubbles, their fragrance tickling her nose. Without warning, her stomach rumbled. The Skimmer took the kettle from her and hung it on the kettle iron above the fire. He flung in a handful of tea leaves and set them to steep.

With a wooden spoon Lally shoved the mushrooms to one side of the pan. Then she took slices of brown bread, poked holes in their middles, and plopped them into the fat to brown. When they were nicely crisped on one side, she turned them over and cracked eggs into the holes—an egg to each slice of bread. Out of a pocket she took some rather rumpled herbs and sifted them over the pan.

Mokie's mouth watered. The combined smell of mushrooms, frying bread, eggs, and herbs was devastating. The Skimmer dealt out battered tin cups, plates, and spoons. Lally poured out hot, strong tea, slid a breaded egg onto each plate, and poured mushrooms and gravy liberally over each piece. With iron control Mokie made herself wait until they were all seated cross-legged around the fire and Lally had taken the first bite. Then she attacked her plate like a yard full of pigs and did not stop.

"Sugar?" said John politely, and passed a dented dish. Mouth crammed full, jaws busy chewing, Mokie had no room to spare for words. She shook her head. Apple sat expectantly at her feet, watching for crumbs.

The others ate more slowly. They were watching her under their eyelids, exchanging an occasional glance but covering their surveillance with a gauze of inconsequent conversation.

Although she seemed to be concentrating on food, Mokie, too, was darting glances from under lowered lids. She was gathering impressions, taking the measure of these new creatures who were suddenly so supremely important in her world.

"You from around here, boyo?" asked The Skimmer casually.

"No. Well, yes. Well, not exactly around here. Not too near. That is . . ." She floundered to a stop, cheeks flaming in confusion.

Lally came to the rescue. "What's your name?"

"Mokie, I guess."

She said it gruffly, following as near as she could the rough tones of the village boys. She was trying not to stare at Lally.

"What you mean, 'you guess'? Don't you know?" said The Skimmer. And then he said, "Ow!" for Lally had surreptitiously jabbed him in the ribs.

Mokie didn't mind. She liked his directness. There was no malice in it, no desire to hurt for hurt's sake, as with the village boys.

"I mean," said The Skimmer, "Mokie. It's, ah, an unusual name. Never met anybody named Mokie before."

There was a little silence. Lally moved into the breach. "I'm Lally Dai," she said. "He's The Skimmer. And this is Dogger John."

"Pleased to meet you," said Mokie, thereby using up her entire store of social graces.

"Hello, Mokie," said John.

Mokie flicked a glance at John, and unexpectedly her eyes met his. She blinked in surprise at the contact, remembering that night outside the hut and how their eyes had also met in the green of the marble. She was intensely aware of John, but she was determined not to show it. Something about him, the dark hair, the darker eyes, reminded her of someone, and the memory teased at her, but would not name itself. More than that, she knew that he had seen her spying on their magic there in the hut. He had seen her watching through the crack and had winked in conspiracy.

She looked away self-consciously.

"And your pig?" asked Lally.

Mokie reached out to Apple, who pushed her head under the girl's hand. She cleared her throat.

"Apple."

"Hello, Apple," said John.

He looked from the girl to the pig and back again. The pig looked at him steadily. Then she blinked. Then she rose and went over to where he sat next to Lally. She settled herself between the two of them. Mokie felt momentarily abandoned, though she refused to let it show, even to Apple. She tried to smile, but her face wouldn't cooperate, so she arranged her forehead in a stiff little frown, the better to seem indifferent and male.

"Had the pig long?" inquired The Skimmer.

"Since she was born," said Mokie. "We're like sis—like partners, Apple and me, like two halves of the same person. This is a special pig. Very smart. Goes everywhere with me." Until now, said her thought, but she would not hear it.

"I knew a pig once did tricks," said The Skimmer. "Walked on his hind legs, did flips and somersaults. Did card tricks, too. Held the cards in his mouth. Brought his owner a lot of money."

"Apple can do tricks," said Mokie proudly. "Fetch, catch, do somersaults, sit up and beg—all sorts of things."

"How about that, now!" said The Skimmer. "And what about you? Let's see you do a few tricks." Mokie blinked, remembering all too vividly her failures in the forest.

"A few—? Me, you mean?" She felt trapped. Her chin came up.

"You, I mean. It's you I'm talking to, boyo. How about you? You're surely as good as the pig, aren't you? After all, who trained the pig?"

"I did," said Mokie faintly.

"Well, then," said The Skimmer. "That proves it. Now, what can you do? Let's see you do a headstand."

"A head—?"

"Like this."

In one smooth movement The Skimmer crouched over the balls of his feet, tipped himself head downward, swung his buttocks skyward, and straightened his legs until they were vertical. His mouth worked grotesquely; it took her a minute to realize that he was grinning at her upside down. His legs twittered nimbly, dancing on the air. He rolled down off his shoulders and sat upright.

"Now you," he said.

TWENTY-THREE

FLYiNG

MOKIE HESITATED. If she failed, they might not want her. They were all looking at her. She would not be shamed.

"Sure," she said. "I've done it lots."

Without hesitation, before her nerve could fail, hoping desperately for beginner's luck, Mokie crouched, rocked forward onto her hands, and kicked her legs wildly. She actually got them into the air, though not exactly at the same time. In the process, her too-big shirt sagged in folds about her shoulders and the baggy, ridiculous pants sagged around her thighs. Unnoticed, the silver scissors dropped from her upended pocket, landing open with the blades crossways on the dust. Unnoticed, Lally reached out a hand and slid them out from under her. She dropped them in her pocket.

For a long second Mokie stayed suspended with the sky

swinging below her; then she overbalanced, floundered awkwardly, and came down flat and hard on her back with the wind knocked clean out of her. Apple trotted over to sniff her and make sure she was all right, but for once Mokie paid her no attention. Satisfied that no harm was done, the pig settled down to watch.

"Looks like you're a bit out of practice," said The Skimmer mildly.

Before Mokie could make a sound, Apple had risen to her four feet, trotted to the center of the circle, lowered her head, and performed a neat somersault. She came upright with a modest air of triumph and lay down quietly again.

"Well!" said The Skimmer. "That's some pig, all right. Now, if we can teach Apple a few card tricks, our fortune's made. Come on now, young Mokie, if that's your name. You're not going to let a pig best you, are you? Try it again. But make sure you get your center before you raise your legs. You're a bit leggier than a pig, and there's a good deal more of you to go up, so there's more to come down. Here, I'll help you."

He came and stood beside her, reaching a hand to support her back. She flinched away as if his hands were clubs.

"All right," he said mildly, "never mind, I'll just keep an eye on you. Take it slower this time. Ease your head down. Now tip up your backside . . . easy . . . easy . . . that's it. Keep your knees tucked in to your stomach. Make sure your shoulders stay even. Now, get your balance before you go any farther. That's it. Now, both legs together—no, don't kick your legs, straighten them slowly. Take your time—first from the hip, *then* from the knee. Both legs together, I said. Keep your middle. No! Too fast! Too fast!"

The horizon tilted. She came down hard again and looked up, breathless and embarrassed, at the ring of faces.

"There, now, see?" said The Skimmer with annoyance. "You did it wrong again, just like last time! Try it again, and this time see if you can follow instructions."

Mokie glared at him and angry tears pricked behind her eyelids, but she refused to let them fall and got ready to try again.

Lally put in a word. "Just let yourself fall if you have to," she said. "When you feel like you're falling, just curl your back and pull in your knees. Roll yourself down in sections. Then you won't slam so hard."

"Brace your shoulders," advised John.

"Pull in your middle," said Lally.

"Tighten your backside," ordered The Skimmer.

No one in all her short life had ever paid so much attention to her. She was determined not to disappoint them. She braced her shoulders until they felt like wood. She pulled in her middle until it nearly touched her backbone. She tightened her backside until it almost came through the front side. She tried again, much too hard, keeping her muscles so stiff and tight that she never got off the ground but tipped over on her side. The Skimmer clicked his tongue impatiently.

Lally intervened. "You're going too fast, Skimmer. Let her watch first, see how we do things. She'll catch on if you give her time."

She was stripping off her shawl and jewelry as she spoke. Laying them on the ground, she rubbed her hands in the dirt to give them a grip. Mokie noticed that John and The Skimmer did the same. Then the two men took up positions facing each other some ten paces apart. The Skimmer half crouched, advanced a bent knee, and held out a cupped hand at waist height. Lally stepped lightly up this makeshift stair, caught his other hand in hers, gave a little spring and a turn as he swing her aloft. And next moment she was balancing upright with her feet on The Skimmer's shoulders, pretty as you please. Now he braced his elbows against his ribs, holding his hands palm upward at shoulder height directly in front of her feet. One foot at a time, keeping her weight balanced, she stepped onto his hands. "Up you go!" he said, and slowly, keeping his arms close to his body, he raised her in the air until she was standing high over his head, arms slightly extended out to the side for balance. It looked easy.

"Ready, John?" The Skimmer called.

"Ready," he answered, and took a wide stance, knees half bent, arms swinging.

Without moving his head, The Skimmer glanced upward from under his eyebrows. "Ready, Lally?"

"Ready."

As The Skimmer lowered his hands to shoulder height,

Lally reached her arms forward. He bent his knees springily and straightened his elbows, propelling her up and out. Lally flew like a swallow toward John, who caught her outstretched hands and swung her up and around until she lighted on John's shoulders. The whole maneuver had taken less than a minute. Lally looked down at an entranced, openmouthed Mokie.

"Do it again," said Mokie.

Lally laughed, a delighted ripple of sound.

"Liked that, did you?" said The Skimmer. Mokie nodded, wordless.

"Once more, Lally?" asked John.

"I'm ready," she said. "Skimmer?" she called. "Will you catch?"

"Right." He nodded. Once more she flew, received by The Skimmer, who this time swung her to one side, caught her around the waist, neatly reversed her, and set her down light as a bird on the ground.

"Want to try?" she asked Mokie.

"Could I?"

"Here, now, Lally!" said The Skimmer. "Slow down. Who's going too fast now? You can't have her fly before she can balance."

But Lally had seen the look on Mokie's face, as if a door had opened. "We can talk her through it. Just to give her the feeling. Can't we, John?" He nodded.

"All right," said The Skimmer. He shook his head and sighed heavily, his unspoken words hovering in the air—don't blame me if she falls and cracks her head.

"Now, Mokie," said Lally, "just hold yourself easy and let The Skimmer and John do the work. Keep your knees a little bent until you're up and safe. Don't hunch your shoulders, and whatever you do, don't look down. Keep your eyes on the catcher. Skimmer, you can take her up."

As she had seen Lally do, Mokie scrubbed her hands in the dirt and flexed her fingers. "All right, Mokie," said The Skimmer. "When I say 'up,' you jump. I'll do the rest. Now, give me your hands."

Hands gripping The Skimmer's hands, calloused and hard as a tree branch, Mokie scrambled to his knee, solid as a block of wood. She wobbled, stepped gingerly onto his offered hand, heard him say, "UP you go!" Propelled up and around, she landed, rocking precariously, on The Skimmer's shoulders. She clutched his head in panic. His hands steadied her. "Got your balance?"

"No," she said breathlessly. "Yes."

Cautiously she released her grip on his head. Slowly she straightened her legs. She was up. She was there. On top of the world. She risked a look around her from what seemed a dizzying height.

"Eyes, Mokie!" yelled Lally. "Eyes on the catcher!"

Too late. Distracted, Mokie looked wildly about her, teetered, lost her balance, and fell forward. The Skimmer caught her, set her ungently on solid ground. She stumbled, but he held her up.

"Told you," said The Skimmer to no one in particular.

"Let me try again," said Mokie. "I'll do it right this time. I will. I promise. Please⸮"

The Skimmer looked at John, who nodded, looked at Lally, who gave him a pleading smile.

"Once more," he grumbled. "But only once."

Once will be enough, you mean old spoilsport, said Mokie to herself. I'll show you. She took a deep breath, rubbed her palms together, stepped briskly from knee to hand.

Up!

SWING.

She landed hard on The Skimmer's shoulders, rocked, recovered. She looked desperately at John, who caught her eyes with his own. The shock was physical, but the very force of it steadied her. All in a moment a connection was made, reinforced, tied into place. Suddenly the air was turned to green glass, and she was looking through green air at John and he was holding her with his glance, his eyes never leaving hers. Locked in John's gaze, she carefully released The Skimmer's hands. Locked in John's gaze, she slowly straightened to her full height. There was a pause.

"Now onto my hands," said The Skimmer. He didn't look upward, but spoke to John, who nodded at Mokie. "Shift your weight as little as you can." He gave her his hands, palms up, and she moved onto them. She could sense him under her making minute adjustments to keep them both in balance.

"Ready?" he asked.

"Ready," she said, and swallowed hard. Slowly, steadily, he straightened his arms and she went up and up. John's head tilted to follow her with his eyes. He looked very small and very far away.

Now, said John's eyes. She tensed and sprang up and out as The Skimmer's hands propelled her, and for one ecstatic instant she soared free of the earth, airborne, triumphant. It was glorious. Then she lost the moment, reached out too late, overshot John's outstretched hands, and slammed into him full force, bearing him to the ground and landing heavily on top of him.

"Ouuff!" he exploded. "Mokie! You're on my stomach."

She rolled over and looked at him tragically. She was earthbound again, the lovely feeling of freedom knocked clean out of her. She would never fly again. He would never look at her again.

Unexpectedly, it was The Skimmer who came to the rescue. "Not bad, considering," he said. "Not bad at all. She flies like a trouper, only she forgot to spread her wings. We'll try it once more. On your feet, Mokie. You all right, John?"

"Recovering," said John, brushing himself off. He grinned at Mokie. Crimson with embarrassment, she did not grin back.

"Who do you want to launch and who to catch, Mokie?" asked Lally.

"Like before," muttered Mokie. She did not trust herself to

144

look at John. But she would have to look at him, she realized, and wanted to.

One more she mounted The Skimmer; once more he swung her up. Shoulders. Hands. It went easier this time. She set her jaw, got her balance, got her courage, and looked at John. And there it was again. The same physical impact, the same connection. But this time she was prepared.

"Ready, Mokie?"

"Ready."

"Don't forget to spread your wings. Here you go!"

She felt The Skimmer gather himself to pitch her. She lifted her arms up and out, pushed against his hands, and took off. Again she rode the air. She was weightless, a bird, a cloud, a puff of wind. John's eyes sustained her. Too soon she met the solid reality of his outstretched hands, but instead of swinging her around and down, he shifted his hands quickly down to her waist, held her for a heartbeat, and set her lightly on the ground in front of him. In all that time, neither had looked away, and still their eyes were locked.

"Well, now!" The Skimmer broke the moment. "That was a way sight better."

Mokie felt his approval and turned to him. It was hard to look away from John, but she needed the relief.

The Skimmer patted her on the shoulder. "Take to it like a natural, you do. We might make something of you yet, Mokie."

"We might," said Lally, but she was looking at John. John said nothing.

"Enough for now," said The Skimmer. "We don't want folk noticing too much too soon."

Gray and empty with first light, the meadow had gradually became bright with sun and alive with people. The gypsies shifted into performance mode—Lally taking her seat in the tent doorway, John squatting before his sand patterns. Crossing and recrossing on their way to this or that booth or stall or exhibit, people in the gathering crowd were busy with their own preoccupations, but not too busy to see again the scarlet tent, the fortune-teller fanning her cards, the juggler tossing and catching iridescent glass balls that flashed fire back at the sun.

To all outward appearances concentrating wholly on their various occupations, John and The Skimmer managed an unobtrusive conversation.

"She's the one, all right," said The Skimmer, tossing a ball and catching it on his elbow. "Mokie. That's no proper name, just the pig word. She's not even sure it belongs to her."

"What did you expect?" asked John, head bent over his sand drawing.

The Skimmer threw him a look. "You'd think they knew something, those folks in her village."

John shrugged eloquently.

"But that's not all." The Skimmer balanced a ball delicately on the tip of his nose. "It's not just her name; she acts like her body don't belong to her either. The minute you touch her—just to give a hand—she tightens up like a fiddle string. Did you see the way she flinched away when I put my hand on her back? You'd have thought I was going to beat her instead of help her. Or something worse."

"That's what she's used to," said John. "Give her time," he added, "and she'll loosen of her own accord. She isn't easy in her body right now. She doesn't like it; that's plain enough. Well, we know what happened. Her body remembers; you can see it."

He paused, reflecting. Then went on.

"But she doesn't want to remember, and can you blame her? That means her spirit isn't easy in her body. She hasn't caught up with herself yet. She's trying to be someone she's not, or else trying to *not* be someone she's afraid she might be. And so her body fights her spirit and her spirit struggles in her body. But you saw her fly, saw how different she was in the air. It's a start."

He broke off again, paused. Then he continued. "Let's keep working. She'll settle out in time."

"Time," said The Skimmer. "How much time? The pig's here, isn't she, and ready and waiting?" A toss of his nose sent the ball skyward to join the two his hands had flung. All three glass balls caught the sunlight as they cascaded back into his waiting fingers.

"Now who's wanting to hurry things?" said Lally, looking up from her cards. "You yourself told me we were waiting for her

147

time. Well, we're here to help her get to it. As for the pig, she knows when the time is better than we do."

John, sifting red and green and yellow circles through his fingers onto the ground, looked at both of them. He swept up the sand and began again. A shape grew under his fingers, a pig face with narrow eyes, a square nose, alert red ears. The face stared at him, and he stared back. Then it changed to Lally, her apple-green glance flashing bright at him. Next moment it was Mokie, looking up at him with wide, startled eyes. The look was so real that for a moment it seemed to be Mokie herself, and so compelling that he felt his heart turn over. He shook his head to clear it of the vision, swept up the sand, and began again. Then it was the pig once more.

For Mokie the rest of the day passed like a half-remembered dream. It won't last, she assured herself, so I'll make the most of it while I can. She watched intently from the sidelines as the gypsies repeated with small variations their performance of the day before. Her muscles felt trembly from their unaccustomed use, and her hands and elbows and knees were sore from falling. There would be bruises tomorrow. But I did it, she told herself. And John caught me. I flew, just like Lally. Nobody in Little Wicken ever did anything like that. I can fly.

She was more than ready for bed by the time they had finished the supper that Lally provided—potatoes baked in the ashes of the fire, hot and floury when you broke them open, fragrant and delicious when you sprinkled them with a little salt.

The crisp brown skins were eaten last, spread with lashings of sweet butter. There were hunks of mellow cheese to follow, toasted in the fire, the whole meal washed down with cups of strong black tea. Mokie was stuffed, her stomach filled full for the second time that day and after a long stretch of sparse meals. Her eyelids began to droop and she yawned gapingly. Yawned again.

"Mokie, you're dropping with sleep," said Lally. "Make yourself a bed out of those pillows and a shawl and lie down. We'll be along presently."

Mokie snuggled down with Apple and watched in sleepy content as John and Lally and The Skimmer scrubbed plates and cups with water and ashes, stowed them in the chest by the tent door, damped down the fire to ready it for tomorrow morning. Then they sat talking softly to one another around the fire pit, the rose glow of the last embers lighting their faces and shadowing the hollows of their eyes. She could not hear their words, but their voices made a murmur of music. The tent smelled of Lally's apple blossom perfume, an incense that wafted her into sleep.

As she slipped into darkness she said their names over to herself, tasting them on her tongue like forbidden sweets.

Lally Dai. It sounded like water falling into a little pool.

The Skimmer. His was a different kind of name, light and clear, like the insistent sound of wind in summer leaves. She liked him. However demanding, however blunt he was, he was her friend. The knowledge was like solid ground under her feet.

Dogger John. There she stopped. She didn't know what to make of him, and she was attracted and afraid in equal measure. She wondered what he thought of her, but her wondering brought her no answers.

Finally, hugging the pig close, she slept.

TWENTY-FOUR

Lessons

"**R**EADY FOR BREAKFAST?" The voice was not in her head, but coming from somewhere above it. Mokie looked up. Lally was standing in the doorway of the tent. Behind her, the dark sky was just beginning to grow pale. Mokie stood up, wincing as her body reminded her of yesterday's unaccustomed exercise. In spite of the pain, she felt remarkably well, better than she had felt at any time since leaving Little Wicken. She hobbled outside into the fresh dawn half-light.

John and The Skimmer had breakfast under way. The Skimmer was feeding sticks into the fire as John hung an iron pot on a trivet to simmer. "Want me to fill the kettle?" offered Mokie.

"That'd be lovely," said Lally. Her glance took in Mokie's stiff posture and cautious movements. "Feeling a bit stiff, are you?

That's not so surprising. Never mind, walking'll loosen some of those kinks. And if you think they're bad now, just wait till tomorrow. The second day's always worse. But don't worry. We'll limber you up."

Mokie whistled for Apple and headed for the brook, dancing to Lally's words. "Wait till tomorrow." There would be a tomorrow—it was a promise. So happy was she that she forgot her pain, even forgot to swagger in her boy's disguise and relapsed into her old swinging walk. Behind her trotted the pig, her ears fluttering in the breeze, her neat little hooves beating the earth in time to Mokie's dance.

Having no past experience to use as a measure, Mokie did not recognize happiness when she felt it. She only knew that she was in some new state of being that was different from anything she had ever felt. It had not the piercingly joyous quality she associated with the Crystal Time, when she had been lifted out of herself into another world. Now, in contrast, she felt grounded in herself and in this world. The Crystal Time had been impossibly high and clear and bright. Now was realer, earthier. "More human," she would have said, if she had been able to describe her feelings. But she was not, and so she simply hugged them to her all the way to the brook and back.

Lally watched her go, then turned to John and The Skimmer, her eyes shadowed.

"All right," said The Skimmer. "So far, so good. She's here, and it's moving, and we can all feel it."

Reflectively, Lally stirred the pot. "It's moving awfully fast, Skimmer. And Mokie and Apple—they're like one person, almost. It's going to be tricky separating them. You were asking yesterday, how much time? Not enough, it seems to me."

"Well, now, Lally," said The Skimmer. "I seem to remember when you were the one wanting things to move. Now you say they're moving too fast. There's no pleasing you, woman. Good thing you're not in charge, or we'd all be slowing down or hurrying up every time you changed your mind."

He gave her a frown of feigned exasperation. She stuck her tongue out at him.

"And don't you worry none about the pig," he went on. "She'll separate herself when the time comes without us doing anything. She knows what she's doing. Better than we know."

"She's an odd waif," said Lally, paying little attention to his words. "But there's something very engaging about her."

"I agree," said John. "I find her rather appealing."

The Skimmer stared at him. "Appealing! What you doing finding her 'appealing'? That's no part of the pattern. You better be careful you don't find her too appealing, boyo. You watch yourself, John."

John shrugged. "Don't worry about me," he said. "She's still very much a child, after all. Let's just wait. Let's wait and see what comes."

Lally shot him a sharp glance. "She's older than she looks."

"Doesn't look any age at all in that ridiculous getup," said

The Skimmer. "Does she really think she's fooling anyone⸮"

"She's fooling herself," said Lally. "I'll find some way to get her out of it."

"I'll loosen her up," said The Skimmer. "Keep her too busy to pretend."

"I found some mushrooms to go with breakfast," said Mokie's voice. She had come up behind them. One hand clutched the kettle, the other held out an offering of some squashed, gray-brown items. Lally looked at them doubtfully.

"I washed them off in the brook," Mokie assured her, "after I filled the kettle. In clear water. I didn't see any sheep around."

Lally took the gift. "We're having bread soup this morning," she said. "The mushrooms will add flavor." She dumped the mushrooms into the pot, took the kettle from Mokie, and hung it on the stand over the fire to boil. "Not long now," she announced.

Mokie folded herself down and sat cross-legged by the fire. Her happiness was almost too great for her to bear. To her this second breakfast was in the nature of a ceremony, a consecration that sealed her membership in the company.

As on the previous day, The Skimmer dealt out dishware and spoons. John poured the tea. Lally ladled the thick, fragrant soup into bowls. Everyone was hungry, and for the first moments, no one spoke. Mokie was too blissful, The Skimmer too busy eating. Lally and John were busy watching.

After a decent amount of steady eating had taken place, The

Skimmer put down his spoon and looked at Mokie. "Mokie," he began.

Apple looked up alertly. Mokie sat dreaming.

The Skimmer tried again. "Mokie!" he said sharply, and Mokie jumped. She swallowed hastily.

"You mean me?"

"Course I mean you. Your name's Mokie, isn't it?"

"I meant, uh, what did you say?"

"I said 'Mokie,' but that was just the beginning, so here's the rest of it. How about if you joined us, you and the pig—you and Apple? Apple knows a few tricks, and you're a fast learner, you've shown that. You're just beginning, but you're not afraid to try, and that's the important thing. We'll make something of you yet, you wait and see. How about it?"

To be offered what she had been bracing herself to plead for caught Mokie unawares, and for a moment she was bereft of speech. Then Apple grunted and butted her with her little hard nose. Mokie looked down at her, then up at The Skimmer. "Apple says yes. For both of us."

Perhaps Apple had some idea of what saying yes would entail, but Mokie had not. She found out when The Skimmer started work with her after breakfast. First he put her through some limbering-up exercises. In view of her inexperience and obvious soreness, he made the going gentle, but Mokie, for whom all such movement was unnatural torture, did not see it so. At first she was afraid she would die. Then she was afraid she wouldn't, for surely death would be easier than the methodical pulling apart of each protesting joint and muscle. It was a grim contest between Mokie's body and her will, for which The Skimmer felt compassion and amusement in equal parts. With detached sympathy he watched the sequence of anguished grimaces that chased one another across her face as she gasped and struggled in stubborn silence.

After almost an hour of such struggle, he felt she needed encouraging, but The Skimmer's way of giving encouragement was better suited to the boy she pretended to be than to the girl she so obviously was. He thumped her heartily on the back.

"I'll say this for you, Mokie, my lad, you're a tough one. Most beginners wouldn't take what I've been putting you through without they'd let out some sort of squeal, or groan, or cry. But I haven't heard a whimper out of you, for all this effort."

"Why would I whimper?" She sat up, face red, lungs pumping. "Crying wouldn't help. It never does. And anyway," she added, "you don't cry. So I won't."

"Ah, but it's different with us." Lally had wandered over and stood looking at The Skimmer and his protégée.

The Skimmer coughed loudly and looked a warning at Lally. Telling too much too soon. Giving the game away before time.

Lally started to say something, then thought better of it, shrugged, and strolled back to the tent.

Well, well, thought Mokie. That's plain enough. Her eyes fol-

156

lowed the retreating Lally for a moment, then she returned to her struggle as if nothing untoward had been said.

"There, that's enough for now," said The Skimmer after a bit. "You got to coax your body, not force it. Give it a rest. We'll try a bit of juggling for a change."

Suddenly there were three glass balls flying through the air, seemingly out of nowhere. She caught one easily enough, reached and caught another, but could not manage the third. Helplessly she watched as it hit the ground and shattered into rainbow shards. She remembered her failure at juggling acorns and despaired.

"There, now," said The Skimmer mildly, "see what happens when you try to hold on to things? Keep 'em in the air, boyo."

He reached down and scooped up the shards, showing complete disregard for possible damage from their sharp broken edges. With no warning he flung them straight at Mokie. In slow motion they came together in a perfect circle, and an iridescent, unbroken ball floated toward her. As she followed its path in hypnotized fascination, the ball shimmered down, hesitated briefly, and came to rest on Apple's nose. With perfect aplomb, the pig balanced it delicately long enough to show her skill, then with a toss of her head she sent it flying back to The Skimmer.

Mokie's eyes widened in admiration and envy, and she dropped the other two balls. They landed intact and rolled back to where The Skimmer waited. He picked them up, juggled all

157

three once, twice, then flung one out as before, straight at Mokie. Light as a butterfly it landed on her nose, and although her eyes crossed with the effort, she was able to keep it there.

"Well," said The Skimmer after a moment, "don't just stand there with your face in front of you. Toss it back."

Without thinking, she gave her head a toss. The ball lofted off her nose and sailed smoothly through the air. The Skimmer caught it on his chin, bounced it to a lifted heel, caught it again behind his knee, and transferred it to the crook of his elbow, where it rested like a nesting dove.

"That's better. You got to keep your eyes on the balls, boyo, not on your hands. Let your hands and your body think for themselves. You got to think like the balls. You got to be the balls. Now, let's try it again."

She tried it again.

TWENTY-FIVE

MiRRQR MAGiC

T HAT NIGHT LALLY PRODUCED DINNER for all out of a rather scrawny rabbit The Skimmer had caught. Combined with a withered onion, some wild garlic, a potato, and a few herbs, it was adequate to go around, even for four hungry appetites. Mokie could never see quite how Lally managed, but there was always enough and it was always delicious. Afterward John and The Skimmer went for a walk, "to have a word with the stars," they said, leaving Lally and Mokie to themselves in the tent.

Mokie was tired after another hard day, so she was content to watch Lally, who sat before her mirror playing with the image that looked back at her. There seemed no end to her invention. She darkened her eyes with paint and reddened her mouth. She draped shawls and scarves to see the effect. She tried out a brass earring for her left ear and a glass one for her right to judge one against the other. With every new decoration her mood seemed to change. Before Mokie's eyes she became by turns ethereal, earthy, brassy, demure, seductive, prim, bawdy. At last, done with adornment, she began brushing out her hair in long strokes that made it crackle and spark and fly about her head with a life of its own.

Mokie sat cross-legged on the ground, watching Lally in the mirror. She was enthralled. She had never seen a woman decorate herself before. The wives of Little Wicken considered themselves dressed up if they put on a clean apron and tied up their hair. Lally's smoky gray-green eyes watched Mokie watching her, reading the longing on her face and in her heart. She caught Mokie's eye and smiled into the mirror. Her own eyes widened guilelessly. Slowly she stroked the brush through her hair, letting the lamplight change it from bronze to honey to amber as the brush passed. Then she held out the brush to Mokie. "Want to try?"

"Yes. Uh, no. I don't need—boys don't bother much about their hair."

Lally looked at her straight. "You are not a boy, Mokie, and if you think you're fooling me, or John, or The Skimmer, you'd better think again."

Mokie's jaw dropped.

"My dear soul, you might fool people who can't see what's in front of them, like the folk around here, but it's not much of a disguise for those with eyes in their heads. You don't stand like a boy, you don't talk like a boy, you don't walk like a boy—

except when you remember to swagger, which boys only do when someone is watching—and you most certainly don't look like a boy. You're too beautiful."

Mokie's jaw dropped lower.

"Beautiful? Me?"

Apple, who had been asleep in a corner, opened one eye, looked at Lally, then closed her eye again.

"Yes, you. Beautiful. Not doll pretty, not all pink and white like these giggly, silly little town females who come to get their fortunes told. I mean beauty in your bones. Down deep. But it would show to more advantage if you dropped the pretense and let yourself be what you really are. Come on, let me show you."

She held out the brush like a lure.

Mokie struggled with buried memory. If she were truly what Lally had called her—beautiful—what would happen? Lally's regard was safe enough, but what of The Skimmer? Or John? Her thoughts retreated in panic.

Lally watched the struggle and waited. Apple woke up, ambled over to Mokie, and lay down beside her.

The battle reached a peak, then ended abruptly in sudden surrender. To be praised, cared for, was so new an experience that Mokie feared to turn it away, though she feared almost as much to trust it.

She shrugged. "I don't care."

"That's good enough for now. Come here and sit in front of the mirror. That's right."

Obediently Mokie sat herself down. Tight as a bowstring, she forced herself to submit to Lally's touch.

"Now, off comes this old head rag. It's such a mess we ought to burn it. Let's have a look at your hair." She shook her head. "A nest for birds—magpies at that. And off comes this shirt so we don't get hair all over it. And off comes the breast band. Oh yes, it does, don't squirm. Let your body be what it is."

As the tight band was released, Mokie let out an involuntary gasp. Freed from its constraint, her chest expanded, and her breasts stood out naturally, young and high. She looked down at them doubtfully.

"Just for tonight, " said Lally coaxingly. "Tomorrow you can go back to being a boy if you want. For now I'm going to wrap you in this to keep the hair cuttings off you." She swirled a flowered scarf around Mokie's shoulders. "Cross it in the front and tie it behind, or it'll fall off."

Meekly Mokie did as she was told. She looked in the mirror—curiously, timidly. Having only Lally to measure against, she despaired at the difference. Beauty seemed a long way off. Her eyes peered warily out from under a matted hedge of hair that overhung her brow and fell raggedly about her head.

"Now." Head on one side, hands on hips, Lally surveyed her critically. "I can't do anything with your hair until I get the tangles out. I'm going to comb it first—if I can, which I doubt, it's so snarly. However did you get it that way?"

Mokie opened her mouth to reply, but Lally kept on talking.

162

"Never mind, it doesn't matter. When the tangles are out, I'll brush it smooth, or as smooth as I can. When I've finished I'm going to trim it a little, just to even up the ragged ends. All right?"

"I don't care," said Mokie. She looked away from the mirror.

Lally took a big wooden comb that smelled of sandalwood and set to work combing out a young lifetime of neglect. It was an ordeal for both of them, with much pulling and tugging punctuated by frequent yelps. It took time to comb out the snarls and smooth the tangles, and even then some bits were too matted and stubborn for the comb to penetrate and had to be cut out. When she had done all she could with the comb, Lally took her brush and went to work. When that was finished, Mokie, to her secret disappointment, looked worse than ever. Her hair stood out all around her head in a shaggy, irregular mane. That it shone red-gold in the lamplight and even showed a tendency to wave was lost on her. Her mouth trembled.

"It's worse than before. It's all different lengths and it sticks out all over. I'm a freak."

Lally smiled gently, careful not to mock. "No, you're not a freak. Have patience. I'm not finished yet. It will be better, I promise. But I'll have to do more than just trim the ends. I'll have to cut it short all over."

She meant no threat, and Mokie's reaction astonished her.

"No, Lally, no!" Mokie clapped both hands to her head. "You said you'd trim it, not cut it off. Short all over—then I *will* look

163

like a boy." She spread her fingers, protecting as much hair as she could cover.

Lally sat back on her heels, her brows arched, her mouth curving in amusement. "Correct me if I'm wrong, Mokie, but haven't you been trying to look like a boy?"

Hands still holding her hair, Mokie's eyes clouded. A long moment passed.

"But you said . . ." she began. Then, "I don't know. Not like . . . not really. I guess it does look that way. But no. I don't know what I've been trying to look like. Just not me. It was a way not to be . . . or a way to not be, maybe. But I didn't think . . ."

Something going on here, thought Lally. She decided to let up for the moment. The subject was too big, too many things were unsaid, Mokie's confusion was too deep to be resolved all at once.

"Never mind for now. I promise you, Mokie, you won't look like a boy. We're working on allowing you to be a woman, remember, and that's quite enough at present. You have to trust me."

She pulled Mokie's hands away from her head. Out of her pocket she pulled a pair of scissors and began to cut. Mokie shut her eyes.

From her place on the floor, Apple watched patiently.

Mokie kept her eyes shut. Clip went the scissors—clip and clip again. She could feel little hunks of hair falling on her knees, her shoulders. Bits of hair got up her nose and made her want to sneeze. The cutting seemed to take forever.

"Keep your eyes closed," ordered Lally.

She took off the scarf and shook out the hair cuttings. She dropped a silk blouse over Mokie's head, pulled her arms through the short, puffy sleeves, patted the neckline into place. Then she draped the scarf loosely over her shoulders, the two ends lightly wrapping her arms. Lastly she turned to her jewel box and took out a necklace, a brass chain hung with little brass disks that clashed musically against one another. She fastened the chain around Mokie's neck. She took out a pair of ear bobs, also hung with little disks, and fastened them in Mokie's small and very pretty ears. Mokie shook her head. The ear bobs jingled.

"Open your eyes," said Lally.

Mokie risked a look at the mirror. Nowhere to be seen was the freak she had feared. Staring out at her was a changeling with tilted eyes, a gypsy princess with brass rings in her ears, a small, proud head of close-cropped, softly curling hair that framed high cheekbones and a wide, generous mouth open now in astonishment. It was a face of challenging, uneven beauty. It was a stranger. It was an enemy. It was no one she had ever seen. The gypsy princess looked at Mokie out of the mirror, and Mokie looked back and met her own eyes. For the first time in her life she saw herself. She was taller than she thought, older than she realized.

At that precise moment John and The Skimmer walked into the tent. Mokie's eyes shifted immediately to their reflected faces as they stood behind her. For the third time she and John locked glances, and as before, she felt the force of it in her body. For a heartbeat their eyes locked. She caught her breath. In the mirror she saw his eyes widen, saw The Skimmer's do the same as both men registered her new appearance and all that it suggested. It took them a moment to react—only a moment, but in that little time Mokie saw herself for the second time in her life, not just reflected in the mirror but reflected in the eyes of John and The Skimmer. Her buried wound tore open and bled.

The two men looked at her and now their look was a physical blow. It was Grime jabbing his finger against her breast. It was the silent stare of the boys in the wood. It was her doom descending. There was no way to escape it except by pretending it wasn't happening. Although she had no way to deal with or even to sort out what she felt, her body remembered and stiffened in panic against what it knew was coming. She radiated terror. Her breasts tingled with pain, her gut tightened, and her body closed on itself. Her eyes were fixed and staring, ringed with white. Her jaw clenched, and the muscles stood out in her neck. It took all her strength to stand still and not to make a break for the door, but the men were in the way and so she held on, frozen, like a rabbit in an open field.

TWENTY-SIX

FANCY

LALLY SAW EVERYTHING—the shock, the terror, the barely maintained control. She put a hand protectively on Mokie's arm and felt her whole body rigid and quivering like a plucked bowstring. John and The Skimmer saw it as well, and though they did not fully understand it, they responded in their separate ways. Both of them backed out of mirror range. Both of them took their eyes off Mokie and turned all their attention to Lally.

"What's going on here?" inquired The Skimmer. His jovial ferocity was meant to be funny, but it had the opposite effect. Only Lally's hand on her arm kept Mokie in her seat.

"Well, well," said John mildly. "There've certainly been some changes made."

"There are more changes to come," said Lally. "We're not finished yet. John, Skimmer, kindly turn around, you two."

Keeping a tight hold on Mokie to prevent her bolting, Lally smiled a promise and signaled a warning—back off.

Obediently the two faced away, looking industriously out the door of the tent. Mokie's breath, which she hadn't known she was holding, came out in an explosive sigh.

"Now, then," said Lally to Mokie, "stand up."

Like an animal coming out of cover, moving slowly and warily and keeping a tight hold on her terror, Mokie obediently stood up.

Lally rummaged in a trunk and held out a drape of rainbow fabric. "Here's a skirt to match the scarf. Put it on. No, no, no! Not like that. You have to take the pants off before you put the skirt on."

Mokie unwound her belt and the pants immediately fell around her feet. She stepped out of them and hesitantly slid her legs into the shimmering, many-flounced skirt that Lally handed her, pulled it up, and fastened it around her waist. Unlike the pants, the skirt fit as if made for her and swished deliciously around her ankles. The colors, lilac and blue, water-green and silver, swirled and melted into one another. She took a few tentative steps, felt her hips answer to the swing of the skirt, and stopped immediately.

"Lally, can we turn around now? I'm tired of staring out the door." Thus The Skimmer.

"Yes, turn around. Well? What do you think?"

Proudly she displayed for their appreciation the new, feminine Mokie, as if she had just invented her, which in a way she had. Mokie said nothing. She was not waiting for acorns this time, but for something so dreadful she could not face it and so did not know what it was. Lally watched her quietly. It was up to the men.

The Skimmer folded his arms across his chest and looked critically at Mokie. "My, my, my," he said judiciously, "that's quite a change. But I think I miss the old Mokie."

Mokie stood still, like an animal blinded by torchlight.

"Lally, what magic have you done? How did you do it?" asked John, stepping back another pace as if to get a better view, at the same time allowing Mokie room to move, space to breathe.

"No magic," said Lally. "Just Mokie."

"Yes," said John, "but it's more than 'just Mokie.' Where's the Mokie we left this morning? Who is this beauty?"

Mokie stood rigid, waiting.

"Well, now, I don't know," said The Skimmer, walking all round her to make a complete assessment. "It's pretty and all, no doubt of it, but it's not a very practical outfit, Lally. She can't do headstands in that flimsy skirt and hung about with all that jewelry." To Mokie he said, "You'd better stick to your old pants for every day and save that fancy getup for special occasions. It's too elegant to wear just for the likes of John and me."

John raised an eyebrow. "And why shouldn't she be elegant? I think the fancy getup is appropriate—and becoming."

To Mokie he said, "That's a very nice outfit, Mokie. But can't we find one for Apple as well? A skirt and scarf? And a pair of earrings? I fancy she'd look good in yellow."

It was a feeble joke, but it got Mokie to laugh and the laugh released just a little the terrible hold she had on her body.

John continued. "Now, why were you hiding as a boy when you so clearly are not one? Did you think we'd bite you?"

The question was playful, but Mokie had never learned how to play. She stood tongue-tied.

"Yes," answered Lally, coming to the rescue. "Of course she did. Us or somebody. Don't be stupider than necessary, John. She might not have liked being a boy"—she gave Mokie a bland, shuttered look—"but if she felt safe being a girl, she'd have let us see her. Use your head."

"All right," said John. "I'll try." He looked at Mokie appraisingly. "No one will bite you, Mokie, and we'll be honored—all of us—to have you be who you really are."

Mokie looked hesitantly at Lally.

"You might say thank you," said Lally.

"Thank you," said Mokie. She ducked a stiff little curtsy. "Thank you, Lally." Her memory let go its hold and the tension in the little tent eased perceptibly. "Thank you, John. Skimmer, you're right. I won't wear these clothes for practice although," she said a touch wistfully, "they do feel lovely."

"Well, now," said The Skimmer, "they're good enough. They're just not for every day. Still, those duds do make quite a difference. I have to say, Mokie, you're more believable as a pretty girl than you ever were as a boy."

She looked at him and shrugged. "I guess I really wasn't a very good boy."

"On the contrary," said John, a smile twitching the corner of his mouth, "you were a very good boy, very proper, very well behaved. Just not very convincing."

Mokie giggled.

That's good, said Lally to herself. Keep it going, John.

"Now that you've got proper clothes," said John, "what about a proper name? Mokie's no name for the pretty girl you are. We should find you another one. Who called you Mokie?"

"They did."

"Who's 'they'?"

"Them. The folk in my village."

"But it's just a word, isn't it? Not a real name at all. Not even a nickname. Doesn't it mean 'pig'?"

"Pig girl," said Mokie. "It means 'pig girl.' That's all I was good for. Nobody ever thought I belonged in a house like real people, so they left me outside and set me to herd the pigs, to be the pig girl. I did all right at that, so I guess they decided I was just another pig."

"You could do worse," said The Skimmer. "Pigs are fine animals. They're smart and they're independent and they understand more than you might think. Wiser than people, pigs are, lots of times. You keep your name, Mokie. You be proud of it. It's

171

a fine name. Sounds to me like the folk in your village are the real pigs, if you take my meaning. You're better off with us."

She was so quiet it took some time for them to see that she was holding her breath and blinking furiously, that unshed tears were filling her eyes and threatening to spill down her cheeks.

"Here, now," said The Skimmer, "No need for that. I mean, we're all friends. No reason to cry." He fished a grubby cloth from his pocket and handed it to her.

"No reason at all," said Mokie, blowing her nose vigorously. "And anyway, I wasn't crying."

A little silence followed.

"It's funny, really," said Mokie after a bit.

"What's funny?" asked John.

"What The Skimmer said, about how pigs are nicer than people and the people were really the pigs. I used to call the folks in Little Wicken the people herd. I didn't mind if I was part of the pig herd; I liked them better."

"Mokie," said Lally, "you're part of our herd now. But is there no one you'll be sorry to leave behind? Anyone in your village? Anyone you care at all about?"

"I left the village behind a long time ago—at least it feels like a long time. Apple and me, we care about each other. And now you."

"Now us. But you must have had more than Apple. Did you never have any friends at all? Anyone?"

Deeper silence, a pool of it widening in ripples out to the

walls of the tent. They let it be, watching and waiting. Mokie's eyes shadowed, looking back to things they could not see.

"There was this boy . . . one time . . . we played once. But then his mother . . . took him away. . . ." Her voice trailed off as images jostled, overlapped, crowded into one another. Janno's face as his mother dragged him away. The same face but older, looking down at her when—something happened. What had happened? Her eyes closed tight, shutting out the inadmissible pains that battered at her memory.

Change the subject. John probed, but gently.

"Your mother? Your father?"

"No father," said Mokie, coming back slowly. "They made sure I knew that. And mother—well, here I am, so somebody must have had me. Somebody had me and then she left. I guess she left. Anyway, she wasn't there when they found me. I was just crying and squirming in the grass. That's what they told me. So I never knew my mother very well."

"Didn't know her very well?" The Skimmer arched an eyebrow. "Sounds to me like you didn't know her at all, if she went away right after she had you."

"Oh." Mokie laughed with some embarrassment. "I used to pretend—I used to try to imagine her—what she might have been like, what she might have looked like, whether she—if she kissed me before she left. When I was little, sometimes before I fell asleep at night I used to try to imagine that I could see her face."

"What did it look like?" asked John.

Mokie looked at him. "I did see it, once or twice," she said. "Or somebody's face. I felt like I knew it."

"What did she look like?" asked Lally.

Mokie hesitated. "Not like me. Beautiful. Beautiful like you, Lally, only with long black hair, like a night with no stars. Wavy. Her hair fell forward around her face when she bent over me to say good-bye. I remember it tickled. Her face was pale and bright, like the moon looking down. Her eyes had shadows around them. When she held me I could smell her, kind of warm and earthy, but sweet. Like babies' sweat. Good smelling. You know?"

"I know," said Lally.

"It was warm in her arms, before she put me down in the grass. She said something, I don't remember what."

"You just imagined all of this?" asked Lally.

"Oh, well." She shrugged. "When you're falling asleep—maybe I dreamed it. I don't know."

There was a little silence, each busy with private thoughts. Apple, snoozing heavily at Mokie's feet, grunted and turned over.

"Well," said The Skimmer. "We'd better all be getting some sleep."

Lally blew out the lamps and they rolled themselves into blankets and settled into their pillows. A little later, the sounds of sleepy breathing sent whispers through the dark of the tent.

Out of the dark Mokie's voice came softly, speaking to no one in particular. "I wish I knew her name."

A hand reached out and patted her shoulder, but whether it was John or The Skimmer or Lally she could not tell. In a few minutes she was asleep.

TWENTY-SEVEN
MOON MOTHER

LATER THE MOON CAME UP, its light sifting like powder through the tent walls. Mokie dreamed that the walls faded, the tent became transparent. The night was a bowl of black glass inverted over her head, the moon riding its curve so near, she could almost reach out and touch it. She stretched up her arms, but out of nowhere a ragged cloud blew across the moon's face, trailing rain like tendrils of black hair, and it disappeared from sight. She sighed in her sleep and turned over, cuddling close to Apple, who tucked her snout under Mokie's chin. The little pig's warm breathing felt like a fall of soft, feathery hair tickling Mokie's neck.

Mokie slept deeply then, in a dreamless quiet without light. Cradled in the dark, she did not see Lally get up and come to stand looking down at her, eyes shadowed, mouth grave. She did not feel it when Apple detached herself from Mokie's encircling arms and went to the door of the tent. Lally followed the pig, and the two of them walked out into the moonlight. A little way behind the tent they stood together, their heads tilted up toward the moon, high overhead. Apple sat on her haunches, her little pig nose pointed at the moon. Lally raised her arms, as if she would touch the moon's circle with her fingertips. She was utterly still, a statue carved out of light, arms lifted, head thrown back, her long, moon-silvered hair rippling like a fall of water down her back. Standing so, no sound came from her, yet her low voice breathed a chant on the air:

> *Shaper without shape,*
> *Seer unseen,*
> *You whose light*
> *is your Self,*
> *whose pity*
> *is too bright to see,*
> *look to her.*
> *Tend to her.*
> *Keep her in*
> *Your old way*
> *and take her,*
> *when her day*
> *goes into dark,*
> *under Your cold*
> *mercy.*

When she had finished, she stood still for some moments, her head high, her arms held stiff and straight. Moonlight spilled from her lifted face down the curve of her throat. Then she felt something go bump against her leg. It was Apple, butting her gently to say it was time to go back inside. Silently they turned their backs on the moon, returned to the tent, lay down, and went to sleep.

Mokie dreamed again. In this dream she was back in the Wickenwood, looking through the window into the little hut. But with the multiple perception that dreamers have, she was also inside the hut somehow, a part of each of the three people at the table. She could feel the rough cloth of The Skimmer's green overcoat against her own skin, under her own toes the rungs of the stool as they touched Lally's bare feet, in her own fingers the curve of the green marble in John's hand. Then with no appreciable shift, she was the marble, rising and rising through the air, falling again to rest as John caught her.

She was at once the marble and herself watching the marble. She could see close up every detail of John's hand, trace the intricate lines of the palm, the fine-drawn whorls on the capable, square-tipped fingers, those fingers that curved so delicately around the falling Mokie marble and cradled its landing. She felt his hand enclose her, felt the warmth where he held her. And then without transition she was in her own body and John's hand was stroking her hair, touching her cheek. His touch was familiar, sweet, it made everything right. He was just going to tell her something of great importance, a word that would reveal the meaning of everything, when a voice she had never heard but had always known said, "Mokie."

The dream ended, and she woke up.

She was staring awake in an instant, wide awake with no hope of snuggling back to sleep. Beside her, Apple woke and raised her head. After a moment Mokie got up and went outside, and Apple followed. The night had clouded over, the moon was hidden. A black wind rushed over the meadow, so dark and heavy as to be a living presence. It pushed against Mokie as she stood outside the tent, whipped her skirt, flattened her hair, took the breath from her lungs. She felt a kind of fearful awe, as if some great invisible being were passing through. She wanted to turn away, but wanted more to stand and face the wind and dare it to do its worst. For a long, long minute she stood so, rocked and buffeted by the wind. Apple leaned against her leg, ears pricked forward, listening for something. Then as suddenly as the wind had risen it dropped. The air was still again.

Mokie turned to go back and saw a dark shape in the doorway. For one breath she thought it was John, and her heart jumped in her body. Then she heard Lally's voice, low so as not to wake the others: "Is that you, Mokie?"

"It's me. The wind woke me up."

"It's stopped now."

"I'm not sleepy. Everything's too new. And I feel so strange in these clothes."

"You'll get used to them in time."

A pause.

Then, "Lally?"

"Yes?"

"I just want—well, thank you. Really thank you, not just because you told me to say it. Thank you for giving me the skirt and the necklace and the earrings. For cutting my hair. For everything."

"Mokie, it was a pleasure," said Lally, and Mokie heard the smile she could not see. Around them the night was still, their low voices fluttering back and forth like the soft flight of moths riding the darkness.

"Lally, I've been thinking—"

Lally was silent, waiting.

"Remember what The Skimmer said tonight, about pigs being so smart and all? And being nicer than people?"

"I remember."

"Well, I think he was right. They are. Nicer than most, anyway. Not you, though. Nor him. Nor John." This was said hesitantly, shyly, an offering whose acceptance she was unsure of.

"Why, thank you, Mokie." Lally accepted the offering and honored it. "I think The Skimmer is right too. I'd much rather be a pig than be like some of the people I've seen."

"And there's something else." Mokie pressed on. "What The

Skimmer said about my name? He was right about that too." The words came out slowly, with difficulty. "Your name ought to say who you are. I am Mokie. I am the pig girl and I should be proud of it, whatever they think in the village. I'm glad for you to know who I am."

They were more words than she had ever spoken at one time to anyone but Apple, conveying more of herself than she had ever given to anyone, even Apple. In the shelter of the dark she felt suddenly light, free of a burden she had not known she carried.

Well, that was easy enough, thought Lally. Well done, Skimmer. She has chosen it. Freely and of herself she has chosen it. So be it.

"Hello, Mokie, you proud pig girl," said Lally gently. "I'm glad to know who you are."

There was silence. Mokie hesitated. Accepted, she wanted to give acceptance, but didn't know how to do it gracefully, didn't know if it should be done at all.

"And—and Lally?"

"Yes?"

She took a breath. "I know who you are too."

The silence lasted so long Mokie began to doubt whether Lally had heard her.

"Who I am?"

"Yes. All of you. You and The Skimmer and John." Mokie took another breath and plunged. "I saw you—in the hut back there in the wood. I was looking in the window. I saw you make magic. I know you're from—from the Crystal Country. Yesterday when The Skimmer was saying how I didn't cry and he thought I would? And you said it was different with you? The Crystal Folk don't cry. You're Crystal Folk, aren't you?"

There was a pause, during which Mokie forgot to breathe.

"Yes," said Lally quietly, "and it's clever of you to have guessed."

"I just want you to know, it's all right. I won't give you away or anything. I won't tell anyone."

"I know you won't," said Lally. "But maybe, just for now, you'd better not say anything to John or The Skimmer. Let's keep it between us."

"I won't say anything," Mokie assured her. "But . . . there's something I'd like to know, if you don't mind my asking. When you were all there in the hut, when everything changed, where exactly were you? Is the hut real? Is it really there?" She went on swiftly, "I mean, of course it was there, I saw it and touched it, but where is 'there'?"

Lally tilted her head to one side, judging how much to tell. Then she said carefully, deliberately, "That's not the way to ask, Mokie. 'Real.' 'There.' Those are just words. What you saw in the hut is what most folks never see—that the worlds touch. Anywhere there's an edge, the worlds meet—if you're in a doorway, or between sleep and waking, or going into a wood or coming out of it—you can touch both worlds. The hut is a place where they touch, and if you're 'there,' in that place, you can see both worlds at once. Some people—not many, but some—live their lives right on the edge. They don't belong to either, but they can see both."

Mokie nodded gravely. She knew about the edge, about not belonging. Lally's words took the sting out of loneliness, made the edge a place of special privilege.

"Oh, and Lally—I have to tell you, Apple knows too. She was with me. She saw you too. And she's a smart pig, like The Skimmer said. She won't talk of course, but she knows."

"It's all right if she knows," said Lally. "Apple is one of us." She hesitated, started to say more, then changed her mind. "I'm getting cold standing out here. I think we ought to go back in. Can you sleep now?"

"I can sleep now," said Mokie.

With no further words the woman, the girl, and the pig went back into the tent and lay down. Mokie slid immediately into sleep. Apple lay awake, looking at Lally. Lally also lay awake, staring into the darkness.

TWENTY-EIGHT

REAL MAGIC

N EXT MORNING MOKIE WOKE EARLY, before the others. In the light of the new day she was more than a little unsure of the person she had become last night, as if that one were a visitor who might decide to leave at any moment. It was safer to banish her, however briefly, than to have her escape. She took off the blouse and the skirt and laid them carefully aside. She unhooked the necklace from around her neck and with some difficulty, for she had never done it, she unfastened the ear bobs. Then she bound up her hair and her breasts and climbed back into her oversize shirt and pants and belted them tight. Their familiar feel was a comfort and reassurance.

To outward appearances the day was just like any other day, but for Mokie every smallest event was charged with meaning, every word echoed, every detail stood out sharp and bright. Her dream haunted her, an unseen companion to everything she did, an invisible part of everything that happened. When the others woke, she wanted to tell them, "I saw you last night. I was with you last night." And even, "I was you last night." Yet for that very reason, she could not say it. It was too close.

She went outside to look at the weather and breathe the dawn-touched air. It was cool and fresh and the sky was slightly overcast, with high, rippling clouds whose undersides the rising sun, just breaking through, touched with incandescent pink. No one else was up, and for a moment the whole world belonged to her. Then folk began to stir. Somewhere nearby a cock crowed. A woman's voice called and a child's shrill treble answered. Inside the tent she could hear Lally getting up and shaking out her skirts, the rasp of The Skimmer's voice, the low murmur of John's.

The men went off to forage for breakfast, to coax fresh eggs from the poultry woman and wheedle new bread from the early baker, while Lally and Mokie built up the breakfast fire. Apple was an eager participant in any camp activity, but she was less than helpful with meal preparations, for her hunger took possession of her and she rooted eagerly into pots, pans, kettles, overturning with her nose whatever might hold a promise of food.

"Keep that pig out of the way, will you, Mokie?" said Lally, after Apple had pricked her nose on the toasting forks and upset the kettle. "She's more trouble than she's worth."

"That's how I got her," said Mokie. "We both were. But she's not really trouble, just curious. Like me."

"Well, get her curious nose out of the kettle."

Mokie hauled Apple out of the work area and told her to "sit" in the tent doorway. Apple complied, but watched Mokie with bright, inquisitive eyes.

There were more immediate things than breakfast on Mokie's mind.

"Lally?"

She was testing. Her experience with village children—and village grown-ups as well—had taught her that what seemed all right to say on one occasion was definitely not all right on another. There were some questions she wanted very much to ask, but if she pushed too far, Lally might shut down.

"Yes?"

"Can I ask—uh—there's something I'd like to know."

"Ask away."

"Well, if you are—who you really are . . ." She stumbled, stopped, started again. "Well—if you know magic, then . . ."

"Then what?"

"Why don't you use it? I mean, here we are waiting for John and The Skimmer to bring us bread from this morning's baking. And then we'll toast it over the fire, when if you wanted, you could just make food appear. Magically. All the bread we could eat, already toasted. Onion soup without onions, like in the hut. Apples of immortality and cauldrons of plenty, roasts that cook themselves. You know."

186

She frowned, not in anger, but with the intensity of what she was saying.

"But you gather real mushrooms and The Skimmer catches a real rabbit, you fry real eggs and brew tea in a kettle and cook in the ordinary way. Why do you go to all that trouble when you don't have to? And back there in the wood, you were got up like tramps—all dirty and raggedy until . . . until you made yourselves beautiful. Why are you acting like ordinary folks when you are— who you really are?"

"All right," said Lally. "I'll tell you. But it must be between us two."

Mokie nodded.

"There are good reasons for us to act like ordinary folks when we are among ordinary folks. If we were to show who we are, if we were to do what you call magic, what would be the end of it? Either people would want us to do magic all the time, which is, to be honest, a bore—or else they would be so frightened and bewildered by what they couldn't understand that they would stay away from us altogether. One way or another, we couldn't move free among people as we do now. Most folks are frightened by the things they cannot understand, and they cannot understand the other world."

"I don't understand the other world either," said Mokie slowly, "but I think I'm not frightened of it. I liked what I saw of it. I thought it was beautiful. I wanted to be part of it. And I like what I see of you. And you've asked me to be part—part of whatever you are here in this world. You and John and The Skimmer—you've been better to me than all the folk of this world I've ever known. However your world is, it's better than this one we're in now, a way sight better. I'd like to go there. I wouldn't care if I never came back."

"Hush," said Lally. "You don't know what you're saying."

"Well, all right. But can I ask another question?"

"If you want to."

"Back there in the wood, when you were in the hut that is the Doorway, you were watching me, weren't you?"

"Yes," said Lally. "We were."

"I felt something odd, but I couldn't tell what it was. I almost saw you sometimes, on the edge of my eye."

"You might have," said Lally quietly.

"And you fed me, didn't you?"

"Fed you? No. No, we didn't. We watched, but we didn't interfere. It's against the rules. You had to seek us. We couldn't seek you."

Mokie's brow wrinkled. "But someone fed me. I used to find little bits of food hidden in unexpected places."

"Then someone else was taking care of you, Mokie. But it wasn't us. Maybe you had a secret friend in the village."

Mokie shook her head. "No, I didn't. I couldn't have a friend in Little Wicken. That much I do know."

"Well," said Lally, "I don't know who it could have been."

"Neither do I," said Mokie, and for a moment she puzzled

over the mystery. But no ready answer came to her, so she gave it up and went on to her next question.

"Last night, when you were fixing me—cutting my hair and brushing it, dressing me up and all?"

"Well?"

"If you can do magic, why didn't you do it then? It was just the two of us alone in the tent. No one would have seen. Couldn't you have magicked me pretty without going to all that trouble? Said a spell, or waved your hand or something?"

Lally looked at her, so eager to know, so ignorant of the real nature of what she was asking about. She nodded.

"Yes, I could have done that."

"Then why didn't you?"

"Because I wanted to do something different."

"But it would have been so easy."

"'Easy' wasn't to the purpose. I wanted something better."

"Better than making me pretty?"

"Better than *only* making you pretty. If I could magic you pretty, I could just as easy magic you unpretty. Magic—real magic, not tricks—is not a shortcut. It isn't something you can use for your pleasure. If you try, it will use you for its own pleasure, and you won't always like it. It's not a toy for playing with."

She paused, took a breath. How much to say, how much to reveal?

"Magic is always present, Mokie, always in the world, only most folks don't see it. Magic doesn't change things; it just

189

changes the way you see what's already there. It's always a part of what's there to begin with."

Mokie was listening intently. She was trying to learn something. Lally continued.

"And so magic was already at work last night, and we were just working along with it. I wanted you to be pretty, not just to show outside but to know inside. So I had to make you see and feel and know that it's real, not a spell, not illusion. If I hadn't done that, you wouldn't believe it. This way you know—or I hope you know—that you are truly pretty, and that it is you and not some spell that did it."

"But it wasn't me, Lally. You did it."

"Mokie, I did not do it. I made you see it, but it was there all along. Don't forget, don't you ever forget, that it was there all along."

Mokie's face still showed puzzlement.

"Well?" said Lally. "What now?"

"All right. I see how it had to be last night. That makes sense. It feels right. But back in the wood—"

"What about back in the wood?"

"Well, I saw you, and I saw your magic. Was that playing? How you pulled flowers out of the air and baked bread out of a penny and made soup out of nothing? The hut changed. You all changed. I *saw* it."

This is going to be difficult, thought Lally, but I've done it now. I've started. In for a penny, in for a pound.

"It looked like playing. To ordinary eyes it *was* playing. But to us it was just—what we are. That's what you saw—us on the edge of our world. There, on the edge, we could be in either world, and so we were—first this world, then the other world, as you saw. We chose to let you see, let you be a part of it. But it was serious, not a game."

"Then you knew I saw you. You knew it all along. I didn't have to tell you."

Now for it, thought Lally.

"Yes. We knew. So you didn't have to tell me, not for our sakes. But for your sake, you did have to tell. It's like you taking off your boy's clothes to be who you are. Like not having to be who you aren't, or pretend not to know what you know."

"Then I did see it—the other world. I saw it as it really is?"

"Everyone's eyes see things a little different. Your eyes saw as they could because of who you are."

Please, Mokie, don't ask me who you are.

"Now, how about getting that kettle filled for the tea?"

Swinging the kettle, Mokie and Apple set off at speed for the brook. Lally stared after them, her eyes narrowed, her expression unfathomable. Too fast, she thought, it's going too fast, it will come much too soon. She's nearly there already and the time's lagging. She sighed and shrugged and put sticks on the fire.

By the time Mokie and Apple returned, John and The Skimmer were still not back with the bread. Lally put in a handful of tea leaves and hung the kettle on its stand. Mokie fed more

191

sticks into the fire. They sat down to wait. The kettle was boiling and the fire had burned itself down to a bed of glowing orange coals before the men arrived. They had only one loaf of bread.

"And we had a hard time getting that," complained The Skimmer.

"Never mind," said Lally. "We'll make it go around. We can always fill in with what's left of last night's stew."

They gathered around the fire, holding out their long forks speared with hunks of bread, carefully turning and turning the bread to toast it even on both sides. At Mokie's side, Apple waited patiently for morsels. To all appearances they seemed to be, as on other mornings, chatting and sipping their tea with easy friendship. But however she seemed, Mokie did not feel easy. Her late night conversation with Lally, her confession that she had spied on the three of them in the wood, made her shy, made her perversely unwilling to trade on what was now a shared knowledge. She worried that she might have trespassed, might have overstepped a boundary and betrayed a secret to which she had no right.

Then, too, sloughing off her boy's disguise had not just made her seem different, it had made the others seem different as well. She felt unaccountably shy and tongue-tied, as if they were all meeting for the first time—as indeed in a sense they were. Shy of Lally, she was doubly, triply shy of John. Her dream of him had been so vivid, his dream touch so tender and intimate, that it seemed he must remember it as vividly as she did, though she knew well enough he could not.

If it was hard to look at him without betraying herself, it was harder still to not look at him. His face, his body drew her eyes like a lodestone. She found herself sneaking glances when she could be sure he was not looking at her. She was fascinated by his hands, watching every gesture, every smallest movement. When he cradled his hands around his cup, she felt them encircle her. When he lifted a piece of toast to his mouth to take a bite, her body went with it. She felt him engulf and swallow her.

Only with The Skimmer was she able to relax and be natural, for the events of the night before had caused no alteration in him or in her feeling for him. He was entirely and always his usual self—blunt, direct, plainspoken.

"Mokie, mind your toasting fork. Your bread's scorching to cinders on the one side there."

Smoke was curling from the end of Mokie's fork.

"Oh. Right you are, Skimmer. Sorry."

"No need to apologize. It ain't my bread that's burning. Keep your wits about you, girl. If all that fancying up last night has turned you silly, I'd as soon have you plain again."

"Sorry, Skimmer."

"And quit saying you're sorry."

"How come no eggs and only one loaf of bread for the four of us?" asked Lally, changing the subject. "You said you had a hard time. Why? What was the trouble?"

John answered. "The one loaf was all anyone would sell, even at Harvest Fair. It's near to closing and food's scarce and getting scarcer. Time was when people around here were ready to sell you anything they had, Harvest Fair or not, but not anymore. Now they're holding on to what they have."

The Skimmer chimed in. "The talk around and about is there's been poor crops these last years, even poorer this year and next year looks worse. It's the weather. All the signs are pointing to a hard winter. Nobody's very happy. If things don't improve by next spring it's going to get ugly."

He hesitated, glancing at Mokie, then away.

"You know what they'll do."

John nodded.

"What will they do?" asked Mokie.

"Pig sacrifice," said The Skimmer shortly. "They'll do more than bury the bones with the grain if it gets really bad."

"What more?" she asked, but she was afraid of the answer.

"Have you never seen it?" said The Skimmer. "Perhaps not. It doesn't happen that often—only in the Bad Year that comes . . . well, it comes whenever it comes and no one can say when that'll be."

"But what is it?" Mokie asked. "What is it that happens in a Bad Year?"

"They choose out the pig they want, and let her escape from the pen. That is, the pig thinks she's escaping. The people know better, for it's all planned. The hunt gets up and they chase her back and forth across a farrow field so as to charge the earth with her heat. When she's clean exhausted, out of strength and run to ground, they stone her to death and leave her body for the earth to take and use for the grain."

"I knew things like that happened," said Mokie slowly. "I saw it in my village once—the pig getting loose and all. But I didn't know it was on purpose. I thought it was just . . . sort of an accident that people seized on, you know, to make the most of it."

"It's no accident," said The Skimmer.

"But why?" asked Mokie. "What good does it do? One pig for all the earth—that's not going to make much difference."

The Skimmer set his jaw.

"Anytime you eat," he told her, "something has to die for it. If it's leeks and mushrooms and grain for bread, well, they don't bleed and they don't squeal. But they die just the same. So you got to give something back. Keep the bargain. Well, the more you give back, the more you'll get, or that's what they think. A live pig, a fertile female who could make more pigs but instead gives back all she is to the earth—blood, bones, heart—they feel like . . . like it richens the earth somehow. Makes it happy. And the earth should be grateful, see? That's what they want. That's what the whole thing is for."

"Yes," said Mokie slowly. "I do see. But the way you say they do it, all that chasing and throwing stones and all. Why don't they make it simpler? Surely they could just . . . kill the pig and then . . ."

She looked down at Apple and shivered.

"Yes," he continued, reading her face, "it's an ugly thing to watch. A quick, clean killing, now—that's one thing. It's needful and you do it and it's over. But this is different. They're afraid. Killing's killing, after all, and sometime it might be one of them. It's not the body they're after, when you get right down to it—it's the spirit, whatever it is that keeps life going. That's what they want, that's what they try to take."

"But you can't catch the spirit," protested Mokie.

"No," said John gravely, "that's right. You can't capture the spirit. It will go free."

"Go free where?" wondered Mokie. "Where does the spirit go when the pig . . . when the spirit goes free?"

Lally looked at The Skimmer and raised her eyebrows. The Skimmer shook his head ever so slightly. Not yet.

Mokie did not notice the pause. Her mind had skipped ahead to other things. "Can—can it be any old pig?" she asked. "Or does it have to be a special one?"

The Skimmer answered her. "It has to be a special one—a sow, a young female come into season. She's the chosen one."

"What makes her the chosen one? How do they choose? Who does the choosing?"

"Ah, that's the mystery. It's the secret of the rite and the strangest part of the whole strange business. She chooses herself. No one knows how. Maybe she doesn't even know herself."

Mokie reached out a hand to touch Apple, lying at her side,

her little pig eyes narrowed on the food that passed so swiftly from hand to mouth.

Apple was running, scraping through vines and under low-hanging branches. Mokie was running after her. Her breath came fast and ragged, harsh in her throat. Her legs ached with the running. In the distance behind her she could hear the cries and the shouting.

They were beating the woods for Apple, hungry for her blood, her death. Voices followed their flight.

Get her! Catch her!

Kill the pig!

Stick her good!

Mokie dared not stop, not for an instant. Someone was behind her, but she could not see who it was. At the sound of footsteps she risked a glance over her shoulder. It was enough to throw her off stride. She stumbled and almost fell.

Up ahead John was waiting. He reached out his hand to her.

Mokie, stop! Stop! It's all right. I'm here. I'm with you. It's all right. He held her steady, and his voice gentled and slowed as she saw him, knew him. They stood so, in the dry field, wind ruffling the grasses all around them. Mokie shook her head.

Oh, John, they want Apple. People want to take her. They want to stone her for the seed grain. I won't let them. I've got to get her away.

"Mokie! Look alive! Are you dreaming, girl?"

The Skimmer's rasping voice broke her reverie. So involved in her interior drama had she been, so completely within the imagined experience, that she came back to the present world with a shock, a dreamer rudely shaken from a troubled sleep. She blinked.

"Where on earth did you go to?" demanded The Skimmer. "I asked you for more tea and you looked right through me as if I was made of glass."

So you are, thought Mokie, but she didn't say it.

"Skimmer, I'm sorry, truly sorry this time. I was, uh, I was just thinking. Here, let me have your cup."

She tipped the kettle, but her hands were shaking, and more tea spilled on the ground than went into the cup.

"Thinking, my eye!" said The Skimmer, taking the kettle out of her hand. "You were miles away. Where, I can't imagine, but you went through the most peculiar gyrations. Do you know what you did? First you ducked your head from side to side. Then you swung your head around as if you were seeing something none of the rest of us could see. And finally you got the most awful expression on your face. And all the time your lips were moving. Who were you talking to? What were you saying?"

He filled his cup and set the kettle carefully on its stand. He took a long sip and cocked his head on one side, like a robin listening for a worm.

"What in the name of common sense did you think you were doing?"

"Oh, nothing," said Mokie. She shrugged. "Nothing important."

TWENTY-NINE

MOXON

THAT DAY, THE LAST DAY OF HARVEST FAIR at Great Wicken, brought the sense of something coming to a close. It was, in a way, for the end of the fair marked the real start of winter. The year was shutting down. The good time, the gathering-in time of harvest, was over for another full round of the sun. Some of the hucksters, getting an early start, had already taken down their stalls, packed up their wares, and loaded them into carts or barrows and left.

Lally and John and The Skimmer chatted quietly as they went about the business of taking down the tent, packing up the equipment. They were moving on, they told Mokie. They did not tell her where they were going, but she did not care. Anyplace, she said to herself, as long as we're together and it's not back to Little Wicken.

She, too, had packed, with some wistfulness stowing away all her new clothes. Carefully, lovingly, she had folded the beautiful ruffledy skirt, smoothing it so it wouldn't wrinkle and laying it neatly in the trunk. She added the pretty blouse, layered the flowered scarf just so on top of these, and returned the brass necklace and the jingling ear bobs to their place in Lally's jewel box. All her finery was baggage now, just more gypsy paraphernalia along with the tent and the pillows and the cooking gear, the stilts and the cards and the colored sands.

Now she was away out on the edge of the meadow behind the tent, where The Skimmer was putting her through body stretches. Once more in her male clothing, Mokie was acutely conscious of her female body underneath it. The skin of her breasts remembered the silky caress of the blouse. Her hips still felt the swing of the skirt, her ankles remembered its soft brushing as it swayed with her every movement. And although she would not let herself look at him, she was conscious as well of John's body, lean and graceful as he moved in and out of her view. She wondered if John, too, might be remembering last night, might be watching her now from the corner of his eye, as she was watching him. She pretended to be too busy to notice. She had just succeeded in a fairly respectable headstand and was anticipating The Skimmer's approval, when there appeared, before her upside-down gaze, several strange pairs of feet. They came to a halt just in front of her, so that she had to dodge sideways as she rolled down. When she sat upright, several pairs of unfamiliar and very hostile eyes glared coldly down at her.

There was a portentous silence.

"What's amiss, friends?" asked The Skimmer.

"That's him," said a scrawny fellow with darting eyes and a ferret nose, pointing down at Mokie.

"He's the one, all right," said a plump woman in a shawl and apron. Mokie sat stock-still, looking bewildered from one to the other.

"Who's the one?" said The Skimmer with an edge in his voice.

"Your apprentice is the one," said the woman.

"Him? Our apprentice? And what is he to you?"

"It's what he is to you that matters. I don't know where you got him, but your apprentice there is nothing but a common thief, a cutpurse, and as far as anyone knows you're more of the same," said the scrawny man. "A lot of things have gone missing since the fair began, and he's the cause. Stealing food, fancy gewgaws, lifting purses right off people's belts—he's a smooth one, I'll say that. But we've been watching. Made off with a pair of my best scissors back there at the fair, silver, with inlaid handles. Worth a pretty penny they were."

"Took my clean laundry right off the hedge," said the woman. "My man's best shirt and a pair of his work pants."

"How do you know?" asked The Skimmer mildly.

"That's them he's got on right now," the woman told him. Her mouth compressed into a thin line as she looked Mokie up and down.

"Stealing is a hanging matter in this part of the world," said the first man, "in case you didn't know."

Sensing trouble, Lally and John had drifted over from the tent.

"We didn't know," said Lally.

Mokie swallowed. She had forgotten her fairground thievery as soon as it was over.

"Know or not, it makes no difference," said the woman. "The law's the law. I've the constable's men to make an arrest."

"Without evidence?" asked John.

"There's the evidence," said the woman with a snort, gesturing at Mokie. "Plain as day." She favored John with a searching up-and-down gaze, as if he might have more stolen laundry stuffed away in his pockets.

"We're the witnesses, and there's the evidence. You! Boy!" She thrust her face up close to Mokie's. "What's your name?"

Frozen into near paralysis like a rabbit in the glare of a torch, Mokie opened her mouth, but nothing came out. The little man took her roughly by the arm and dragged her to her feet. Lally made a sharp movement of protest, but The Skimmer stopped her with a look.

"She said, 'What's your name?' you ruffian!" said the scrawny man angrily. "Answer, can't you!"

Mokie said nothing.

"Moxon," said John, pronouncing the name slowly and clearly.

"His name is Moxon." He gave Mokie a straight look. She stared at him uncomprehendingly.

"Moxon?" said the woman. "'Pig's son?' That's a laugh!"

"A piggish name for a piggish thief," said the little man. "I'll give you pig!" He looked hard at Mokie, then at John, his eyes narrowed with suspicion.

A crowd was beginning to gather, drawn by the raised voices, the tension that quivered in the air.

"Getting it now, aren't they?" said a voice. "I thought they was too clever for their own good."

"How'd they get here, anyway?" asked another. "I'll wager they don't have no permit."

"Thieves, all of you, I'll be bound," said the woman. "A right pack of rascals with stolen goods in your possession and on your way to steal more. I've seen your kind."

"Have you, now?" said John silkily. "And what is our kind?"

"The kind that gaols were made for, fellow, and that's where you'll go, right beside your pig friend, if you don't watch your tongue."

"No offense," said John. He turned to Mokie.

"Go along with these people, Moxon." Again he articulated the name carefully and gave her another straight look. "And don't be frightened. No sentence without trial. We'll see you get justice."

The woman snorted. "Justice! We'll see you all in gaol if there's any justice."

204

"Take him away," said the scrawny man, gesturing to the two burly constable's men standing behind him.

They took Mokie by either arm, turned, and marched her across the fairground and into Great Wicken. Stumbling with fear, she cast one anguished, desperate look back at the three standing in the field and gave herself up to her fate. They watched her small shape diminish in the distance. The crowd that had gathered stood about indecisively for a few moments, then, sensing that there would be nothing worth watching for a while, gradually drifted away.

There was a little silence while the three looked at one another.

"Well, now!" The Skimmer whistled between his teeth. "That was a close one. Quick thinking on the name business, John."

"Quick talking, you mean," said John.

"Thinking, talking, whatever. It wouldn't do to have them smoke what she is before her proper time."

"We have to get her back," said Lally urgently.

The Skimmer looked at her inquiringly, startled by the intensity of her tone.

"Aren't you taking this a bit too serious, Lally? It's only a delay, not even that, really. There's a few days yet. We'll get her back, and she'll keep safe and quiet in the meantime."

"I don't trust 'meantime,'" said Lally, "and I don't trust mean folk. And it's certain those are mean folk. Ugly. How do we know what they might do with her? Or do to her? Didn't you see their faces? Didn't you see her face? She's frightened near to death. She has no one but us."

John was silent.

"Where's Apple?" asked The Skimmer. He looked warily about him. One or two fellows were still hanging about, hoping for excitement.

Lally twitched her skirt and out trotted the little pig, who had taken refuge there when the trouble started. The Skimmer snapped his fingers invitingly, and Apple trotted over and sat at his feet. He stroked her soothingly. Coaxing her with tidbits of leftover stew, he got her to sit. The Skimmer kept one eye on the remaining hangers-on, the other on the pig.

"That's my Lady." His voice caressed her. "That's my wise Lady. Here, catch." He tossed a scrap of meat in the air. She caught it deftly.

"Ahhh, good Lady." His voice was a caress. "Try again."

He held the tidbit under her nose, flung it high. She caught it again and snapped it down. There was a spattering of applause.

He scratched her between the ears. "Good Lady. Very good. Want another? You'll have to work for it."

He held out another lure, this time a mushroom. Apple sniffed it eagerly, ready to snap. He held it above her head, dangling it just out of reach. She strained to catch it, sitting up on her hind legs, front hooves beating the air. It was still out of reach. Then she stood up, erect on her hind legs.

"That's it," crooned The Skimmer. "Good Lady! Come on, now! Off we go!" He walked a few paces away, holding out the prize.

"Come along, now," he coaxed. "Let's go for a walk."

He held out the mushroom and took a few paces. The pig, as if making a decision, stood upright on her hind legs. Step after step she followed him until they had crossed the meadow, gathering spectators as they went. Applause followed them as they reached the perimeter, and the bystanders waited for them to come back, to gather the pennies they had ready to throw.

But they did not come back. As soon as they had reached the road, the pig dropped to all fours again, caught up with The Skimmer, and trotted at his side. They stopped near a cluster of outbuildings on the edge of the meadow. The Skimmer looked around him carefully, saw no one, and slid through the half-open door of a granary. The pig followed. The air inside was light and dusty, the floor scattered with husks and chaff. Half-empty sacks, their tops rolled down like collars, sagged against the walls. The dark of the shed was spiked by shafts of sunlight that splintered through the cracks and caught the dust motes, turning them into golden spangles. Apple and The Skimmer were nowhere to be seen, but two glittering dust motes hovered in two slender, parallel sunbeams lancing down from a roof that had no gaps in it. Silent voices rode the sunbeams.

THIRTY

SUNBEAMS

What now, my Lady?

Need you ask? What will come. John saw it in the sand. Lally saw it in the cards.

She's only a child, after all.

No child. Not any longer. But not quite woman, either. That's why we're here, to see her through it.

You know what Lally wants.

Lally's part is up, she isn't in it, not anymore.

Ah, but you know her, she's that stubborn, she won't give up easy.

A cloud passed over the shed, graying the sunbeams to empty air. The Skimmer and the pig emerged from the granary and walked slowly back to the now deserted fairground, The Skimmer deep in thought.

That night Apple disappeared. They looked under the cart. They looked in the ditches and hunted through the weeds. They called, they whistled. She was gone.

"Leave her be," said The Skimmer. "I reckon she knows what she's doing."

PART THREE
MOKIE

THIRTY-ONE
A Hanging Matter

"**N**AME?" The voice was brisk, impersonal, expressionless.

The prisoner made no answer.

The man behind the tall desk spoke again, his eyes huge behind his spectacles, his bald head shining.

"I asked you for your name."

Still no answer.

Irritably the man rapped with his knuckles on the desk, commanding attention.

"Speak up, can't you? What's your name, boy? You have got a name, haven't you?"

"Mok—Moxon."

It came out in a whisper, barely audible.

Her mouth was dry, her throat clogged with the dust and damp and old, stale air of the cell where they had flung her last night. Her body shook with chills from lying on a bare stone floor. She was empty and dry, for no one had bothered to bring her food or water. It was only a day since she had been taken, but the unutterable, bleak emptiness of it stretched the time to forever.

As she stared at her interrogator, struggling to keep her tired eyes focused, his face blurred and changed. Suddenly he was Grime, the owner of Red Sorcha, the would-be killer of Apple. She shook her head, blinked hard, looked again. Now the face was a boy's, sullen and angry, suspended above her and blotting out the world, blotting out her very self.

"Moxon, is it? Well, Moxon, stand straight, can't you? Come forward here so they can see you."

She took a step forward, staggered, and almost fell against the desk. She propped herself against it.

"Now, then, now, then, is this the person you observed, the person you saw?"

She saw that he was not speaking to her, but to a little cluster of people ranged opposite her, looking her over with hostile, inquisitive eyes. "Is this the boy you say took your property?"

"It's him, all right," said the scrawny little man. "Saw him with my own eyes."

"I don't know whether it's him or not," said the plump woman, more cautious in the presence of the law than when she had accused Mokie, "for I didn't see anyone. But I know my husband's breeches when I see them, and that's them he's wearing."

214

Her voice was shrill and sharp. She might have been bargaining for a length of muslin rather than identifying a thief.

"How about my scissors?" demanded the little man.

The bright daylight hurt Mokie's eyes after the dark of her prison cell, sun shining through the windows as if the world were still going around. The air was close and stuffy. She couldn't breathe. Her mouth felt dry as cotton wool. The man's lips were moving again, he was saying something. She blinked. What was he saying? She tried to focus.

". . . the scissors."

She stared at him dumbly.

"Did you hear me? I said, hand over the scissors. Hand them over. They're evidence."

"I . . . I haven't got them. I haven't got any scissors."

Mokie could not look at them, but she felt how they looked at her, with bright, incurious eyes, as if she were not a fellow human creature but a dumb animal with which they had no kinship.

"Haven't got them? Haven't got them? Where are they, then?"

"I don't know."

"A likely story!" squeaked the little man. "You ought to search him. If he hasn't got them, the others do. His gang."

She was trying to hold on to herself, to keep her recollection of Apple, to keep her remembrance of Lally and John and The Skimmer. But the harder she tried, the more insubstantial they became. The more desperately she clutched them, the quicker they slipped out of memory. Nothing was left but this man looking down at her from his high desk, propping his elbows in front of him, tapping fingertips to fingertips, making a little cage of his hands. She was inside the cage, a tiny, helpless figure peering out between his giant fingers.

"Wha—what? What did you say?"

"I said, do you know the penalty for stealing, Moxon?"

She tried to find her voice, but all she could manage was a whisper. "No. Yes. He said, the man said it was—"

"Hanging."

A great hole in the world opened in front of her.

"Catch the boy, somebody, he's going to fall."

Hands gripped her shoulders, a stool slid under her, she was lowered onto it. Her head spun. Everything was bright black in front of her eyes, pinwheels whirling, tracking fire across her eyeballs. The hands kept a tight grip on her shoulders.

"Now, then, Moxon! Now, then!"

The man was talking again. She forced herself to pay attention, to look up at him no matter who he was, to meet his enormous, staring eyes. This time his face stayed fixed. She did not know him. He was a stranger.

"Listen carefully to me, boy. Listen carefully."

He says everything twice, she thought, as if he doesn't believe it the first time.

"You're in serious trouble, serious trouble. It's sad, it's very

216

sad to see someone so young so far gone in crime. But you're young, and you've had no one to guide you. We're in mind of that. We're prepared to be lenient with you, very lenient, if you help us out. Now, it's possible, you know"—he peered over his spectacles—"it's possible that this crime, this stealing of personal property, wasn't of your own doing. Perhaps you were, shall we say, 'persuaded' into it? We're prepared, I say we're prepared, to take that into consideration. Your, ah, former companions are most unsavory characters. Most unsavory. Just see how they've abandoned you. Typical."

The black faded from Mokie's eyes. The pinwheels stopped whirling. She raised her head and looked directly at the man.

"And you're here, a prisoner, and they're free. With a little cooperation, you could go free. Free. Just tell us their names."

She opened her mouth, shut it, swallowed.

"Come along, then. Tell us their names."

She spoke, but no sound came out.

"Yes," he said encouragingly, "that's the way. Just tell us."

She shook her head wearily.

"No? You surely don't mean no. You're dizzy, aren't you? Take your time. Some water? Someone bring him water."

Mokie found her voice. "No, no water." She took a deep breath. "No names. No."

"You're being very foolish."

"No."

"Veerrry foolish." Coaxing.

Somebody had fetched water; someone was holding out a cup. She pushed it away. She closed her eyes and shook her head. "No" was all she could manage. She had said no, and now she had nothing left.

The man at the high desk peered down at her. "You're simply asking for trouble, you know that."

Again she shook her head.

"Very well, then."

He shook his head sorrowfully, as if deeply disappointed at her intransigence.

"Take him away. Take him away. We'll see how he likes hanging."

The hands gripping her shoulders tightened, pulling Mokie to her feet. Her accusers stood staring at her like wooden dolls.

Empty words drifted across her consciousness, vague, void of meaning.

—vagrant—

—no kin—

—he'll do—

—time's right—

The dizziness came back, the whirling pinwheels. She stumbled drunkenly wherever she was pushed, feeling only the hands on her shoulders, the floorboards under her feet. When the boards changed to cobblestones, when cool, fresh air blew in her face, her head cleared a little, and she looked about her. She was in the town square, a wide, open space closed on two sides by the stone walls of the magistrate's court and the gaol. The other two sides were fronted with shops and stalls. The square was crowded, as if on a market day, but the people were not moving about, just scattered in little clumps. They were staring at her. Why?

The answer came in short order. A large wicker cage suspended on a long chain was lowered jerkily from an iron ring fixed in the wall several stories above the main doorway of the magistrate's court. As she watched, the cage came to rest on the cobbles. She was manhandled toward it, and the door swung open. Scarcely understanding what was being done to her, she was pushed inside and the door closed and latched. Then the men who had pushed her in pulled down on the chain and the cage rose correspondingly, rocking unevenly. She staggered and fell against the wicker side of the contraption, causing it to rock even more wildly as it rose up and up through the air.

When the cage had reached almost the height of the iron ring, the lower end of the chain was wound several times around a post and attached to a massive hook set into the pavement beside it. There Mokie hung, swinging to and fro, captured and held like a cricket in a jar. Still bewildered, she clutched the wicker bars to steady herself and peered down at the watching crowd. Bodiless voices floated up to her.

"That'll teach him."

"Birdie in a cage, can't steal now, can he?"

"Nobody'll steal him, that's for sure. He's safe enough there."

"He'll be safer still where he's going."

They were laughing, pointing, making jokes. It was the village boys all over again, but now she had no acorns to throw, no place to run, no place to hide. A flung cobblestone hit a corner of the cage, rocking it violently. Last night, lying abandoned on the floor of the gaol, she had rediscovered the loneliness of her childhood, all the bleaker for the warmth that had so briefly replaced it, all the sharper because she was no longer a child. She had thought no pain could be greater. She found out now that it could get even worse. Her eyes stung, her chest heaved, the back of her mouth ached, every muscle tensed against the despair that came down on her like a wall falling, against the grief that wanted to overpower and betray her.

She would not give in to it, and she fought back with all that was left of her little strength. Breath by breath she choked down the sobs, she swallowed the tears, she battled with the pain until it retreated back and down into the center of her body. She won at last. Gradually her breathing smoothed and lightened. She yawned, a convulsive, juddering breath. Her eyes closed of themselves, and at last, worn out by trouble, she fell into a shallow, troubled sleep.

When she woke, stiff and chilled and aching in every bone, night was all around her. The square was deserted. How long she had lain there she had no idea. She shivered, pushed herself up to a sitting position, and looked about her, wondering what the time was. Through the bars of her cage she could see the sky dusted with bright, cold stars. Silence echoed in her ears, no voice, no footfall to break it. So bare, so empty was that silence that she might have been the last human on earth. The buildings of the square leaned toward her, stone giants with gaping doorway mouths and shuttered eyes—blank, closed windows with nothing behind them. It was too quiet. A nameless dread crept over her, and she shrank back into a corner of the cage for shelter. From what? She didn't know, only that something was coming.

From somewhere out in the darkness came a faint sound, a brittle, staccato patter as of somebody tapping lightly, rapidly on a distant drum. The sound reverberated off the stone walls, barely audible, yet seeming to come from everywhere at once. Mokie looked apprehensively about her but could find nothing, only the darkness holding its breath, waiting for something. Mokie held her own breath and cowered in her corner.

The tapping was coming nearer. It was getting louder now, drumming a brisk tattoo through the empty night. Closer it came, and closer, like the drumming of little thunder when a storm approaches. Out of the dark mouth of the street and into the starlit square trotted a little white pig with rust-red ears. With no hesitation, knowing exactly where she was going, she trotted to the center of the square, came to a halt, and looked up at Mokie.

Scarcely daring to believe what she saw, Mokie gave a lurch that set the cage to swinging wildly. The square rocked and tilted sickeningly, and she grabbed at the wicker bars to steady herself, her stomach heaving.

"Apple?"

It came out a hoarse croak. Apple made no sound, but she stood upright on her hind legs and step by step, precisely and delicately, walked forward until she was directly in front of the cage, where she performed a neat somersault, righted herself, and sat up.

"Oh, Apple!" said Mokie with a little half-hysterical laugh, "I always said you were the star of the family."

Apple beat at the air with her forelegs as if it were a solid barrier, and Mokie reached her arms through the cage as if there was nothing between them, trying in vain to bridge the distance. The little pig stood at stretch for a moment, then she shook her head wisely, dropped back to all fours, lay down on the cobblestones, put her chin between her forelegs, and, with slow deliberation, closed her eyes. She opened them once and gave Mokie a long look, as if to say, "Nothing can be done right now. Wait. Go to sleep." Then she closed her eyes again. This time they stayed closed.

Mokie's reaching hands clutched a moment longer at the empty air, then she pulled them back and hung her fingers through the wicker barring of the cage, resting her forehead against the backs of her hands. For a little while she struggled to keep her eyes open, warming herself with the sight of Apple. Finally they closed of their own accord, and she gave in. Relaxing her hold on the cage and herself, she brushed her fingers help-lessly down the side of the cage, lay down, pillowed her head on her arms, and fell deeply asleep.

Not a shadow stirred in the square.

THIRTY-TWO

THE CAGE

LALLY SAT CROSS-LEGGED in the little willow coppice beside the hedge, sheltered in the lee of the cart, her fingers sifting and sifting a handful of dirt. She was scooping it up from the dry ground and letting it trickle to earth again, watching it catch sparkles from the setting sun that lighted her face and dyed the world with molten bronze.

"All right," said The Skimmer. "What's eating at you?"

"Nothing." She stared at the dirt dribbling through her fingers as if within its little cascade was hidden some immense, incommunicable secret.

"Nothing, my eye! Don't you give me 'nothing'!"

The Skimmer was exasperated and impatient as only a man can be when he does not want to know what the trouble is.

"You've not said a word since we found the pig gone. John

and me might as well be having a nice long talk with the air. Come on, now. What's up?"

She flung the dirt up to catch the light, let it fall in a shower of false brightness, dusted one hand against the other to rid both of any clinging fragments, took a breath, looked The Skimmer full in the face.

"All right, if you will have it. I hate this."

"Hate what?" he asked.

"All this." She gestured widely at the world around her. "I feel like I'm caught in a cage and there's no way out."

"Out of what?"

"This—this that's happening now. It's way past the reckoning and it frightens me. I hate it, that's all."

"Talk sense, can't you? What frightens you, the seely creature that you are? What don't you like?"

"You'd know if you thought about it."

"If you mean what happened to Mokie, it's a surprise, I grant you. But you know as well as I do, Lally, that it can't be out of the reckoning. It's got to be a part of the pattern, same as always."

"This isn't 'always,' Skimmer. It's now. And I never minded the pattern before, because I could see it plain. I followed it, but I never felt like I was stuck in it, caught."

"We all followed it," said John.

"Yes, but now . . . now—I don't know—" She paused, searching out the words. "I feel—" The Skimmer broke in.

"Feel? Feeling's not in it. Things will be the way they have to be. Times before you've never bothered. What's different about this time?"

She answered him slowly, feeling out the words. "This time it's Mokie." She shook her head, knowing that was no sort of answer, and tried again.

"I didn't know, truly, until I saw the way she looked at us as they took her off. I mean, I knew she was in it for us, for the game, but I didn't know how much we were in it for her. She loves us. I've never been loved before; it's a funny feeling. So it's this way, Skimmer." She shrugged an admission. "I love her."

The Skimmer looked at her sideways, and she bristled.

"Dare to laugh and I'll bite you, so I will."

He pretended to cringe in fear, but stopped the play when he saw her face.

"Well, now, 'love,' that's a pretty strong word, Lally. Goes along with hate, don't it? They're a pair, as you might say. Myself, I don't know much about either, and I shouldn't think you would. I can't say I love her, though she's a taking child, no question, and I will own I've got fond of her. But fond or not, love or not, taking or not, it makes no difference. There's no use in fighting what you can't change, and you can't change the pattern. You know that."

"Can't you see it at all, Skimmer? How this is different from all the other times? How Mokie is different from all the others? So gawky and awkward, wanting so much, not even half knowing what it is she wants."

Lally turned from The Skimmer to John, not asking his help but wanting his understanding. "It's like she's my daughter. My sister. She's my other self that I never saw till now."

"All the more reason," said John quietly.

"I don't want it to happen."

"Now, Lally," said The Skimmer patiently, persuasively, "Mokie's the chosen, we can't change that. The pig knows it, Apple knows it, that's why she come into it. And we were to follow, and we have. Whether we can see it or not, the pattern's going just the way it's meant to go."

"What about those others?" said Lally. "The ones who took her away? They don't know about the pattern and they wouldn't care if they did. They've got their own game, and it's one I don't like. Those mean-eyed, mingey-faced rats, so smug, so glad to catch her out, so glad to have a victim, somebody to punish for all their troubles. They didn't know who she was, what she was, not really, they're not supposed to know, but they're enjoying it just the same. They liked having her helpless."

"Well, they're human beings, ain't they?" asked The Skimmer. "Stands to reason. What you expect from humans? All this talk about love. People got other feelings besides love, see? They have likes and dislikes. They have greed and jealousy and fear."

"Ah," said John, "and fear is the strongest. That's really why folk need someone else to catch, why they need someone else to blame."

"Well, there has to be someone to blame, John." The Skimmer tried to be reasonable. "That's how humans are. That's the system. It's part of the balance. We can't change that, we're part of it, just like they are. We're the other part, as you might say. And it's come round the Bad Year and we're part of that, too, nor we can't change it neither. The time come around and Mokie is the chosen."

"She's something more than that," said John, half surprised at his own vehemence. "She's more than just the chosen one. Lally's right. She's different. It's different this time."

The Skimmer sighed, a deep breath with the weight of uncounted time behind it. "And I tell you it isn't any different this time from any of the other times. It can't be different."

"Why can't it?" asked John unexpectedly.

The Skimmer threw up his hands. "I don't know what's got into you, John. I never saw you like this before. And you, Lally. You say you like her—"

"Love her," said Lally.

"Love has nothing to do with it."

At that she flashed out. "Then will you kindly tell me what does 'have to do with it?' If what I feel makes no difference, if what she feels makes no difference, then why are we here? What are we following? A pattern's got a meaning, hasn't it, beyond its own design? It's for something. It *means* something beyond itself. Or is it just a cage and we're caught in it and can't escape?" Her voice rose. "Like pigs in a pen."

"Pigs in a pen, motes in a sunbeam, caught in a cage—you've a power of names to call us, but it don't change things, Lally. I'm sorry, but it just don't."

"I hate this," she said again.

"I hate it too," said John. "This time. This Mokie time."

She looked at him, astonished.

"What is it that you want, Lally?" asked John quietly.

Her face contorted suddenly, as if she were going to sneeze, but no sneeze came out. Instead a silent cry, a despairing, wordless protest drifted on the air like a torn scarf, taking the place of the tears she could not shed. Her body shook under the pressure of feelings she could not name.

"How can I tell you what I want when all I really know is what I don't want? I don't want her . . . I don't want it all to end now, to be over when she's just started, when she's just finding out that it can be good. She's just beginning to find out who she can be if she tries, and that's when . . ."

"That's *why*, Lally. And you know it just as well as I do." The Skimmer gave up, his hands flung wide, his shoulders eloquent of frustration.

"What do you want to do, Lally?" asked John. "What it is you want us to do?"

She looked at him straight, her face flushed red-gold with the last glow of the dying sun, her eyes shining in its light. Then the sun sank out of sight, her face shadowed, and her eyes filled with night.

"Get her out of it before it's too late," she said.

"It's already too late, Lally," The Skimmer said with unaccustomed gentleness. "Don't you see that? You must see it. The thing is moving. I wish it weren't, but it is. We can't stop it; it's out of our control, as it always has been. Even if we could break the pattern it would re-form, find a new way to fit into the old shape. If it doesn't happen one way, it will happen another. We—can't—change—it."

"We could try, couldn't we, Skimmer? We could try."

She faced them both and stared them down. The Skimmer let out a noisy, frustrated breath, halfway between a sigh and a grumble. John held her eyes for a minute, then dropped his eyelids and shook his head. No one said anything.

The silence held while night gathered around them.

It was The Skimmer who spoke, finally.

"So that's what the pig is doing."

Lally looked at him. "*What's* what the pig is doing?"

"She said she had to see her through it. I thought she meant . . . but now I see . . . so that's where she is."

"That's where *who* is? Skimmer, if you don't start talking sense, I'll never feed you again."

"I can't take a chance on that," he said with a grin. "I'll talk sense on the way, if you like, but let's get started. We haven't much time and we don't have much of a chance, but needs must. We'll do what we can."

He set off walking back along the road to town. When

nobody moved, he swung around, hands on hips, and jerked his head, beckoning, commanding.

"Come on, then, you two, what you waiting for?"

Without stopping for an answer he turned on his way again. John and Lally followed.

THIRTY-THREE

OPEN DOOR

TWO STARS WERE TALKING. Mokie could see them set like gems in the velvet sky above her. They glittered each in turn as they spoke.

One said, "The Door is opening."

The other said, "She will not see it."

"She may," said the gentle voice of the first star. "Give her time."

"There is no time," said the second star irritably. It sounded like one of the wives in Little Wicken.

If there is no time, it doesn't matter, thought Mokie. If there's no time, the Door is always open.

But she thought she would look anyway, just to see, and the gate of her cage opened, swinging outward into the starry dark, then banging back against the doorframe of the hut. She hesitated in the doorway, her hand on the silk tent flap, feeling with her fingers the ropes of shimmering beads. John and Lally and The Skimmer looked up from the table and saw her. They rose to greet her and bring her in, putting their arms about her in a three-way embrace, and quite suddenly and easily they were all dancing, and then she was Lally, tossing her silver hair, whirling and swaying while the girl Mokie watched through the window and The Skimmer played his glass flute and John's hands banged a rhythm on the table, but it was the door banging and Mokie went to latch it, but, "Not that way," said Lally, and held out her hand and Mokie took it and together they walked deeper into the wood, where the trees stood tall, their silver-green leaves ringing against one another with the smallest of sounds, or was it the air itself that chimed as its colors shimmered from silver to scarlet to sapphire to violet to emerald and then to silver again?

Hands clasped, Lally and Mokie made a progress down the aisle of trees that dipped their branches in salute as they passed, and the music of the air sang a welcome. In the brightness at the end of the aisle a throng of people waved a welcome. They were beautiful, shining, elegantly dressed in bright, clear colors with light shimmering all around and through them. They smiled and beckoned to her, laughing with eager anticipation, and Mokie felt the breath in her lungs bubble swiftly up to catch her throat in answering laughter. She knew that something inexpressibly wonderful was about to happen. Someone she could almost see, someone she almost knew, was waiting for her. Something wonderful was about to come to her, borne on an apple blossom wind. She knew, almost, what it would be. The light before her eyes brightened unbearably as she drew near, and her heart trembled on the brink of a loveliness too great to take in.

And then the light dimmed as if some hand had wiped a dirty cloth across a clean window, the music ceased, wind shook the branches of the wood, and the silver-green leaves rang sharply against one another, their voices shards of broken glass that cut so that the blood ran.

—What's your name, boy—
—Slut—
            —I'll look like a boy—
   —Thief—
                   —Beauty in your bones—
—Hey, piggy, want an acorn—
        —Birdie in a cage—
             —I wish I knew her name—

The voices rose shrilly, following her as she ran frantically toward the swift-receding light and the door swung wide and the voices at her back pushed her and she stumbled inside as the gate slammed and the wicker cage rocked wildly. The floor came up to meet her and she fell awake.

All was quiet. The cool rose and silver of a winter dawn flushed the eastern sky. Mokie's waking eyes saw a square quiet and still, saw houses and shop fronts settled in their proper level where a moment before they were tilting crazily in giddy opposition to the swinging cage. Shreds of the dream clung to her memory like torn cobwebs—a faint music she could almost recall, a lilt of irrational happiness tied to a panicky need to escape, to run away, to find someone. . . .

But even as she tried to hold these moments fast in her mind, they drifted away like mist in a sunrise. The rainbow light was gone, the voices were gone, the people were gone. Lally was gone. Cold morning light showed her an empty square—Apple, too, was gone. She was alone again. The cage floor beneath her was all she had to hold on to, a frail raft on which she rode precariously, halfway between earth and heaven.

The town was waking up, getting ready for the day. A few early risers crisscrossed the square on their various ways to somewhere or other, eyes squinted against the brightening sun, footsteps clacking loud in the morning quiet. A gangly schoolboy in cap and knee britches, his books dangling by a strap from his belt, came running out of a side street and skidded to a halt just below the cage. He looked appraisingly at the cage and its contents, as if he were calculating the throw of a stone, but finding no stone ready to hand ran on his way.

The sun was full up now and shining down on the increasing activity in the square. Shop fronts were opened, shutters were flung wide, water was sluiced on the lintel stones and briskly scrubbed into the gutters. The merchants of Great

235

Wicken were ready for buyers. With loving hands the cheese vendor set out a tempting display—thick wheels of pale gold with beads of moisture pearling on their sides; blue-veined wedges whose aromatic smell proclaimed their tangy taste; hard, sharp cheddars; curded kitchen cheeses done up in cloth bags; and cool, creamy little heart-shaped cheeses wrapped in green dock leaves.

An apple woman set up her stand in a corner of the square. Great collops of flesh wobbled under her stubby arms as she worked. Her large, loaf-shaped bosom threatened to burst out of her bodice, and the tightness of her apron strings and the girth of her hips made her look like a sack of laundry tied in the middle. Her little pig eyes and squat, pushed-up nose were almost buried in fat cheeks chapped as red as her own apples by the cold air. She began laying out the last of the autumn picking, round, hard russets, yellow-green pippins, and small, tawny winter pears to tempt passersby. On the opposite corner a farmer in a smock displayed his cages of chickens, scrawny, bedraggled birds past laying, their feathers drooping as if they knew they were too old for anything but the pot, and a long simmer at that. They clucked to one another dispiritedly.

The pinched, skinny milliner's assistant was busy behind the display window artfully draping embroidered petticoats, setting out needlepoint pincushions, smoothing fragile laces, flouncing a cascade of satin ribbons—all ready for the wives and girls looking for a fancy. Down the way from the milliner's shop, the

236

bookseller wheeled out his cart of cheap bargains and positioned it directly in the way where folk would pass. In the midst of the commotion, the schoolboy came wandering back, having apparently decided to give lessons a miss in favor of the greater enjoyment of the square. In the way of boys, his curiosity drew him to the cage and he came and stood directly under it. Mokie retreated as far as she could from his gaze, huddling to the center of the cage. I'm like the chickens, she thought, and sank her head between her knees.

"Mokie."

Out of the air a voice quietly said her name. Her head came up. The voice spoke again, irritably, from directly underneath the cage.

"Mokie! Pay attention, can't you?"

She pushed herself upright and looked about her.

The schoolboy?

"Keep still, dummy. Don't rock the cage."

The Skimmer?

"Where are you?"

"Here, just below you."

She peered over the edge, her shifted weight tilting the cage. It rocked gently.

"Keep still, can't you? Did I say don't rock the cage?"

The Skimmer, sure enough, giving orders like always. By now he was halfway up the wall and climbing like a lizard, his round, monkey head in its schoolboy cap tilted to the sky, his bare knees at right angles to keep his body flat against the ashlars, his finger-tips and toes clinging with simian strength to invisible crevices between the stones. As she watched, he crawled silently upward course by course, nimble as a squirrel, until he was directly behind the cage and on a level with the hook over her head.

"Stay in the center of the cage and sit *still*."

Carefully she held herself immobile, scarcely breathing lest it disturb the balance of the cage.

"Now. Keep just where you are."

Iron creaked rustily over her head, and she knew without seeing that The Skimmer was letting himself down the chain to land on the cage roof. A moment more and he was there, poised just above her though she could not see him.

"Well and good. When I say, slide yourself as far as you can to the side away from the wall. I'll balance you on the opposite side. You got that?"

"Yes."

"Right. Go."

Pressed as flat against the floor as The Skimmer had been against the stones of the building, she snaked herself along to the outside of the cage, feeling, though she could not see, that The Skimmer was using his weight to balance her so that the cage did not tilt.

"Now make yourself as heavy as you can and keep stone still. I'm coming in."

Mokie held her breath.

The square was filled with folk tending to their own busy-
ness, shopping and browsing, looking and buying, but how long
would it be before someone glanced up and saw what was going
on just over their heads? The cage, though holding still, was
creaking ominously under the combined weight of Mokie and
The Skimmer, but she willed herself into the floor for ballast,
and in a moment more The Skimmer's legs dangled into view
between the cage and the wall. His body followed, and there he
was, hands and feet clinging to the bars and his blessed, ugly face
peering at her like a monkey on the wrong side of his cage. She
opened her mouth and he stilled her with a look.

"Now, stand up where anybody can see you. But do it
slowly or we'll both land on the cobbles."

She slid her back up along the bars, pushing herself upright
and leaning against them. With her body as screen and balance,
The Skimmer began to work his wiry frame through the bars.
It was a treat to see, and she wished she had the leisure to
appreciate his skill, for so neatly and so quietly did he insinuate
himself that nothing moved but an arm, then a head and one
shoulder, then a leg, and the rest following. He melted into the
cage, slid to the floor, and came to rest.

She moved carefully toward him and risked a whisper.

"What do we do now?"

"We wait."

He tilted his cap down over his eyes, closed them, and went
to sleep.

THIRTY-FOUR

ESCAPE

WAIT? THOUGHT MOKIE. What for? The Skimmer slept solidly beside her, as if nothing in the world would disturb him. But he had said wait, so she waited. By now the square was crowded with people. Tired and fearful though she was, Mokie could not keep her eyes from the ever changing pattern of folk passing to and fro. She tried to imagine their errands. Some were easy. Mothers doing the day's marketing shushed the small children who clung to their skirts. They poked judicious fingers at the cheeses or hefted the apples and felt the pears for ripeness. Those with money to spend were easy to spot, their eyes scanning the shop windows, their faces set with purpose.

The browsers were more entertaining. They strolled carelessly along, pausing now and again to admire a display, finger an apple or a pear, poke the center of a cheese, or idly leaf through the pages of a book. One stoop-shouldered, scholarly-looking fellow with gray hair straggling down over his collar got so taken by the book he picked from the bargain cart that he began to read, nosing his wire-rimmed spectacles so close to the page that he was unaware of the annoyance, the sharp glances and irritated coughs of those who had to step off the curb to walk around him.

Out of a side street came a bald little man in a rusty black coat with a great ring of keys jangling at his side, his eyes rimmed in spectacles half the size of his face. He walked over to the magistrate's building. On his way, he glanced up at the prisoner sitting slumped against the cage, head on knees, and shook his head. A massive iron key, bigger than his hand, or so it seemed, was inserted ceremoniously into the gaping keyhole of the door and turned with a great shriek of metal against metal. The door swung slowly back, revealing a hallway dank with the dead, chill air of the law. The little man went inside. Another day was beginning for the magistrate's court, and the forlorn figure in the cage was its first concern.

Mokie's eyes suddenly widened, and she sat bolt upright and stared. A little red-and-white shape at ground level was busily moving in and out and around the legs and feet that crowded the cobbles. It was a pig. As Mokie started to call out, she felt The Skimmer's hand close like iron around her ankle.

"Not a word, understand?"

She nodded.

"Right," said The Skimmer, never moving or opening his eyes. "Now, do *exactly* what I tell you, exactly *when* I tell you. Don't ask questions. Don't wait. Just go. Got it?"

"Got it," she breathed.

In one smooth movement he snaked over to the wall side of the cage. His hands slid through the bars, his elbows crooked outward, and two of the bars broke, but the noise of the crowd blanketed the sound.

"When I'm out and on the wall, you follow me and hold fast to my back. Stick like a cocklebur and hold tight, no matter what happens. But don't go till I tell you. Right?"

She nodded.

He gave a wriggle and a kind of jump, and suddenly he was on the wall, arms and legs spread and clinging like a lizard. Freed of his weight, the cage rocked violently.

At that precise moment the pig trotted head-on against the scholarly reader's legs; he stumbled, still clutching his book, and fell against the book cart, knocking it over and sending three shelves of bargains toppling out and down to land helter-skelter on the cobbles, leaves fluttering, spines cracking, corners crumpling. The bookseller erupted out the shop door in a frenzy.

"Now," said The Skimmer.

"Catch that pig!" cried the scholarly man, book still in hand, giving chase in the opposite direction to where the pig was going.

Trying not to think, Mokie slid out through the bars, raking her ribs on their broken ends, and fastened herself monkeylike to The Skimmer's shoulders, wrapping her legs around his hips.

The pig's chosen course sent her squarely into the apple stand, overturning it and sending apples and pears rolling treacherously under feet, cascading and bouncing in every direction. With a cry, the apple woman made a dive for the pig and managed to smack her rump and send her zigzagging into a forest of legs and feet, tripping their owners, who lurched cursing into one another. Continuing her trajectory, the pig careened into the chicken cages, springing the wicker doors and loosing the occupants. Amid a great flapping and squawking the chickens hopped free, adding their voices and feathers to the confusion. The noise rose to a clamor.

Paying no heed at all to the turmoil below him, The Skimmer lowered himself and Mokie foot by foot, stone by stone down the wall. Something banged against her leg. She looked down. It was a packet of schoolbooks hanging by a strap.

The square was chaos, with chickens flapping under everyone's feet, people chasing the pig, others the apples, others trying to gather the scattered books and pile them back on the cart. In the confusion the pig ran one way and the book reader another. The apple woman left her stand to give chase. Skirts billowing, she ran past the cheese shop, knocking loose a wheel of cheese, which came careening like a juggernaut after her. It caught up and passed her as with a last whisk of her apron she disappeared round a corner.

Landing on the cobblestones, face inward to the wall, The Skimmer turned to find himself nose to nose with a man who stared at him openmouthed. He swung aside only to near collide with another. They were hemmed in and there was no way through. "Right," said The Skimmer over his shoulder to Mokie. "You'll have to fly. Can you do it?" He felt rather than heard her "yes."

"Up you go, then." He cupped his hands for her feet and heaved her onto his shoulders. She scrambled upright, swaying as he tried to steady her against the movement of the crowd. "John!" he called across the square. "Catch!" It was an impossible distance. She would never make it across. But there was no time to think. The scholarly man turned and held out his arms, The Skimmer platformed his hands, Mokie stepped onto them, and without a pause The Skimmer launched her over the heads of the crowd.

She was flying. John's eyes held her up, his hands caught hers, and with no break in movement he set her down and said, "Run!" Together the two of them zigzagged through the press, ducking, dodging, heads down and feet moving. Like divers they surfaced out of the swirling chaos before the bouncing apples had rolled to a stop. On they raced, ducking through side streets, dodging down alleys, twisting around corners, making for the edge of town and the open fields.

Then they were out on the road and running pell-mell. Gradually the noise from the square and the sounds of pursuit—if any pursuit there was—faded. But still the road was too bare, too exposed, if any were after them, and no sooner did he think it than John veered sharply off the road, vaulted a ditch, pulled Mokie scrambling up a steep bank and through a thorn hedge that raked her ferociously, and they ran pelting through the dry grass of a sheltered meadow.

"Stop, John, please stop, I can't breathe."

John pulled up under the thin shade of a copse of willows, their yellow leaves fluttering like little banners in the fitful breeze.

Mokie stood gasping. Her mouth was dry, her lungs were pumping, she had a stitch in her ribs, her side ached where she had scraped through the cage bars, her arms and legs were scratched and bleeding from the thorns. Her chest was constricted in iron bands, and she felt as if her breath would never come back. Suddenly, overwhelmingly, it all caught up with her—the arrest, the bleak night in gaol, the magistrate, the dreadful cage, too little food, too little sleep, despair and hope taking turns with her heart, the fear and tension of the escape. The world turned black. She staggered and would have fallen had not John caught her and eased her to the ground. Then Lally, still in cap and apron, was bending over her.

Her eyes wouldn't open, but there was something she had to know.

"Where's . . ."

"Mokie, don't talk. Rest now. All's well. I've a fire here, and the kettle on to boil. What you need is some tea and a bite to eat."

Mokie shook her head.

"Where is . . ."

She couldn't get the words out, but she had to say them, had to ask. Then she felt something warm and solid against her leg and she looked down to see Apple stretching herself at length beside her. The pig had an apple in her mouth.

Mokie sighed and closed her eyes. "Make it real tea and not sheep piss," she murmured to no one in particular, and slid immediately into sleep.

Lally covered her with a shawl. Yellowed leaves from the willow drifted softly over her.

THIRTY-FIVE

The River

I<small>T WAS DUSK</small>. Mokie awoke to the friendly crackling of Lally's cook fire, to the smell of wood smoke and cheese toasting, to early starlight and the warm glow of flames.

"Where are we?" Even as she asked the question and before anyone could speak, she knew where they were.

"Here," said John.

"Together," said Lally.

"Well away, and safe for now, but not for long," said The Skimmer.

Lally, John, and The Skimmer were near, sitting companionably around the fire, the dancing flames sending alternate lights and shadows across their faces.

"Like the candle," Mokie murmured drowsily.

"What's like a candle, Mokie?" John.

"You are. Your faces. It's like when I saw you first back there in the wood; your faces were flickery in the candlelight." She smiled at the memory. "I didn't know you then."

"And now you know us." That was John.

"Now I know you," she agreed drowsily.

"Now we know each other." That was Lally.

"I'd say that's enough about knowing and we'd better think about going," said The Skimmer briskly. Going where? thought Mokie sleepily, and Lally echoed her thought.

"Going where, Skimmer?"

"We can't stay here forever, not even for very long unless we want them to find us and take Mokie back. Folk like that won't take kindly to us making fools of them with our breaking her out of gaol."

Blinking against the firelight, Mokie heard only a comfortable buzz of voices that hummed around her head like sleepy bees. She was exhausted still, content simply to breathe in great deep breaths that felt as if they filled her heart, content to feel her muscles ache with the relaxation that follows the strain of effort, content to listen without having to reply, without having to make sense or understand. They were talking across her.

"Let's head toward the river." That was John's voice. "They'll be looking everywhere but there. Overland, off the road, in the woods, maybe."

"The river's a ways." That was The Skimmer. "Take too long to get there."

"We could try it."

Was it Lally who said it, or Mokie herself? It didn't matter. She was floating into sleep.

Someone who sounded like The Skimmer said, "It's as good a start as any, and better than some, and we've got to go somewhere. We'll take the cart."

Carts don't float, thought Mokie, and then she remembered. The world is magic, magic is the world. It's always there, you only have to know it.

"Tomorrow?"

"Tonight."

"Get her into the cart," ordered The Skimmer, "and we'll wrap the tent around her. It'll keep her warm and hide her if anyone comes along."

Mokie felt a warm hand under her rump and another under her shoulder, felt herself lifted and heaved onto the piled stuff that filled the cart almost to overflowing. It made an unexpectedly cushiony resting place, and smelled old and sweet and a little musty. A silken substance soft as night was lapped round her and she gave herself into its protection, content to lie cradled, listening dreamily to the night noises of crickets and cicadas and the occasional chirp of a sleepy bird, listening to the voices that wove a web over her head and covered her.

Through a fog of sleep she could feel the cart roll bumpily over the meadow. Presently she heard the sound of water. As they came closer to the creek, a low-lying mist enveloped and hid them. It was dank and chilly, and Mokie snuggled deeper into the cushions. Then they plunged into the wood, still following the water, and she could feel the cart scraping against stones and underbrush. The wood closed over their heads. The water noises mingled with the noise of their passage, and the tumbling splash became a smoother, deeper-running, quieter sound. Then it fell below hearing altogether, but she knew it was still there.

"Here's a place," said The Skimmer. Mokie felt the cart tilt and roll unevenly. Then it was jerked to a stop.

"Right," said Lally.

The cart rolled forward again; there was a sound of water slapping against the sides, and then a floating feeling as the water took it.

A certain amount of thumping and bumping followed as the wheels were pulled off the axles and jammed down in the back of the cart, completing the transformation from road vehicle to water vessel. The new-made boat rocked precariously as first Lally, then John, then The Skimmer jumped aboard. Apple gave a surprisingly nimble leap off the bank and landed neatly against Mokie's ribs, shipping water and soaking the cushions. No one said anything, for voices carry far in a mist, over water.

The channel was narrow here and edged with overhanging trees on both sides. Mokie saw a latticework sky of woven branches passing continuously over her head, a black lace canopy through which stars glimmered like diamonds caught in a web. The last thing she saw as sleep claimed her was her mother's face framed between two intercurving branches.

She woke to daylight. Above her, the dark lattice swayed gently, and for a drowsy minute she was back in the cage, looking with sleep-fogged eyes at the wickerwork of the roof and the sky beyond it. She could feel the floor rock ever so slightly under her, and she knew if she moved, it would tilt sickeningly. Then everything shifted and she couldn't tell where she was and that was almost worse than being back in the cage. She lay suspended in a confusion of light and shadow, disoriented, disembodied.

"Good morning, Mokie." Lally's voice rang like a glass bell. She was crouched on the narrow foreshore just beyond the boat, hovering over a fire as usual.

"Lally?" said Mokie. She still felt suspended, but held now in some clear transparent substance that was neither air nor water, but the atmosphere of dream. She raised her head to take a look around her, but her head weighed heavy on her neck, and the exertion was all she could manage. She could see that they had pulled the boat up against a bank under a stand of trees whose twisted roots reached into the black water, digging into the muddy bank like gnarled hands. Exhausted by the effort, she dropped her head back onto the comforting cushions. Water slapped gently against the sides of the boat.

Lally spoke again. "It's a bit swampy down here, but I found a

251

field away back yonder and there'll be food shortly, though whether it's breakfast or dinner I leave to you. Roast potatoes, anyway, enough to fill you up. It's past harvest, but there were a few left to dig."

The thought of roast potatoes, steaming hot and fragrant, brought Mokie back to herself.

"Where's The Skimmer?" she asked.

"Up here," came a familiar, raspy voice, and she turned her head to see him standing just beyond the boat.

"Skimmer. Are we there yet?"

The Skimmer looked at her.

"Wherever 'there' is," he said, "we're not there yet, just on our way, just letting the river carry us. We'll lie up here for the daytime and travel again tonight. Night's our best concealment."

She nodded, content to know they were all there, to let them carry her.

"Good morning, Mokie," said John's voice, low and vibrant like the sounding of a deep glass bowl when a finger runs around the rim. "I hope you're sleeping well."

He was standing so near that she was surprised she hadn't noticed him before. His hands were holding sticks he had gathered for Lally's fire, and Apple was leaning against his leg. Shadows of tree branches fell in ragged bars across his face.

For the first time since her escape, Mokie let herself look directly at John.

"Yes," said Mokie. She wanted to go on, but she couldn't think of anything to say. She felt strangely blank, even transparent, as if she wasn't really there.

A confusion of memories overwhelmed her. The pig girl, the village target. A stranger in the mirror. Lally's Mokie, the beauty with the brass earrings and the gypsy necklace, the new-found Mokie in the ruffled skirt and pretty scarf. A prisoner named Moxon, dumb and tongue-tied before the magistrate. A birdie in a cage perched helpless and exposed high above the square.

Now John was looking at her and she wasn't anybody at all.

For the first time since her arrest—but that was years ago, she thought—she remembered how she had felt on that last morning before they took her away, covertly watching John, wondering if he watched her.

"That's good," said John.

His words floated loose in the air between them, refusing to connect to any meaning.

"What's good? I mean, what did you say?"

"I said, 'that's good,'" said John gravely. "That you slept. It was hard back there in the town."

She frowned, struggling to recall. There were crowds, and confusion, riding pick-a-back on The Skimmer, flying, running for the dear life—was there anything more? Her eyes blurred and John's dark face came and went like something recalled in a dream. Everything ran together. She closed her eyes and immediately felt the cage tilt under her; voices buzzed in her head, shouting, accusing.

"Hey, piggy!" A child's voice.

"Take him away. " A sorrowful voice.

Shrill voices cried out, "It's him, all right!"

Loud footsteps rang on the cobblestones. A hail of pebbles pattered against the cage. The old feeling of sick hopelessness clutched at her stomach. She opened her eyes and brushed away the skeleton leaves the wind had whispered onto her face.

John was still there. Greatly daring, she let her eyes meet his, and as if it were the first time, the sudden, strong connection took her breath away. Memories washed over her—a cracked window and that same dark gaze catching her through the green glass marble, the smell of soup and wine and bitter weeds. Her face in Lally's mirror, her eyes and John's meeting for one heartbeat. John's eyes holding her up, keeping her in the air. Past and present overlapped, and for a brief moment she understood.

"Dinner," called Lally. "Or breakfast. Or whatever you want it to be. Anyhow, it's ready."

The thread loosened, the moment passed. She sat up. The boat rocked with her movement and once again the world spun around her and she had to shut her eyes again. Sick and dizzy in a whirling darkness, she clutched for anchor at the side of the boat. She felt herself lifted, carried up the bank, and put down softly beside Lally's fire. She knew it was John, but it was over before she had time to really feel it.

"Well, now," said The Skimmer, rubbing his hands briskly. "I'm ready for some food. Anything to go with those potatoes, Lally?"

"Just tea," she said, "and you should be grateful for that."

He looked around him at the tangle of trees, the empty water.

"Nobody about but us. Come on, now. Couldn't you conjure anything more than tea and potatoes? Something a little tastier? Some cheese, maybe? A bit of cake, say? Or fritters and honey?"

"No," said Lally. "We're living off the country, Skimmer. You know that. And you know why. Now, don't fuss me. I got you a bit of cheese yesterday, in all the excitement, but I can hardly go back to town for more. As for fritters and cake . . ."

She raised her shoulders, expressive of astonishment. "My goodness, don't you think of anything but food?"

"Not if I can help it." He grinned and squatted by the fire.

Afterward, Mokie was never sure how much time had passed. She lost count of hours and days and weeks. It didn't seem to matter. Day and night moved into each other as seamlessly as a river flowing, as endless as a dream while you are dreaming it. The narrow, swampy channel led them through a maze of waterways that met and parted and flowed into each other. It was a world beyond the world. Strange birds nested in the shallows, whose calls echoed eerily down the twisting corridors of the dank and dripping trees. Fish jumped with little splashing sounds and fell back, leaving ripples on the water. Tiny frogs sent clear high trills to one another through the night, making it seem as if the air itself was singing. In what seemed almost another world the boat wound by night along the twists and turns of narrow channels, suspended out of time and space on the black glass water, a second sky that held the stars in its deeps.

The water seemed to hold their voices too, disembodied sounds like the whispers of stars, that came from shadowy selves they could barely see. Their words were quiet, inconsequential. They talked of where they would go next, of how they would travel. Of rain and sunshine, of autumn's touch that they could see in the dry grasses, of the hope they had that spring would come again. In the half-light of dawn they pulled up on some little beach or sheltered cove and their faces glowed with the rising sun as they cooked and ate, drank and laughed with one another. They never stayed long on any shore, for the inconstant river was their one secure and constant place, the solid banks on either side a shifting flow that passed them by as swift as water running, the boat their cradle wherein they lay like careless children while the world went on its way without them.

All her life before seemed to Mokie like a story she had once heard but was forgetting. Another story, better and richer, was unfolding and she followed it unquestioning. All the hurt of her young years, the hidden-away pain and loneliness, the unremembered, never-to-be-forgotten injury and insult of Dommel's assault, all dropped away like a cloak that fell from her shoulders and was left on the ground. Slowly, cautiously, she began to explore the Mokie that Lally had uncovered, to feel within herself the presence of the girl with beauty in her bones.

And outside herself that girl felt the presence of John as an almost palpable sensation against her skin. If she looked at him directly, his eyes were always looking elsewhere, yet she was aware of his gaze resting on her when she was not looking. She felt, too, when their glances involuntarily crossed, which happened more and more often, the invisible thread that vibrated between them. Nor was it their eyes alone that seemed irresistibly drawn to the other. As if by accident their hands would brush one against another, and a streak of winter lightning would jolt through her body. It could be anytime—building a fire, handing a mug of tea, maneuvering the boat in and about the shallows. When it happened it was almost more than she could bear, but she waited for it and wanted it and longed for it to happen again. And when it did happen again, every time it happened again, it was as sudden as the first time, without warning, like thunder from a clear sky.

Yet if she closed her eyes and tried to picture his face, she could not see it. Or if she tried when he was absent to remind herself what he looked like, she could not remember. It worried her, that she could not imagine his face. But the harder she tried, the less she could conjure him, and so she stopped trying. What that might mean she would not allow herself to wonder. It seemed safer to accept whatever came without trying to tease out a meaning, to live moment by moment without any regard for what the future could bring.

But all things end, and one day The Skimmer said, "We've rested on the water long enough, I think. We're going in circles, never getting out of the wood. We'd best go back to the land."

"Why?" asked Lally. "We're safe here. No one's followed us."

"I like it on the water," offered Mokie, scratching Apple under her bristly chin. "It's peaceful."

John said nothing.

"The year's coming to its end," said The Skimmer to no one in particular. "Time's passing."

"What time?" asked Mokie idly, but Apple distracted her by pushing her snout against Mokie's hand for more scratching.

"We can't stay forever; sooner or later we'll have to go back, and now's as good a time as any," said The Skimmer, as if he hadn't heard her.

John looked at The Skimmer and both looked at Lally. Mokie saw that something passed among them, but she didn't understand what it was, and she was too content to wonder.

Lally dropped her eyes and looked down at her fingers, laced in her lap. She shook her head.

THIRTY-SIX

MOONLiGHT AGAiN

MOKIE CAME AWAKE INTO A STILLNESS. The lack of motion felt strange after the soft rocking of the boat. The air felt different—drier, thinner, harsher in her lungs than the water's soft breathing. A voice said, "She's still asleep." Another voice said, "We'll have to wake her. We can't hang about any longer."

Her eyelids felt intolerably heavy. With a tremendous effort she dragged them open only to find that she could not see; they were still closed. Why wouldn't they open? She tried again with no more success and heard someone say, "She's waking up."

I'm already awake, she said, but she knew that no one heard her. She gave up the battle to open her eyes and let herself drift back into sleep, back into the boat, back into the rocking—

"Time you stirred, Mokie. We've got to be moving."

Lally was bending over her.

But we have been moving, thought Mokie, we've been moving forever. Something light as a bird feather tickled her face. She put up her hand to it, and as she did her eyes flew open. She plucked a slender, yellowed leaf off her cheek, and while she looked at it in bewilderment a puff of wind loosened a little shower of leaves that fell all around her. She glanced up. Overhead the willow coppice swayed and whispered, and beneath her the ground was suddenly hard. Covered with Lally's shawl, she was lying right where she had fallen asleep, in the shelter of the cart with Apple warm against her.

"You've slept long enough, Mokie—clear through the night and half the day too. We mustn't hang about here any longer. Time's passing."

That was The Skimmer, impatient as usual, his voice rough with anxiety and something else she couldn't put a name to.

"Are you hungry? You were too tired to eat last night, but there's leftover tea, and apples and a little cheese."

That was Lally, holding out a cup filled with tawny liquid.

Mokie looked at both of them and then at John, but he said no word. She felt like one exiled from fairyland—a stranger in a world she didn't know. It was all sliding away, going faster and faster as she tried to pursue it, to recover the lovely feeling of utter rightness, of unutterable, quiet joy that said without words all is well, everything is in place, this is how it is supposed to be. And then it was all gone beyond recall and the loss and the emptiness were more than she could bear. She took the cup, felt it cold and hard in her fingers, held out her hand for cheese and apples. The workaday world, actual, solid, plain as bread, rearranged itself around her.

"Hungry. I guess—yes. Yes, I am."

She drank the cold tea thirstily, crunched into the apple, felt the cheese mellow and tangy on her tongue. There was nothing else to do.

"Where are we going to?"

She wasn't really curious; it was just something to say, something to distract her from looking back toward the hollow where the dream had pulled away.

"Away from folk," The Skimmer told her, "at least for a while, till this fuss blows over. We've got some options. We might be able to circle around the other side of Great Wicken and cut across to the Forgotten Inn up in the hills. We could lie up there for a while. Nobody much goes there and we'd be out of sight."

"But the inn's a ways," objected Lally, "and the track runs right across the plain. We'd be seen before we got there."

"Well, that's out, then, let's stick with what we know. I say the Wickenwood's closest, it's easy to get lost in there, and it'll be no trick to dodge pursuit, especially if we know where we're going and they don't."

"Back to the hut," said Mokie.

"What hut?" The Skimmer looked at her sharply.

"Not to the hut," said Lally quickly, "not yet. At least— I mean, it's not time for that. I mean—" She stopped in midsentence, her mouth clamped shut on whatever she might have been going to say.

John moved smoothly into the awkward moment. "Let's just get started, shall we? We'll be on our way and we'll see where our feet take us. Finished eating, Mokie? Good. You can ride for a while. Pile yourself into the cart. No, not you, Apple. Good girl. She wants to walk—look at her trotting ahead of us already."

Gently, persistently he talked them through it, got the cart rolling, got them moving, the whole procedure oiled and smoothed by his soft voice and ready smile, his easy words that flowed over them like warm water. They were on their way.

Mokie felt it all falling farther and farther behind—the gentle meadow, the murmuring willow coppice, the angry town, the cage, the turbulent square, the arrest and imprisonment, the heart-stopping escape. Time and distance rose up like an invisible wall, making a barricade between today and what was past, and she was content to have it so. The beautiful dream of the time on the water was gone too—let it go. There was nothing but the present moment. The sun was filtering down out of a sky with a thin dusting of clouds, its chilly rays scarcely warming the cold, crisp air. Winter was on the way sure enough.

Ahead of them trotted Apple, ears pricked, nose lifted, rump bobbing in and out of the tall grass of the meadow. She was heading straight for the wood.

"Looks like she knows right where she's going, don't she?" The Skimmer grinned. "We'd better follow the pig."

Follow her they did, not stopping until they reached the wood and were well within its deep shadow and shelter. There they made camp, parking the cart in a little glade with a narrow thread of stream glittering through it. John and The Skimmer cast about for stones to build a fireplace. Lally went to fill the kettle. Mokie, who had journeyed in a half doze, cradled in the cart, came out of it into an earlier being, and for a lightless moment she was once again the person of no place and no people that she had been so short a time ago. She reached a hand to touch some present reality, to reassure herself that she was changed, no longer that person. Her fingers encountered a hard little snout and she looked down to see Apple regarding her thoughtfully.

Supper was a quiet meal in spite of Lally's efforts. She brewed tea, stirred up a good hot soup out of field greens thickened with late grain gathered from the heads of the wild grasses, the whole flavored with wild onion. It was not a banquet, but they were all hungry, and it should have tasted delicious to their starving appetites. And perhaps it did, but they had no savor for food. The Skimmer tried a few jokes but realized soon enough that no one had any laughter left, all of them alone with thoughts they were unwilling to share.

Sleep was no better. The long day's walking should have tired them all, and when they snuggled down next to the fire they were ready to close their eyes. Yet they found themselves lying awake, sensitive as skinned fingertips to one another's presence and reluctant to acknowledge it. The night noises resounded unnaturally loud and clear through the dark, cold air. Insects sang high and shrill to one another. A late cricket chirped, slow and stridulent. From some distant pond a bullfrog thunked, low and flat over the water. A hunting owl sent his harsh, hollow call rebounding from tree to tree. Gradually the noises faded. One by one, John, Lally, The Skimmer, even Apple gave in to sleep.

Only Mokie lay wide-eyed, staring into the silver moonlight that sifted down through the dark branches. She felt curiously set apart from everything around her. She listened to Lally's light breathing, the deep breaths that were John, The Skimmer's regular snore. Beside her Apple snuffled in her sleep, dreaming perhaps of a paradise of acorns. At last Mokie could lie still no longer. She got up, crept softly to the dying fire, and stirred the coals. They flared up, and a little dance of sparks went fluttering upward—miniature butterflies of the night on their way to some starry flower. The cricket was quiet now. The owl had found his prey or flown to other hunting grounds. The bullfrog was silent. Mokie stared into the heart of the fire, trying to read the pulsing glow of the coals, looking for a message. She did not see Apple open her eyes and look at her. All was still.

Yet not so. Some energy outside the fire was astir in the night, or in Mokie herself, something that made her creep to the edge of the clearing and beyond it. Scarcely aware of what she was doing, following no direction but her feet that followed one after the other, she stole away from the fire and the cart and her sleeping companions. Apple woke and trotted quietly after her. Someone else woke as well and softly followed. It seemed to Mokie very much like that other journey she had taken so short a time ago, walking through the wood in simple curiosity toward a flickering light to find the hut and look through the window to see Lally and John and The Skimmer deep in talk.

And it seemed somehow also like the dimly remembered journey before that one, when she had walked away from the pit of darkness opening at her feet, walked away from self and memory into the wood, which offered the only refuge, blindly seeking a gentler dark in which to cushion her injuries. And now all the journeys became one journey toward an unknown destination. She walked as in a dream, though she knew it was no dream, but something more real than she could put a word to. She walked and walked, unaware that someone was following close behind her.

After a while—she took no measure of time—she came out of the trees into a little clearing in the wood that shone silver under a full moon. She walked quietly, purposefully, sensing rather than feeling or hearing the little sound of wind, moon's breath, that sang among the long grasses. In front of her the hut sagged against its rise of ground. No sound came from it. Behind her the trees made a dark barrier between her and all she had left. Slowly now, feeling the brush of dry weeds like reaching fingers against her ankles, she went toward the hut, toward the door that banged insistently in the wind. She swung it open and went inside.

The hut was empty, its shadows receding into unknown distances that she could not see. A candle was stuck in its own wax in the middle of the table. Dried leaves scattering in the wind. No sight nor sound of anyone; no imprint of bodies against the emptiness, no voices hanging like moon dust on the air. She went to the table, touched the candle gently, absently, feeling with her finger where the burned wick was cold and brittle. Where the moonlight struck it a moon flame flowered ghostly silver. I have done that before, she thought. I have been here before.

The door creaked, and she turned toward it. Someone stood in the open doorway.

She said with no surprise, "John."

"Hello, Mokie," he said, and came to her.

"Why did you come here?"

"Why did you?"

Their voices intermingled as their glances tangled and they both laughed at the same time.

"I wanted to walk."

"I heard you get up."

Again they spoke in concert, and again they laughed at themselves. It was funny. It was inevitable. Nothing else could have happened.

"This isn't the place to be," he said. "We must go from here," and he took her hand, lacing his fingers into hers. She nodded.

266

Hand in hand, they left the hut and the moon flame died behind them and the restless door squeaked and banged against the empty air.

They came out into a world of fairy glamour, a magic light that bathed the little clearing and shape-changed all it touched. The moon glimmered the landscape into strangeness, making a world of colorless light against lightless black. Every detail, every leaf or blade of grass or ragged weed, was edged with silver that shone like cold fire. Every cast shadow was a doorway into darkness. In a wonder too deep for words John and Mokie felt themselves part of the enchantment. The moon robbed their faces of human expression, replacing the familiarity of eye and nose and mouth, of cheekbone and throat, with abstract geometric patterns of light and dark. They knew each other more by touch than sight, for they made less impress on the air than weightless specters, their shadows more definite than their bodily selves.

At the far edge of the clearing Apple was sitting quietly, just under the trees. Neither John nor Mokie was surprised to see her here on this enchanted night. She belonged to the moonlight, as did they. The moon's light shone full on the little pig, silvering her into something unearthly, an apparition, not a part of daily life. At their approach she turned and trotted into the wood and at once the silver disappeared and there was no pig at all, but her red-tipped ears were the flags that marked a path they could not see. They followed her, not the way they had come, but in a new direction.

For Mokie it was an enchanted journey lifted clear of time and space. Apple trotting ahead of them, John's hand in hers were the only realities, the only guides she wanted to wherever they were going. It seemed she could walk forever, a journey that was its own goal. She felt the path rather than saw it, her feet making little sound on the soft forest floor. Darkness flowed around her like a river, broken by little patches of moonlight that glittered like water over rocks. She could not tell how long they walked so, but it seemed a very long time. Somewhere above the trees the moon was going home, riding its arc down the western sky. In the eastern sky the dark was thinning to gray, dawn coming outside the wood. They neared a looming presence and saw Apple sitting quietly near it. Their footsteps slowed and halted.

THIRTY-SEVEN

The Witness Tree

T HEY WERE FACING A GIANT TREE of such width and height that it seemed as if it were a separate world. Its massive trunk blotted out anything that might lie beyond, and its branches towered up and up, the arching pillars of the sky. Dried leaves curled against the moonlight, clinging to the branches like the hands of dead babies as the wind tugged at them. The sound of it whispered a threat, a foreboding that Mokie feared to name and didn't want to know, that was battering against her memory for entry. The wind grew stronger, roaring through the wood, and the trees around her creaked and groaned in answer. The branches of the great tree lashed to and fro in the gale like arms waving, and the heart of the tree gave a great crack as if it would break in two.

In that instant Mokie plummeted from uneasiness through

dread to terror as she recognized the holly oak, her story tree, the tree where . . . Her memory fled from itself and she felt rather than knew that something awful had happened was about to happen was happening. She had to get away or the tree would swallow her. The gaping mouth of an unknown wound would open, she would fall headlong and the blackness would close over her. The wind took her and shook her like a rabbit in the jaws of a great wolf. But the wind was inside her and on some level she knew it and she fought to get free of it, tugging at John's hand in panic, dragging him with her into headlong retreat, a mad flight from being swept away, from total annihilation.

"Mokie, what is it? What's the matter? What's wrong?"

"The wind—so strong! I'm afraid! Let's go! Let's get away from here!"

"Mokie, there's no wind, nothing's happening. Stay still."

"John, let me go! Please!" She tugged frantically at his hand.

"No. Stay."

"I can't. It's here. I can't—"

"What's here, Mokie? What is it?"

"I don't know, I don't know!"

It came out as frantic cries, the terrorized whimpers of an animal caught in a trap.

"Mokie, stop. Stop now, it's all right. You're safe. You're with me. I'm here. I'm with you. It's all right."

He took her into the circle of his arms, holding her gently, firmly, feeling the desperate pull of her body, arched like a bent bow as she strained away from his hold.

"Let me go! I've got—got to get out of here! Please! John, let me go!" She struggled frantically to break free.

"Mokie, don't run away. Stay, and I'll stay with you. Stay."

Slowly, slowly she ceased to struggle, accepting the wardship of his embrace. Carefully keeping her in the circle of his arm, he tilted her face up to the growing light that sifted through the branches.

"Now. Tell me."

"I don't know."

She took a long breath and pulled free of him, reaching out her hand to touch the tree.

"The tree . . . it's the tree, there's something. . . ."

Out of the dawn a bird called—three plaintive descending notes. What she had given to the tree to hold, it now gave back. She was drowning in memory. It washed over her, filling her mouth, her lungs, engulfing her bones. The boys were holding her arms and legs, he was dropping his pants and kneeling over her, he was . . .

She gave an explosive gasp, as if she had been punched violently in the stomach, and doubled over in agony. Clutching the tree with one hand and her middle with the other she gagged convulsively, possessed by her body's need to cleanse itself. Her belly heaved, and in one rush all the stored-up years of hurt and anger and frustration came spewing up and out and the taste of it filled her mouth, sour as vinegar, bitter as bile. Again and again she vomited, until there was nothing left to bring up, and still she gagged and retched as if her body would turn itself inside out. John held her head as she bent helpless, but she took no heed of him. Emptied at last, she sank to her hands and knees, head hanging, swaying like a stunned animal, breathless and panting.

"I can't . . . I can't . . ." She rocked in agony.

"Can't what? What can't you, Mokie?"

Her voice was low and tortured, dragged out of her in anguish. He could hardly make out the words.

"I can't bear it. I don't want . . . I don't want to be me. I want to take off my skin, I'm dirty where it touches me. I hate it. I hate myself."

She shuddered in a convulsion of self-loathing, clawing at the earth as if it were her body. Her breath came ragged from her lungs, ripping out her very soul to get rid of it. The breaths became howls, the howls gut-wrenching, throat-choking sobs, and with the sobs came the tears that would not be stopped any longer. She cried from deep inside, from her heart and her belly. She cried with her whole body and her soul. She cried as if her heart would break in two and bleed out its life at the very center of her being.

John watched it happen, and from her place near the tree Apple watched as well.

Much later—a lifetime later—Mokie lay spent and strengthless, stretched out on the forest floor with Apple, ever watchful, lying beside her. The storm had passed. Mokie's eyes were closed peacefully, and her breathing was deep and even. John sat quietly beside her, not touching her, not speaking, simply making himself a part of her world, waiting for her to come back to it. She was so quiet for so long that he thought at first that she had fallen asleep, and was grateful for the respite it would give her. When after a while she spoke, still with her eyes closed, her voice seemed no human expression but thin sunlight murmuring to itself.

"John?"

"Here beside you."

"Don't go away."

"I won't. Are you all right now?"

"Yes, but my mouth tastes awful."

"I'm not surprised. Here."

He rummaged in the brush and plucked some mint leaves. "Chew on these. They'll make your mouth taste better."

She sat up then and took them in silence, put them in her mouth and chewed solemnly.

"There, now. Does that help?"

"Yes. Thank you."

"Swallow them, they'll sweeten your stomach, too."

She was silent, swallowing obediently. Then, "John?"

"Yes?"

"Apple led us here. Do you suppose she did it on purpose?"

"It looks that way. She certainly seemed to know where she was going."

"Did she know what would happen?"

He took a long breath, let it out. Now for it, he thought. It's up to me now. I have to see her through this. I love her. I didn't want that to happen, but it has. How can I help her and still do what I have to do? How can I get her to the crossing? She'll be alone at the end, everyone is, but somehow I want to be with her until then.

"What did happen, Mokie?" he asked quietly. "Can you tell me? Something happened to you when you touched the tree."

She frowned, remembering.

"It's funny, you know, I had forgotten all about it, like it never happened."

"What had you forgotten?"

"The thing . . . the thing that happened. I only remembered it after we got here. And not even then, not at first."

"Not at first. But then you did remember."

"Then I began to remember. And I was so afraid. Something awful was in it, but I didn't know what. And when I touched the tree, everything came rushing back all at once."

"Tell me, if you can."

"Yes, I can tell you." She took a deep breath.

"On a day . . . I don't know how long ago. It seems like forever . . . I was . . . here. I was here with the pigs like always, and I was telling Apple a story and . . ." She swallowed. "And some boys came. They . . ." She shut her eyes.

He waited, watching.

"They held me down and the biggest boy, Dommel . . . he . . . I don't know how to say the thing that he did to me. I mean, I know all the names, I know what animals do, I know what people call it. But it was more than what he did. It was how. It was how he—hurt me, how he broke into where I was. He stole me from . . . from myself."

She shivered in involuntary recoil as she relived it.

"It was so awful. So awful." She closed her eyes against the memory. But then she opened them, allowing it.

"I know now how awful it was, though at first all I remembered was the pain and I tried to forget that. But when I—when it all came back just now, it wasn't just the pain that I felt, it was more than that—I was angry. I was angry at myself. Yes, and ashamed. So ashamed. I felt ashamed that someone could just do that and I couldn't stop them, that someone could take away my . . . my . . ."

She shook her head. "My something. I don't know what."

"Your self."

"My self. Yes. And I felt it all over again just now, everything that I felt when it happened, only I didn't know it then. I didn't know it."

"You know it now."

"I know it now."

"Now that it's over, now that you've let it out and told me about it, how do you feel?"

There was silence for a little space, then she fetched a great sigh that seemed to come from somewhere deep inside.

"I feel better. I'm better now, lighter. I feel like I could float away. But, oh, John, I'm so tired."

"That's not so strange, Mokie. Fighting is tiring, and you've been fighting for a long time. You can stop now."

She yawned prodigiously.

"I know it's morning, but I think I'm falling asleep."

"Sleep, then, Mokie. I'll keep watch over you. Come here and let me hold you."

He scooped her up and cradled her in his lap. Scarcely aware of what she did, she pillowed her head on his shoulder and her arms went about his neck. She came willingly, without any of her old resistance, snuggling into his arms like a sleepy child. But she was not a child, and the sudden heat she felt along her body where it touched his was not the warmth of comfort, but a new sensation—an unfamiliar, insistent ache. John bent his head and kissed her cheek. His mouth was gentle, his lips touched her as lightly as a butterfly's wing, yet she startled like a frightened bird, her body tensed, and her breath came quick and fast. Her head jerked back, and her eyes looked a question compounded equally of alarm and wonder.

If it will be now, then let it be now, thought John. I love her and I will not hurt her. And, "Yes," he said, and kissed her again, but on the mouth this time and firmly. She stiffened as she had before, but did not pull away, and he felt the quality of the tension in her body change under his hands. Gently he undid the belt that wound twice around her. Softly, with infinite care, he slid off the too large, ridiculous shirt and pants, freeing her girl's body finally and forever from the boy disguise it no longer needed.

She followed every move, watching warily until it was done and she felt herself emerge from the wrappings like a new butterfly from its discarded casing. She came to him cautiously, guardedly, step by step, testing every new advance, every touch of hand or mouth or body against her memories until she let go of them at last, until she gave in to herself at last, and joined with him and took and gave in equal measure. And he was someone new and strange but still John, and she also was a stranger to herself, born new each moment and discovering for the first time the self she had always known was there.

John knew it all. He knew her terrible fear of her own body, and he knew how that warred with her instinctive need to know herself. Her trust, when it finally came, was put into his hands wholly and without reserve, and he held it gently. His love was so tender, so intent on giving, not taking, that what the boys had done to her was—not erased, for now that she had acknowledged it she had no longer a need to forget—but overwritten. It became an old story buried under an even older story—old yet always new. John's face leaned dark above her open eyes, blotting out

277

the wood and the sky and the other face that had haunted her unremembered nightmares. Never in her short life had she been touched with gentleness, never had she been caressed or kissed, never had she been taught how to love, yet she came to loving as her proper element, as the fish to the water or the bird to the air, as if she were just now recovering what she had always known, but had somehow lost the memory.

THIRTY-EIGHT

The Window

THEY LOVED AND SLEPT AND WOKE TO LOVE AGAIN, becoming with each waking more deeply a part of each other. At last, fulfilled, completed, they lay tangled like two children, arms and legs entwined, heads leaning toward each other. For a long while they were content to rest in stillness, asking nothing, giving all. After a little time, drowsily, Mokie spoke, filled to the brim with a happiness larger than any words could hold.

"Remember that night in the tent at Great Wicken? When The Skimmer told me it was all right to be Mokie?"

"I remember."

"I told Lally that night I knew who she was, I knew who you all were."

"Yes."

"Well . . . I mean, I knew who you were, and I thought I

knew who I was. And I guess I did know. For right then. But now I know and it's different. It's so funny."

She stopped, thinking it through, working it out slowly and for perhaps the first time.

"If everybody treats you a certain way, then you have to believe them, you have to believe that you really are what they believe you are. But that's just put on, isn't it? What people say? It's all on the outside, not from the inside. Or maybe . . . I don't know. . . . I'm not saying it very well. . . . I haven't got the words. . . ."

But she did have the words. They came groping shyly out of her, with sudden stops and starts and long pauses. It was more than she had ever said to any one person in her life.

"Or else you try to be *not*—to be *not* what they think, *not* what they tell you. . . ." She fell silent.

"How was it, being *not*?"

She considered the matter gravely.

"Well, *not* isn't real either, is it? You can't be *not*; that's being nothing, that's being invisible. But even if it isn't real, that's how I felt. Not real. Not really real. That's how I was, all my life till now."

"Not really real? Invisible?"

"Not exactly invisible, no. Well, yes, sort of, I guess. As if people were looking right through me, as if I were only glass in a window, something to see through, something transparent. As if . . . as if . . . it was like they were always looking beyond me at something else."

She was silent again, lost in some memory. Then she spoke again, hesitantly.

"There was one once. Only one person in Little Wicken ever looked at me as if I was really there, ever looked right at me and saw me. And when he did, he closed his eyes."

John pulled her closer. "Who was that?"

"A . . . a boy I played with once, a long time ago. So long ago. I'd forgotten. It was before I found Apple. Before those boys . . ." She stopped.

"Before they hurt you and used you?"

"Yes." A leftover shudder ran through her and she shut her eyes. When she opened them again, she looked not at John but downward, at the ground.

"A long time before. But he . . . I remember now, he was with them that day too, he was there. It's like a picture now, when I think about it, all frozen and still. He looked right at me and for a minute I thought he was going to help me, I thought he would make them stop and not do anything. But then he closed his eyes again, like he did the other time. But after, when the others went away, he came back. He pulled down my shift to cover me. So I guess he saw me then too."

John was silent, knowing the boy through her words, seeing him and seeing Mokie as the boy had seen her.

Some moments passed.

"And then the women . . ."

"What women?"

"The women in the village."

"What about them?"

She spoke hesitantly, working it out.

"Well, they knew right away. What had happened. I don't know . . . maybe the boys told them. Or maybe they could just tell somehow. But the way they looked at me then . . . the things they said . . . They said awful things about me, things that weren't true, things that hurt. I told myself that I wasn't what they said I was, that I didn't care what they thought or how they talked. But I did care. I always have. I pretend not to, but I've always cared."

She looked at John then, and her eyes were wide and undefended.

"It's different now. Lally didn't look through me, or see me the way the women did after . . ." She stopped, then went on.

"Lally didn't even see what I tried to make her . . . to make you all see. What I thought I wanted her to see, when I was pretending to be a boy. She saw through that. I guess that was really just part of the window, the not-me. Anyway, she really saw me and she made me see myself, and then she fixed it so you and The Skimmer would see me. And that night The Skimmer gave me my name like it really was a name and not just what they called me. He made me see that I truly am Mokie. I am the Pig Girl."

Hearing it so suddenly and unexpectedly, and from Mokie herself, caught John unawares. So simple a statement to carry such a burden of meaning beyond the meanings of the words. Her innocence, all unknowing of the portent, momentarily stopped his breath. He could say nothing.

His silence caught at her, and she looked away then, shy and awkward, a little self-conscious.

"I guess it does sound silly. I don't know what I'm saying. . . . I'm babbling nonsense, I think. Now you're laughing at me."

He must say something.

"I'm not laughing at you, Mokie. I'm smiling because you say so much with so few words. It wasn't nonsense, and even if it was, that's all right. Sometimes nonsense is wiser than sense."

"Yes. But I never talked like this to anyone before. Especially not you. And now . . ."

"And now you talk to me."

"Now I talk to you."

Like an animal she snuggled herself against him, fitting into the curve of his arm that tightened immediately around her. She let out a sigh.

"I talked to Lally a little bit, and that was nice. I never had a woman to talk to. Those other women, the ones in the village . . ." She let the thought die.

"But talking to you is different. Being with you is different." She tilted her head up at him. "I want to say something more, but it feels . . . I don't know . . . strange somehow."

"What do you want to say, Mokie? You can say anything you want, anything about yourself to me."

"But it isn't about myself. It's about you. But about me, too. In a way. Sort of."

He waited.

"Well, then, it's this. When that boy, not the one I played with but the one who . . . When he . . . hurt me, I just thought it must be always like that. Must always hurt. Because it did then. And it hurt again just as bad a little while ago, when I remembered. But then, but just now, with you . . . it didn't hurt."

She looked at him, a wonderful look somewhere between shy and brazen, and he felt his heart inside him break loose from its moorings.

"It didn't hurt with you and now I know that the hurt was wrong, that how it was with you is how it ought to be."

"And with me it was . . . ?"

"You know. Don't you know? You must know."

"Yes," he said. "I know. But I'm glad you told me, because now I'm sure that you know as well as I."

"I know. After what happened with the boys I was angry at myself, remember, I told you?"

"Yes," said John. "I remember. But shouldn't you be angry at the boys? At the boy who did it?"

Mokie looked at him, her face a blank; then a little puzzled frown appeared between her brows. "Angry at Dommel? I don't know. . . . I didn't think of it. I didn't want to think of him. I just wanted to get away.

"But now I feel . . ." She groped for a word, for the right word. "I feel . . . proud. I am proud of myself, I am proud to be myself. Like when The Skimmer gave me my name and said it was all right to be Mokie. You gave me back to myself. And I . . . love you. That's it, isn't it? Love? What the stories are about?"

"Yes," he said gravely. "That's what the stories are about. And I love you, Mokie. I do love you. I want you to remember that, whatever happens, whatever comes."

"What do you mean, 'whatever comes'? Is something coming? Something more? Is something bad coming?"

She sat up abruptly and looked at him with startled eyes.

He shrugged. "I don't know." He pulled her down to him again and hugged her close. "Perhaps not. You never know. Things are always coming."

"As long as we're together I don't mind whatever comes," she said contentedly, and relaxed against him and fell almost immediately into sleep.

But John lay awake for a while, staring wide-eyed into the future. Then he, too, dropped into sleep.

THIRTY-NINE

THE FARROW FIELD

"WELL, NOW, a proper pair you turned out to be, the two of you. Thought you gave us the slip, didn't you?"

Mokie opened her eyes to early evening. The day had passed while they slept, and beyond the wood the sun was going down in a glory of gold and green and amethyst, and the earth, charged with color, glowed under the light of it. She looked up to see The Skimmer and Lally. She could not read their faces.

Surprised, flustered, a little shy, Mokie scrambled to her feet, John just behind her. His hands on her shoulders told them—and Mokie—all that anyone needed to know. Lally and The Skimmer exchanged glances. They looked at John and he returned their look. It had happened. For better or worse was something none of them could know yet, only that it had happened.

"Oh, I am glad to see you, but how did you find us?" asked Mokie.

"We have our ways," said The Skimmer, looking mysterious. "You're not that hard to track."

"How—how long have you been here?"

"A while," said Lally.

"Long enough," said The Skimmer, quirking an eyebrow.

Mokie looked back at John for reassurance. He came forward to stand beside her, sliding an arm about her waist.

Lally regarded them appraisingly. In some indefinable way, both of them were changed. John appeared younger, boyish, almost—human, thought Lally with a sense of shock. More like one of them than one of us. More has happened than was meant to happen. His smile was incandescent, a challenge to the glory of the sinking sun. But his eyes were as black as ever.

In contrast to John, Mokie seemed older. Released from its old defensive twist, her mouth was curved in the mysterious half smile of a woman with a happy secret, and her eyes shone with new knowledge. No darkness there. She was all joy. She looked full at Lally and The Skimmer, open and unabashed and jubilant. Her glance met Lally's and their eyes locked. Something passed between them, old and secret, a hidden knowledge, a recognition.

"I see you," said Mokie.

Lally nodded, but found no words to match. Her glance held Mokie's for a long moment. Then she closed her eyes.

Well, Lally, she told herself, you got what you wanted. This is what you went and broke the pattern for. Here's Mokie all new. She's found out what you wanted her to find out, she's learned how it can be. It's John who taught her that. But it's you who made her ready for it to happen. And she knows now who she is. But she has forgotten the other. She has forgotten the pig. But the pig has not forgotten. The pig knows what she knows. So is it finished now, Lally Dai? Can you go home now? Or must it still play out? She looked at Mokie and John, standing in the low-slanting sunlight with their arms around each other. She looked at The Skimmer, who stared back with shadowed, expressionless eyes.

Is it as bad as that? asked her look.

He shrugged. Yes, said his answering look. It's as bad as that, if you only look at human time, at moving time. No more motes in a sunbeam. She's ready now. She's new made. That's what we came to do and that's what we've done. She knows who she is, if she doesn't yet know why. She's a woman grown and the time's come. Can't you feel it? Can't you hear it?

It was at that exact moment that the muffled thunder of many hooves suddenly filled the wood. It was the sound of a herd of animals running, grunting and squealing, tearing through the underbrush. Startled, Mokie looked about her. Not a branch stirred; the wood was still. She looked at Lally, The Skimmer. They were frozen still as statues, unmoving, like figures caught in crystal, suspended out of time. She looked at

John. He, too, was frozen. First hesitantly, then insistently, she tugged at his arm.

"John! John? Look at me! Lally! Skimmer! What's the matter? What's happening? Look at me! Where are you? Please look at me! Oh, what is it? What is happening?"

They stood immobile while Mokie's world fell into turmoil. The rush of the Phantom Herd was all around her now, a roaring in her ears like wind in the trees, a mass of movement not to be stopped. Terror took her. There was no escape. They would run her down, they would trample over her, they would crush her underfoot. Pursued, possessed by the sound, she abandoned the unmoving figures who made no move to help her and fled in panic, running helter-skelter out of the wood and out onto the Farrow Field with Apple running at her side.

The brightness of the setting sun dazzled her, and she stopped abruptly, blinking and shielding her eyes. Apple skidded to a halt beside her. The Phantom Herd passed on. There was no sign of its presence now, only a far-off memory of thunder in the wood beyond her. There was no noise but the riffle of grass, the sound of voices borne by the wind. At the bottom of the field near the orchard, boys were tending a brush fire whose smoke lay on the air like a dirty blanket. A man's harsh voice cut through the silence and the smoke.

"Catch that pig!"

It was Grime, the owner of Red Sorcha, just emerging from the wood with the village herd, driving the pigs down toward the orchard. The boys around the brush fire looked up at the commotion.

"That one! There! With the red ears. She's mine, out of my red sow. The pig girl stole her, took her into the wood, but she's mine by rights. Catch her!"

Leaving the herd to its own devices for the moment, he ran heavily, purposefully toward Mokie and Apple. Coming dizzy out of her fear and dazzlement, Mokie made a clumsy grab for her pig, but Apple, aware of Grime's pursuit, eluded her grasp and dodged frantically across the Farrow Field, her red-tipped ears fluttering like little pennons above the tall grass. Mokie ran after her and Grime bore down on them both. Whooping with the joy of the chase, the boys deserted their fire for headier excitement.

They strung out in a ragged line, then circled around, herding Apple down the Field toward the orchard. She doubled back and headed up to the Wickenwood with the boys in hot pursuit. Abandoning his pursuit of Mokie, Grime swung wide to meet the pig. The bonfire was directly in her path and without swerving she ran straight through it, scattering ashes and embers in all directions. Mokie followed. Massive and intent on the far side, Grime was waiting. He scooped up the pig, crushing her struggles against his chest and muffling her squeals with a large, dirty hand. The boys crowded around, shouting in triumph.

It all happened before Mokie could take it in. She looked back at the wood, at the motionless figures standing dark under the eaves. Then she started after Grime and the boys, her passage thwarted by the heaving, grunting mass of pigs that swirled like a river in spate between them. She could not pass it. Apple gave one frantic, desperate squeal as Grime knelt beside her and knotted a rope fast around her neck. Rising to his feet, he spared a look for Mokie.

"You," he said. "Think you've got free, do you? Just wait. Your time's coming. Wait till tomorrow. First we'll take care of her. When that's done I'll get you too. See if I don't."

Then he dragged the pig, struggling and protesting and digging in her hooves at every step of the way, back to Little Wicken. The other pigs followed, straggling as the boys herded them down through the trees. Mokie's last glimpse of Apple was of two ears and a little snout turned desperately in her direction as she disappeared into the village.

Mokie stood irresolute between the village and the wood. The Phantom Herd was gone, the village herd was gone, all the forces that had conspired to separate Apple from Mokie. She was suddenly alone, cut off not just from Apple but from Lally and The Skimmer. And from John. It was all gone as if it had never been—her trust in The Skimmer, her bond with Lally, the never-to-be forgotten union of soul and body with John. She turned and saw them standing at the wood's eaves. Heavily, as if weighted to the earth, she plodded back to them. They moved, breathed, rejoined her world, reached out their hands to her. She stood alone and separate, as unmoving as they had been.

"I have to get her out."

"Wait till tomorrow," said The Skimmer. "Wait till the pigs come up to the wood for grazing. We can cut her out then easy."

"No. I can't do that. I have to go to her now. I can't wait. She came for me when I was in the cage. She stayed with me that whole night. I have to do what she did for me. I have to be with her."

"Mokie, don't. Don't go down to the village," said Lally. "He said you stole her. They'll take you too. It won't help Apple to have you both locked up."

She shut her eyes against unwanted knowledge and went on. "We've done this before. We did it with you. We can do it again. The Skimmer's right. Wait until tomorrow."

"They didn't really see me," said Mokie.

"Grime did," said The Skimmer.

"Yes, but the light was fading. Most of them just saw Apple. She'll be frightened. She'll wait for me. She knows I'll come for her."

"At least wait until night before you go. Wait until full dark. We'll watch out for you going in. We'll wait for you at the top of the field."

"It's almost night now. I have to go. I know how to hide; I won't let anyone see me."

"All right," said The Skimmer. "If you're set on going, go. Stay close to her tonight. But don't you try to get her out by yourself. Let her come up to the wood with the rest of the pig herd in the morning. You follow. We'll cut her out after they've started feeding. Watch how you go. And don't get caught."

As once before and from the same dark ownership, from Grime and everything he stood for, Mokie set out to save her child. They watched her go, slipping down through the orchard, using the trees to hide. Their last sight of her was a shadowy form almost hidden by the long grass.

"She wasn't listening," said Lally "She'll try to do it by herself. Being without Apple is like being cut in half for her."

"You know what day tomorrow is," said The Skimmer.

"I know," said Lally.

John said no word.

Dark fell over the world.

FORTY

HOMECOMING

THE GATHERING DUSK SETTLED over Mokie like a cloak as she moved cautiously, reluctantly down into Little Wicken. She had thought never to return, and here she was of her own free will walking back into the trap from which she and Apple had turned away that day. So long ago. In the fading light the village looked smaller than she remembered, and poorer. But it felt just as unfriendly. The cottages crouched at the edge of the road like animals ready to pounce. The dimly lighted windows were like half-shut eyes staring at her. The dust dragged at her feet as if she was walking through a quagmire of meanness and ill will and petty cruelties. A mire of acorns.

All at once she felt as if she had never left, as if all the past days of freedom and joy and comradeship were nothing more than a happy dream, and now the dream was fading. She was the lost 'un once more, standing alone and lonely on the village street. The familiar smell of Little Wicken filled her nostrils—acrid, pungent, redolent of animal dung and human sweat and kitchen refuse and wood smoke and dust all mingled—bringing with it with a flood of memories, echoes of voices.

A jump rope slapped the dirt and a group of girls giggled and squealed.

There goes the lost 'un,
crying in her shirt!

A boy and girl fought and scuffled over pebbles in the dust.

—the road don't go like that—
—not your road. I can make it how I want—

Her cheeks stung from two hard slaps, and a voice like a rusty spoon scraped at her.

—field brat—
—nothing but trouble—
—don't you ever say that again—

The sound of rustling leaves was like raindrops pattering as a wind came up.

—if you're wanting to cuddle, there's better ways to do it—

The voices were insistent, clamoring so loud inside her head they threatened to drown out everything else. She was overwhelmed by memories, by a past that was suddenly more real and immediate, more alive in her than the actual present in which she stood. Then somewhere out of the dark a pig grunted, and with the sound she heard her own voice.

—you can be my lost 'un, my orchard baby with red ears, my little red windfall apple—

She looked about her to get her bearings. It was full dark now. The road, a shade blacker than the sky, was dotted here and there with little patches of faint gold from windows where folk were sitting down to the evening meal. There was Ammie's cottage. She passed Janno's front window. Then she came to Grime's place. Grime's place. The only home she had ever known. The door was ajar, and from the back kitchen came the remembered sound of Grime's bad-tempered growl, angry over some trifle as usual. She heard his wife's complaining reply. For an instant her knees went weak and she felt the old isolation, the old feeling of invisibility possess her once more. Who am I? she wondered. Why am I here? What is it I'm supposed to be doing? Then she remembered. Apple. I've come back to get Apple. That's what I'm here to do, she told herself. To take back my pig. I am not the lost 'un anymore. I am Mokie, and I am going to rescue my pig.

She thought of John, and Lally, and The Skimmer waiting for her up in the wood. They are my folk, she told herself, not these other people. The realization broke on her like sunlight coming sudden after rain. Grime can't hurt me anymore, she told herself. That was long ago. I am not the same person, she realized, and marveled at the discovery. Then an even newer thought dawned in her, a revelation so unexpected, so bold that it almost frightened her. I don't belong here, she thought. This place is not my home. My real home is—is the Crystal Country with John and Lally and Skimmer. The current of joy that thought sent surging through her bones was so sudden and strong it nearly knocked her off her feet. The notion was almost too wonderful for her to risk looking at for very long. She put it aside to explore later, and settled down to attend to the business of the moment.

With a precautionary look around in case anyone might be observing, she slipped silently behind Grime's cottage and felt her way along the rear to the fence rails of the pigpen. Inside the pen fence, sloped up against the back wall of the cottage, was the wattled lean-to where she had slept nestled close to Apple. She could hear the familiar noises of the pigs grunting and snuffling and see their dark shapes rolled against one another like sausages as they settled to sleep. Mokie had no very clear idea of what she was going to do or how she would get Apple away, but she trusted that some idea would come to her in the course of events. The first thing to do was to tell Apple she was here.

Crouching by a corner, she scratched softly at the fence.

"Apple," she whispered. "Can you hear me?" There was no answer from the pig yard.

"Apple!" she whispered again, more urgently. "Apple, it's me."

From the lean-to came a thump.

"Apple. Are you all right?"

A harder thump.

Mokie put her hands on the top rail and was about to swing a leg over the fence when the cottage back door opened and a beam of light fell across the pig yard. Grime's wife came out, holding up a lantern, and at the same time Grime's voice spoke from the kitchen behind her. "I put her in the lean-to and tied her up tight on a short rope, but she might 'a worked it loose. Don't want to risk her getting out, not with tomorrow coming. Just see it's made fast, will you?" Mokie stood motionless in the dark outside the yard. She could see Grime's dark shape silhouetted against the firelight, peering out of the doorway. Then her vision blurred, and she blinked to clear her eyes. It wasn't Grime.

It was Dommel.

Her hands on the fence rail were all that kept her from falling. Then everything turned black and there was nothing in the world but Dommel outlined in the doorway as he had been outlined against the sky that day. At the sudden, unexpected sight of him, the first since that afternoon, something happened to Mokie for which she was completely unprepared—an erupting volcano of rage that exploded out of some locked-away place deep within her, buried layers below her conscious mind. It took her by storm and swept through her like a cyclone, filling every part of her with fire, searing her veins. Her eyes burned dry and hot, her breath scorched her lungs, her heart pounded hammer strokes against her ribs. She felt as if she were made of flame.

then she was screaming at him running toward him
beating him smashing him
kicking and hitting exultant in the thud of her fists
against yielding flesh in the jolt and crack of breaking
bone

In the yard a pig grunted and turned over in sleep and her hands loosened their convulsive hold on the fence rail. With the sound came the picture of Apple's little pig face, clear and bright in her mind, displacing Dommel. As swiftly as it had come the raging storm departed, leaving her stunned and shaken by its violent passage. And I told John I wasn't angry, she thought in amazement. How could I not know? Her discovery of herself astonished her. I would have killed him, she realized, only I remembered Apple. I really could have done it. I couldn't before, but I am different now. I could have killed you just now, Dommel, she told him silently. With my bare hands. I could have got back at you for what you did to me. But I didn't. And you don't even know it.

For the first time in her life Mokie knew what power felt like. The figure in the doorway turned back and disappeared into the light.

Dancing and swinging along the fence line, the lantern beam shone stripes of gold against the ground where the light broke against the fence rails. The lean-to door creaked protestingly on its crooked hinges as Grime's wife went in and set the lantern on the dirt floor. Mokie could see her huge shadow-shape grotesquely rippled against the wattles. Beyond her, tethered by a heavy rope to a post against the back wall, Apple lay disconsolate, her head in the dirt. Grime's wife bent over the apparently sleeping animal and gave a tug or two at the rope.

"It'll hold," she called into the house. "Must've been something else making that noise. Pig's asleep. Wore herself out with all that running, I shouldn't wonder." She gave a short, mirthless laugh. "Well, she'll need her rest when tomorrow comes, that's for sure."

"Make certain the door's shut proper, good and tight," said Grime.

His wife came out and shut the lean-to door firmly, wedging it tight with a propped board. Mokie watched the swinging lantern retreat to the house and disappear behind the kitchen door as it closed. She let out a long breath. She hadn't known she was holding it. The routine sounds of a household getting ready for the night drifted out into the pig yard, the shuffle of feet and creak of floorboards, the scrape of chairs, the rattle of cutlery and clatter of dishware, a sudden bar of light and a slosh and splash as Grime's wife emptied the dishwater out the back door. The lamp was lowered and blown out. Silence settled on the family Grime.

Controlling her impatience, Mokie waited until enough time had passed for them to fall asleep before she tried again. She was aware of little night sounds all around her—the chirp of a sleepy bird, the scrape of a cricket, the creak of tree branches, the heavy, snuffling breathing of the pigs. At last, all within the cottage was quiet. Taking infinite pains to make no noise, she climbed quietly over the fence railing and, treading cautiously around the sleeping pigs, approached the lean-to. She put her mouth right against the wattled wall and called softly.

"Apple? Apple, can you hear me?"

There was the softest of squeaks from inside, and the muffled sound of eager grunting.

"Now, listen carefully, Apple. You have to chew through that rope. But you have to make sure nobody hears you. Can you do it?"

An affirmative grunt was her answer.

"Good girl. Get to work on the knot, and tell me when you've got it loose. I'll be right here. I won't leave until I've got you. I promise."

Mokie crouched against the lean-to wall, considering what to do next. It was impossible to open the squeaky door without the noise waking the cottage. If she couldn't get in, Apple would have to get out. She settled down to make a plan while Apple chewed at the rope.

Only a very suspicious eavesdropper could have determined from the suppressed thumps and scrapes inside the lean-to that a very small pig was gnawing slowly and persistently at a very large knot that she could not see. It took a long time, and more than once Mokie found her eyes closing in spite of her.

At last there was silence, then a grunt of satisfaction. It woke Mokie up with a start.

"You got through it? You're loose?"

Another grunt.

"All right. Now, here's the next thing. We have to dig a hole clear under the lean-to wall from inside to outside. I can't do it by myself; I don't have anything to dig with. So you dig from inside and I'll dig from out here. When we meet, we'll have a tunnel. You squeeze out and we'll be away before they know you're gone. I'm going to start here at the corner, where the dirt is softest."

She began to dig. The earth was not as soft as she had supposed. It was loose on the surface, where the pigs rooted, but underneath, the dirt was hard. Her fingers were sore and her finger ends raw before she could make any headway. She looked about her for a rock, a stick, anything she could gouge with, but the pig yard was bare of any implement, and she had to use her hands. She heard Apple digging inside, rooting with her hard little nose, scrabbling and burrowing with her hooves. It seemed to take forever. The night was passing and the sky beginning to pale. Just when Mokie was ready to despair, the thin barrier of earth crumbled and a snout poked through.

The sight of Apple was all Mokie needed. She clawed furiously with both hands, widening the tunnel to fit Apple's girth. Fortunately, the earth was softest where it was closest to the wall of the lean-to, where it had not been tamped down by the tromping of pigs' feet. The girl scraped and dug, and the pig wriggled and squirmed, and in a surprisingly short time, Mokie was nose to snout with a very dirty Apple, who sniffed her all over and squeaked with joy, but softly, so as not to wake her captors.

"Now for it, Apple. And you mustn't make a sound."

The sky was very light now, and Mokie knew the village would be waking soon. Even as she reached Apple over the pig yard fence and dropped her, the other pigs were stirring. Somewhere a shutter banged open. Somewhere a child cried and a mother's voice answered. Mokie eased herself over the railing, grabbed her pig, crossed the road, and started up through the orchard. As she walked, she talked, as much to herself as to Apple, as much as anything else to reassure herself that everything was going to be all right, that she really had Apple and the two of them were on their way to the wood and freedom.

"That's my brave Apple. That's my clever girl. You did it. We did it. But we still have to be careful. We're not out of danger yet. We've got to hurry. We have to be away back in the wood before they discover that you're gone. John and Lally and The Skimmer are waiting for us. Come on."

In the relief of suspense and the letdown after furious activity, a sudden desperate fatigue swept over her. Her feet felt leaden. The weight of Apple in her arms was almost too great to be borne. She plodded on.

FORTY-ONE

MOCCA

HUDDLED IN THE SHADOWS, Lally faced away from the field, her hands on the rough bark of Mokie's tree. I cannot, she told it. I will not. If it is to happen then it will happen, but I will not watch it. I will not look. And perhaps it won't happen.

Standing at the edge of the wood, The Skimmer had an uninterrupted view down the slope of the field directly below him, of the orchard beyond the field and the village after that with the curve of the river shining in the distance. The smoke of yesterday's burning was gone, the air was diamond clear, the light hard and cool edged, outlining every last dried leaf on a branch, every sere finger of grass in the field. The morning was advancing, the sun climbing above the village. The villagers were moving purposefully about their business, making careful preparations for this day that came so seldom, that was meant to bring so much. No one left the confines of the village. No farmer went out to a field. No one went down to the river. All the activity was concentrated in the village, and folk were beginning to cluster now in twos and threes around the pen where the pigs were kept.

It's too late, The Skimmer thought, a way sight too late. Of course they won't be taking the herd up to the wood. Not today. They're a herd themselves, and that's how they'll act. So she won't get out now without being seen, even if she does get the pig. There's going to be trouble. What good are all your questions now, Lally? You said it yourself, we're threads in the web. We're part of the pattern, just like Mokie and the pig. He shrugged. No help for it. Come on, Mokie, he thought, time's passing and we can't wait forever.

Oh, can't we? asked a voice in his mind. Isn't that just what we always do? He looked to see John standing beside him, John's thoughts the voice he had heard, John's eyes a despairing mirror of The Skimmer's own.

At the same time, both glimpsed a figure toiling up through the orchard carrying something in her arms. Her head was bowed, and she was moving clumsily, heavily, as if weighed down by a burden far greater than a yearling pig.

Come *on*, slow coach, he urged her silently. Put the pig down and run for it. She'll take care of herself. You haven't all the time in the world; they'll soon enough find the pig missing and raise the hue and cry. He looked at John and read his thoughts—

Mokie, Mokie, my very dear. I would spare you this if only I had the power. But I will watch for you and watch with you and see you through it however much it hurts us both.

Even as they watched, there was a yell of discovery from the village and then a babble of voices. That's done it, thought The Skimmer, and moved out into the Farrow Field, ready to grab her hand and pull her in as soon as she came near enough. John was right behind him. Mokie heard the yell also, and then she did begin to run. John and The Skimmer could see terror and panic impel her into flight without conscious thought, following a blind impulse toward the safe place, wherever it might be. The Skimmer fairly danced with impatience. Why was she so slow? This way, Mokie! To me! To me!

Silent by his side, John watched.

Mokie was running as fast as her legs would carry her, faster than she had ever run in her life, dodging and doubling through the trees, crouching low to the ground. Her hands and arms ached from the weight of Apple, her feet were bruised against stones. Her breath came fast and ragged, harsh in her throat. Her legs ached with the running. Sometimes she stumbled. Always she caught herself and ran on.

In the distance behind her she could hear the cries and the shouting. They were hungry for blood, for death, for vengeance against what they could not know and would not understand. Voices followed her.

"Get her! Catch her!"

"Kill the pig!"

"Stick her good!"

She dared not stop, not for an instant, not to breathe, not to look about her, not to think. The ground rose under her. This is a dream, she thought, like my dream of the water and the boat. It isn't real and presently I'll wake up and Lally will hand me a cup of tea and The Skimmer will ask me where my wits have got to and everything will be like before. She kept on running, as one does in a dream.

Anyway, I've got Apple. She's safe in my arms. They were going to kill her, going to stone her in the field, but I won't let them.

John and The Skimmer could see her running clear now, slip dodging among the orchard trees, emerging suddenly out into the open field. Behind her, the ragged crowd, carrying no burden heavier than their own blood hunger, was closing the gap between them.

Getting there. She looked ahead, saw The Skimmer step forward so she could see him clear, saw his hand outstretched, ready to take her arm and draw her in to safety.

A villager, a dark man in a cap and cloak, appeared out of nowhere and stood in front of her, arms outspread to divert her.

It was Grime. Their eyes met. She shook her head frantically. No! she shouted soundlessly. Yes! he mouthed, and smiled in grim reply. She swerved away, running parallel now, outdistancing him.

Oh, John, they'll take Apple. People will take her. They'll leave her body for the crows, leave her bones on the ground. I won't let them. I'll get her away.

Oddly, Grime didn't give chase, just stood watching. She looked up to see another body blocking her path, Grime's wife, standing with arms outspread like her husband. Mokie doubled back and saw Dommel in the distance, standing at the far edge of the field. Just standing, no more, but he held a stone in his hand. Near him stood Ammie, and she, too, held a stone. The air was so clear, the sun so bright it made them look unnaturally brilliant, as if they were carved out of light. Mokie swerved again, looking for a way through, a way out.

It will be all right—we'll make it. It has to be all right.

She ran on, harder now, her breath laboring, dragged harsh and painful out of her exhausted lungs. A stone winged through the air. It landed just short, only a little behind her.

Someone behind me . . .

The Skimmer saw her hear the thud, but it was John who winced, John who saw her turn to look over her shoulder at Ammie. She changed direction again, swinging back across her own path, and again her enemies didn't close in, just stood in position, quartering the field.

She could make no headway, her feet moving slow and heavy, as in a dream,

Another rock, this one smaller, struck Apple on the nose. She let out a squeal and wriggled loose from Mokie's arms, hitting the ground and rebounding like a ball, running in an erratic zigzag back and forth across the field.

She felt the pig leave her arms. Suddenly the field was full of pigs—half-glimpsed, ghostly figures milling and trampling, jostling against one another, pushing and shoving so that she nearly lost her balance among them. She could hear the drumming of many hooves on the dry earth of the Farrow Field.

In an agony of tension The Skimmer willed her to hear his thought. Leave her! Leave the pig! She'll be all right.

Apple!

Swinging away from the wood, Mokie took off through the

310

empty grass after Apple, running in crazy zigzags, stumbling and recovering as if she were part of a jostling crowd. A village boy stepped forward, and The Skimmer winced at the size of the stone he held in his hand.

"Mokie!" he shouted. "Don't stop now, girl! You're not safe— not yet!"

The voice she heard was The Skimmer's, but it was John she saw standing still as stone, his eyes calling her.

Stooping toward Apple, Mokie hesitated. Girl and pig turned just as the village boy launched his stone.

Far off, in another country, a bird called—three plaintive, descending notes, over and over.

Time slowed down. Everything happened at once and in slow motion. The stone traced a deliberate arc across the air.

It was a dream.

The Skimmer's throat opened in a soundless cry—*No no no no no*—that went on and on. It will be now, said John inside himself.

Mokie's mouth opened and her eyes widened as she saw—not the stone, but who had thrown it.

The village boy stood frozen as he saw the stone hit and

he saw her and knew her and remembered who she was.

The pig herd overran her and she was knocked off balance. She felt the side of her head explode, felt herself hurled sideways, her arms flung out to break her fall.

John, The Skimmer, and Janno felt in their own bodies the impact of the stone as it slammed against her head just above the ear, shattering the bone and driving it inward. All three felt her lose her balance, all three felt the sickening lurch as she reeled and stumbled under the force of the blow.

Earth came up to take her, and the herd trampled over her.

The Skimmer and Janno saw her flailing for balance, legs still trying to run, arms thrown wide in a grotesque parody of welcome. They saw her knees give and buckle while her body's momentum threw her forward. But it was John, never moving from where he stood, who held out his arms as if to catch her as she fell.

With whatever part of her was left in that instant, she knew at last and finally that it was no dream. It was real it was happening she could not stop it. She felt John catch her.

The Skimmer and Janno saw her pitch headlong and land

312

spread-eagled, an awkward, ungainly scarecrow in a barren field.

They reached her at the same time. They halted, one on either side of all that was left of Mokie. They looked at each other across the gulf of her body. There was no bridge. It was John who spoke.

"You can leave her now," he said to Janno. "Go on back home. She doesn't belong to you anymore."

Far off, in another country, a bird called—three plaintive, descending notes, over and over.

Apple had disappeared. Janno stood quiet. He looked down at the pig girl fallen in the grass, then up at John. "I didn't mean . . ." he began. "She . . ." He stopped. "I remember . . ." he said, "we . . . we played once. A long time ago."

His voice trailed into silence, and his eyes, dark as a rainy night, fell before what he saw in John's face, a look from which there was no appeal. He stood just so for a long moment, staring down at Mokie where she lay in the grass. Then he turned and walked away, motioning with his hand to the straggle of people still standing irresolute in the field below, robbed of their quarry and left with their hunger unsatisfied. Then they, too, turned away, drained now of the energy that had fueled the chase, and by two and by three they walked back down the slope to Little Wicken, back the way they had come. The silence they left behind was made emptier by the sound of the wind hissing in the grass.

FORTY-TWO

CRYSTAL FOLK

WHEN THEY WERE GONE, JOHN KNELT to the poor broken body, gathered her into his arms, and carried her back to the useless shelter of the wood. Her head rested against his shoulder, her long legs dangled. Apple, reappearing in the long grass, trotted after them. It was there, a little while later, that The Skimmer and Lally found the three of them. John was sitting propped against a tree, his shoulders bent over Mokie, her head cradled in his lap. A track of blood from her temple down one cheek showed where the final rock had struck. Apple was lying quietly beside him on the forest floor, her head rested on her forefeet, as comfortable with him as if she had never belonged to anyone else in her life.

When The Skimmer and Lally came up, John raised his head and looked at them. His round eyes were dry of tears but deep welling with the sad wisdom that knows too well the way things are, and how it is that they have to be that way.

Lally looked at him. Her face was set, her mouth bleak, her eyes deep shadowed.

"It didn't work," she said.

"No," said John. "It didn't work."

She started to raise her hands, then let them drop, a helpless protest. "There's no way out of it, then, is there? It doesn't matter what you do, what anyone does. There's no way to break the pattern because any break becomes part of the pattern."

"The pattern is in the break," said John. His expression was unfathomable.

"And so it's finished," said Lally.

"For now," said The Skimmer.

"Now is all there ever is," said Lally. "Come on. Time to go home."

John nodded. He rose and very gently, with careful tenderness, he lifted Mokie up and brought her out of the cover of the wood. Kneeling, he set her down so that she lay out at full length on the edge of the Farrow Field. Apple followed. John had thought Mokie was gone, but as he looked down he saw the slightest, nearly imperceptible leaf flutter of her eyelids. Her eyes opened and Mokie looked up at him, her green and brown gaze clear and bright in the last moment. Her voice came to him faint as grasses whispering in a summer wind.

"Where . . . where is Apple?"

315

He bent his head to hers.

"You are Apple," he said.

"I know," she said. The ghost of a smile flitted across her face like cloud shadow on a hillside. Then she closed her eyes and the breath sighed out of her and she was still. Lally and The Skimmer stood for a long moment, gazing down at her. At last they turned and walked away, not waiting to see if John followed.

John watched them go, motionless until they were deep in the shadows among the trees. He waited until they were out of sight and he and Mokie were alone. When they were gone everything was still for a long minute, as if the world held its breath. The Skimmer had done his best to break the pattern for her. Lally had loved her. But what was between him and Mokie was private, not to be shared, not to be witnessed. Dropping to his knees, he took her lax, unresponsive hand in his. Turning it palm up, he laid the green glass marble in her hand and folded her fingers tightly around it. He held her hand in his for a minute. Then he got up and walked into the wood.

The herd was all around Mokie now, but they did not touch her, only stood watching, silent and waiting. She got up and Apple followed her, leading the herd. She thought her head would hurt, but she didn't feel anything. With Apple following, she walked deeper into the wood, where the trees stood tall, their silver-green leaves ringing against one another with the smallest of sounds, or was it the air itself that chimed as its colors shimmered from silver to scarlet to sapphire to violet to emerald and then to silver again? In the brightness at the end of the aisle a throng of people stood waving a welcome.

They smiled and beckoned to her, laughing with eager anticipation, and Mokie felt the breath in her lungs bubble swiftly up to catch her throat in answering laughter. She knew that something inexpressibly wonderful was about to happen. Someone she could almost see, someone she almost knew, was coming to her, blown on an apple blossom wind. She knew, almost, who it would be. Then she knew them—John and Lally and The Skimmer. They were more beautiful than ever, shining, elegantly dressed in bright, clear colors with light shimmering all around and through them. The light before Mokie's eyes brightened unbearably as she drew near, and her heart trembled on the brink of loveliness too great to take in.

Anyone watching—but no one was—would have seen how the shapes melted into the shadows that moved and flickered on the tree trunks and then disappeared, all of them on their way to the hut in the clearing, all of them passing through the Door, all of them returning home, going back to where they came from.

When they were gone, it was very quiet. Overhead a sky of burning blue arched like an inverted bowl. In the crystalline air the dried grasses and the last leaves seemed both transparent and edged with light, and their little clashing in the wind was like faint music from another country. One solitary leaf clinging to a parent branch suddenly let go its hold and spiraled lazily down the still air, etching a path against the sky like a pattern cut into clear glass. A sudden, vagrant gust out of nowhere caught it in midflight and sent it spinning around and around in a frantic dance. Then, as abruptly as it had risen, the wind fell, abandoning the leaf to whatever fate would take it.

Like a planing hawk it rode the air, circling down and down and lighting soft as a kiss on all that remained in this world of Mokie, lying in the long grass where her mother had left her.

FORTY-THREE
COMING HOME

ONCE SAFELY INSIDE THE HUT, Lally closed the door behind her, latching it firmly to shut out memory and desire and the recollection of sorrow. With her back to the door and the wood and the world, she looked the other way, out into the Crystal Country. There the orchard trees were just coming into bloom, the pink blossoms freshly opened with deeper pink at the center, the colors light and airy against the new green of the leaves. They nodded delicately, swaying in the wind, and as they blew there was a chiming, so fragile and far away it was like the memory of bells.

The faintest of scents floated on the air, the echo of apples whose blossoms were petals of delicate tinted glass thin as soap bubbles, crystalline and opalescent and shimmering.

The apple trees themselves were spun out of black glass, and their twisted boles and gnarled branches glittered in the sunlight. The leaves were sharp green spear points of glass, the sky was a green glass bowl. The whole world was glass, clear and bright as a river pool when the sunlight strikes into its depths.

And she knew once again and at last that she was in the heart of it; she, too, was glass and filled with light, bright, transparent. She was Mokie and she was brought back through it all, after it all, to her proper self. Clearer now, she heard the chime of every separate crystal bell and the notes were like tears falling one by one and dropping into silence, no music, only single moments, each alone and only itself, each of such piercing beauty it hurt her heart.

I am home at last, she thought.

She felt a soft weight press against her leg and looked down to see Apple looking up at her, and for a moment their gazes locked, eye to eye. Then they merged, and then there was only Apple looking at her home country with shining eyes, one eye the somber brown of winter fruit, the other the hopeful green of apples in summer.

She knew that something inexpressibly wonderful was about to happen. Someone she could almost see, someone she nearly knew, was coming to her, blown on an apple blossom wind. She felt in her heart how it would be. Then she saw them—John and The Skimmer. Laughing with delight, they led her away from the hut and out into the Crystal Country, and she felt the breath in her lungs bubble swiftly up to catch her throat in answering laughter. They were more beautiful than ever, shining, elegantly dressed in bright, clear colors with light shimmering all around and through them. The light before her eyes brightened unbearably as she joined them, and her heart trembled on the brink of loveliness too great to take in.

"Welcome home, Sorcha," said John.

ABOUT THE AUTHOR

VERLYN FLIEGER is a professor at the University of Maryland, where she teaches courses in modern fantasy, medieval literature, and comparative mythology. *Pig Tale* is her first novel.